The Borribles
Go For Broke

THE BORRIBLE TRILOGY by Michael de Larrabeiti

Available now
Book 1: *The Borribles*
Book 2: *The Borribles Go For Broke*

Coming Soon from Tor Teen
Book 3: *The Borribles: Across the Dark Metropolis*

The Borribles
Go For Broke

MICHAEL de LARRABEITI

TOR

A TOM DOHERTY ASSOCIATES BOOK
NEW YORK

This is a work of fiction. All the characters and events portrayed in this book are either products of the author's imagination or are used fictitiously.

THE BORRIBLES GO FOR BROKE

A Tor Book
Published by Tom Doherty Associates, LLC
175 Fifth Avenue
New York, NY 10010

www.tor.com

Tor® is a registered trademark of Tom Doherty Associates, LLC.

ISBN 0-765-35006-8
EAN 978-0-765-35006-0

First Tor Teen Edition: November 2005

Printed in the United States of America

0 9 8 7 6 5 4 3 2 1

I

It was the hottest Sunday in the hottest July for a hundred years and Chalotte Borrible crouched in the cool shade beneath a greengrocer's barrow in Petticoat Lane market and munched a stolen apple. It was just about noon and all over London the pub doors were opening, even though the streets were as yet silent and empty. Nearly all the inhabitants of the great metropolis were hiding away from the heat, lying undressed on their beds, turning their eyes into the dark because it was too hot to get up and they were too idle to know what to do.

But in Petticoat Lane it was different. That was the busiest place in the world. Chalotte peered between the wooden wheels of the barrow and watched the feet trudging by, feet which belonged to thousands of Londoners, come from all over the capital on a Sunday morning jaunt, up early so they could push and jostle against each other in sweat and swelter as they struggled to examine the goods on every stall. They shouted and shoved and wrestled and the costermongers shouted too, opening their loose mouths to show stained and broken teeth.

Chalotte loved Petticoat Lane, it was such a marvellous place for a Borrible to live; a place where you could steal enough food on market day to last the rest of the week. She pushed her hand up and, unseen, took another apple. The fruit was warm to her touch as her fingers closed about it; the sweet flesh was warm in her mouth as she began to chew.

She ate the apple, right down to the core and the pips, then she ducked out into the open and stood poised, ready to run, but no one had noticed her. On the opposite pavement a group of men stood outside a green-tiled pub holding large glasses of bitter in their hands. Their eyes glinted with pleasure as they upended the amber jugs and poured the liquid into their throats. When the ale reached their stomachs they made loud sighs of happiness and looked at each other with surprise, as if beer had only been invented that very morning.

Not far from the apple barrow a man was selling stolen watches out of a suitcase, in a doorway. Just beyond him Chalotte saw a pickpocket take a wallet from a lady's shoulder bag. Above the noise of people talking and walking came the sound of a man breaking crockery, whole dinner sets. It was his way of making the passers-by notice him. Chalotte smiled to herself, stole one last apple and moved on.

As she took her first step a rough hand wound itself into her long fair hair and seized her. A voice shouted into her ear. 'You thieving little bleeder,' it said, 'got you, haven't I?'

Chalotte twisted her head and looked up at the adult who had caught her. What she saw made her heart jump. She'd been captured by a plain-clothes policeman, of that she was certain. She didn't need a uniform to tell her who was a copper and who wasn't. She fought against the hand, cursing herself for carelessness, but its grasp did not slacken. One short moment of inattention and now her whole existence was in danger.

'Ow, leggo, you're hurting me,' she said, allowing the tears to come to her eyes in the hope that this would encourage the officer of the law to let her go. All round the barrow the busy street became blocked as the curious stopped to gloat and goggle; they looked down at the slender girl with her second-hand clothes and her dirty face, and they grinned.

'Go on, kid, run,' said a man, but the others in the crowd only grinned again and waited to see what the policeman would do. But he did nothing and shouts were heard in the side streets, coming from people who could not see what was happening and who were growing impatient at being hindered in their progress.

'Get a move on, can't yer?' said some and the shoving became fiercer.

The policeman took Chalotte to the end of the barrow. 'What's your name?' he asked, and Chalotte, like a true Borrible, had her answer ready.

'Chalotte Jenkins,' she said, 'and my mum's waiting down the end of the street and she'll worry if I'm late . . . I'm sorry about the apple, honest, she'll pay for it. I'm sorry, mister, I was thirsty.' This she said to the costermonger, who wasn't particularly concerned about the theft of an apple anyway.

'Oh, let her go,' he said. 'She can have another one if she likes.'

'Yeah,' said somebody else, 'an apple a day keeps the coppers at bay.'

The policeman hesitated and Chalotte felt his hand relax in her hair; he was going to release her. She sniffed and tried to look as miserable as possible, but then, on a sudden thought, the policeman tightened his grip. He raised his free hand and, with a confident movement, swept back Chalotte's hair so that he and the crowd could see her ears. There was a gasp of surprise from the bystanders; Chalotte's ears were long and pointed—they were ears that showed great intelligence and daring—*Borrible* ears.

The policeman hooted with delight. 'Look at that,' he shouted. 'I've caught one, a Borrible, a real live Borrible,' and from the back pocket of Chalotte's trousers he pulled a catapult. 'And look at that,' he added, his face red and beaming with satisfaction, 'the Borrible weapon.'

'A Borrible,' said those in the front of the crowd, and they passed the word to the people behind them. 'A Borrible.'

'I ain't letting this one go,' shouted the policeman. 'I ain't letting her go! Quick, clear the road, you're causing an obstruction, move along there,' and he thrust the gawping spectators from his path, shouldered himself between two barrows and up on to the pavement.

Chalotte howled. She struggled and flailed her fists at the policeman, but he was too strong for her. He strode onward, clearing all before him, dragging his prisoner by his side.

'Back off, out of the way,' he bawled, 'police, police, stand back, out of my way!'

Chalotte continued to yell at the top of her voice but there was no one to help her. The policeman barged on through the shoppers and strollers, bursting open the groups of men who lounged outside the pubs, making them spill beer over their fingers and down their shirt fronts. And as policeman and prisoner went along the pavements and crossed the alleys of Petticoat Lane the hubbub quietened as they passed and men and women turned to look and laugh. Why shouldn't they? Not one of them knew how serious the matter was; they did not realize that Chalotte was a Borrible and that for a Borrible to be caught is the very end.

Borribles are thin as a rule and their ears are always pointed; apart from that they look like normal children although they may have been Borribles for years and years. They are tough-looking and scruffy but are renowned for their quickness of wit and their speedy running; a life lived on the streets sees to that.

Normal children become Borribles very slowly, without being aware of it. One day they wake up and there it is, the transformation has taken place. It doesn't matter in the slightest where they come from as long as they have had what other people call a bad start. A child disappears from school and the chances are that he's run away to become a Borrible. Sometimes it is said that a child has been put into care. It's more likely that he has been Borribled and is off caring for himself. One day a shout is heard in a supermarket and a child with stolen goods on him is arrested by a store detective. If that child manages to get away he'll join the Borribles and make sure that he isn't caught again, ever.

So Borribles are outcasts and runaways and they value their independence more than anything else because they take a deep delight in being what they are. They avoid adults; they don't like them and make no effort to. In fact the only people to get close to Borribles are ordinary children and that is because Borribles mix with them in order to escape detection by the authorities. Any child may have sat next to a Borrible or even talked to one, never noticing the ears on account of their long hair or the hats they wear, woollen ones, pulled well down.

Their greatest enemies are policemen—the Woollies. Woollies represent the authorities and the authorities cannot abide a Borrible. They don't like the free and easy way the Borribles choose to live. Running away from home, squatting in derelict houses and taking orders from no one is not neat, nor is it tidy.

For a policeman the capture of a Borrible is a rare and great achievement, it is also the end of freedom for the captive. That is why Chalotte struggled with all her strength. Once that Woollie got her inside the police station it would be curtains.

The policeman came to the end of Brick Lane and stopped on the edge of the Whitechapel Road, waiting for the traffic lights to change colour. He maintained his tight hold on Chalotte's hair and she continued to yell in pain. A small group of men, staggering gently from one pub to another, gathered on the corner and stared.

'Stop that bloody row,' said the Woollie, and he crouched so that he could push his big face into Chalotte's; she jerked her head backwards, the policeman's breath was damp and offensive, like mouldy bread. He laughed, spraying the girl with his saliva.

'Struggle all yer like, Borrible,' he said, 'it won't do you no good. I'll get promotion for this, I will.'

'What are you going to do with me?' asked Chalotte.

'Oh,' said the policeman, 'that's easy, got special orders for Borribles, we have. You see, about six months ago there was a rag-and-bone man killed over in Southfields, and his son, slaughtered in their own home, murdered with catapults, and we all know who uses catapults, don't we?' The policeman shoved Chalotte's weapon under her nose and tugged at her hair so fiercely that she wept, her tears making furrows down the dirt of her cheeks. The policeman smiled. 'Three of our men were injured, nearly killed one of them was, and ever since then Borribles have become top priority . . . Make no mistake, me girl, we'll be taking good care of you. You'll be going to see Inspector Sussworth, you will.'

The lights switched from red to green and the policeman stood upright and charged towards the traffic island in the middle of the wide road, pulling Chalotte along so quickly that her feet barely touched the tarmac.

'Who's Inspector Sussworth?' asked Chalotte, and she wiped her tears away with the back of her hand.

The policeman stopped on the island and looked down at her. 'Sussworth,' he said, 'he's a wonderful man, and since those Southfields murders he's formed a group of specially trained officers, all dedicated to the elimination of Borribles. They investigate Borribles, they study Borribles, they know more about Borribles than Borribles know about Borribles. You'll be sent to him, you will, and when he's asked you every question he can think of and made you answer them, why then he'll clip your ears and that'll be another Borrible less for us to worry about, won't it?'

The policeman laughed with profound enjoyment and spying a gap in the stream of cars he pulled Chalotte forward once more, hauling her to the far side of the road.

'You sod,' said Chalotte, 'you sod.' But the bravery of her words belied the fear she felt. She dreaded being sent to this Inspector Sussworth. If he clipped her ears she would revert to being an ordinary child; she would grow up. Left to themselves Borribles do not become adults and their small size is their pride and the source of their freedom. It means that they can always pass themselves off as children and yet they are often as experienced as the oldest person alive.

'Don't you swear at me,' said the policeman, 'you little savage. I've got strict orders; you're going to the SBG and that's it and all about it.'

'The SBG,' said Chalotte, 'what's that?'

'The SBG,' said the policeman, 'that's the Special Borrible Group, Sussworth's outfit, over Fulham way. That's where you'll be going, all in your own van. If you're lucky I'll come with you.' Laughing at his own joke he strode along all the faster with Chalotte trotting by his side, her mind spinning.

What the Woollie did not know was that this small female Borrible, accidentally captured, knew all about the Southfields murders and what she feared most of all was a severe interrogation. She might, under pressure, divulge valuable Borrible secrets; it would be disaster for her, disaster for her friends. She had seen Dewdrop Bunyan and his idiot son done to death, she knew those responsible, but even if she told her captors that the killings had been richly deserved it would make no difference. They would never believe her.

Chalotte and nine other Borribles had been kidnapped and held in slavery for months by this loathsome Borrible-snatcher. They had been beaten and starved and had only got away by luck. It had been her friends Knocker and Adolf the German who had killed Dewdrop and Erbie, slain them with catapults and well aimed marbles, so as to escape from torture and slow death themselves. Now Knocker and Adolf were dead too, killed during the Adventure of the Great Rumble Hunt, and so were Orococco, Torreycanyon and Napoleon; good Borribles gone for good, and soon she would be gone too. Was every Borrible who had been involved in the Great Rumble Hunt doomed to die? It certainly seemed so.

Despair welled up in Chalotte's heart and her mind misted over with it. She stumbled and the Woollie caught her with his rough hand.

'Come on, chummy,' he said, and then Chalotte heard herself shouting, as if from a great way off, shouting for help, knowing that only one of her own kind could save her now.

'A Borrible,' she screamed, 'a Borrible.' And away on the other side of Whitechapel another Borrible heard her; it was Twilight, the black-haired Bangladeshi from Folgate Street, up near Spitalfields.

Twilight was thin and fragile but he could run like a train. His clothes were ragged and his hair was cut unevenly, long and thick and so black it looked blue. He had a sharp nose and one eyebrow that was cast higher than the other, making him look curious and sly at the same time. His eyes were big and dark and often full of thought, he was cheerful and determined; he was muggins for no one.

Twilight always roamed the streets with a band of Bangladeshi friends, about half a dozen of them, and they stuck together for protection. He only knew Chalotte by sight but he had heard some of the stories that were told about her and her part in the Adventure against the Rumbles. All that didn't matter now; the sight of a Borrible, any Borrible, being taken away by a Woollie was enough to inflame his blood. He called his friends to him and they ran as fast as they could along Whitechapel, on the opposite side to Chalotte, crossing the road eventually some three hundred yards ahead of her, positioning themselves in ambush between the officer of the law and his police station.

There was no time for elaborate schemes. Twilight knew that if he did not rescue Chalotte immediately she would disappear into the cells and never come out again, at least not as a Borrible. Round a corner, where Stanton Street meets the main road, he and his friends waited. When the policeman was only a step or two away Twilight gave the word and he and his gang charged into Whitechapel at top speed with all the energy they could muster. They ran straight at the Woollie, shouting, jeering and yelling.

'Watch out, Woollie; watch out, Woollie!'

Twilight rammed his hard head into the policeman's soft stomach and there it almost disappeared, like a fist punched into a cushion. His mates followed on like a pack of street dogs run wild; tearing, pushing, and laughing too. Everybody went over, the Borribles letting themselves fall forward, using their speed and weight to topple the big policeman to the ground. They stuck to him, jabbed him, butted him and covered his eyes with their hands, and so this strange gyrating lump of noise rolled along the pavement forcing passers-by to leap into the roadway to escape injury. Hands, legs and heads appeared and disappeared as the lump turned once or twice, then whole bodies disengaged themselves. Chalotte felt herself grabbed under the armpits; there was a Bangladeshi Borrible on each side of her, another ran in front to clear the way. The policeman lay groaning on the ground, sorely winded, his mind utterly drained by the suddenness of the attack. It had only taken ten seconds and Chalotte was free.

Once more her feet hardly touched the ground but now she was borne along by friends and there was hope, not despair, in her heart. Nobody said a word, reserving every ounce of breath for flight. They were just a tight knot of brown Borribles carrying a white one to freedom.

The Woollie lurched to his feet and swung round, his arms stiff and straight, and then, with his boots banging the pavement slabs, he set off after the runaways. But he wasn't in the race; by the time he reached the traffic lights the Borribles had disappeared. They had re-crossed the main road and lost themselves deep in the market, hiding like they always did where the crowd was thickest.

The policeman knew full well that he had no chance of finding them now; they could be anywhere, under stalls, in their ruined houses, down side alleys, and they would be watching for him. The word would have gone abroad and every Borrible within a radius of ten miles would be taking cover.

The policeman stood and swore at his failure. He had imagined himself walking proudly into the police station with his captive. He had seen himself telephoning Inspector Sussworth and receiving congratulations and thanks; he might even have been invited to join the SBG, a real plum of promotion for anyone in the Metropolitan Police Force. Ah well! It was not to be. He'd best say nothing about the incident; he didn't want to be laughed at. Sadly he turned and retraced his steps. Nothing to report.

Back in the hustle of the market the Borribles slowed the pace of their escape, walking at first and then loitering to see if the Woollie was still in pursuit.

'We'd better split up for a while,' said Twilight to his gang. 'I'll take Chalotte back to Spitalfields while you others keep your eyes open for that copper; he may have gone back for help.'

Chalotte thanked the Bangladeshis and walked away from them, following Twilight. She found it hard to believe that she was safe and she smiled, taking pleasure in the business of the market and the feel of human bodies as they pushed past her. The sun, high in the sky, warmed the whole street, and the smells of strange spices drifted on the air. Sandalled Indian women went softly by, enveloped in saris that sparkled with gold. The costers still shouted at the passers-by, their voices vulgar and outrageous and cracking under the strain of many hours of bawling. Chalotte touched Twilight on the arm. The shirt he wore was gaudy, orange, sickly and luminous. His trousers were blue and too big for him, torn in several places; stolen trousers. His feet were bare but in the hot summer that was how he preferred to be. After all, the pavements were warm and cushioned in dust.

'Yes?' he said.

'Thanks for rescuing me,' said Chalotte. 'I was just looking at all this and wondering where I would be now if it hadn't been for you.'

Twilight tried to appear unconcerned. 'Well I heard you call out, didn't I? No Borrible can resist that. Besides, I was sent to look for you.'

'Look for me?' said Chalotte in surprise. 'I never saw you before. I don't even know your name, even if you've got one.'

'Course I have,' said the brown Borrible.

'What is it then?'

'Twilight,' said Twilight.

'Twilight,' said Chalotte. 'That is a good'n and I bet a good adventure lies behind a name like that. You must tell me how you won it some day.'

It was quite normal for Chalotte to speak to Twilight in this manner. Names and how they are won are important to Borribles because for them a name is not given but earned; it is the only way. An adventure of some sort must be completed and out of that deed will grow a name. An adventure of any kind will do. It doesn't have to be stealing or burglary, though it often is because that's what Borribles prefer.

Chalotte studied her companion. 'And while we're on the subject, how come you know my name?'

'I know your name,' said Twilight, 'for the simple reason that everyone knows your name and how you won it. It is one of the greatest Borrible stories ever told but I have never met anyone before who was on the Great Rumble Hunt. When we get home I'd like you to tell me about it. I have heard things that are hard to believe.'

Chalotte's face became stern. 'They were probably true,' she said. 'It all got a bit nasty. Borribles should not have been involved in such things. Five Borribles were killed, five good Borribles. It was a waste. I don't mind telling you the story in return for you rescuing me, but it is not a happy story.'

Twilight smiled and his teeth were bright against his dark skin. Like all Borribles he loved stories, both the telling and the listening, but for the present there was no time and he led Chalotte away from the market into less crowded streets. He took her past rows of shattered houses and dingy blocks of buildings where Bangladeshi families, half-hidden among the bright colours of the week's wash, stood on balconies to keep an eye on their children as they played in the glass-strewn streets. But the Borribles walked on across a derelict stretch of ground that had been bombed flat in the war and not built on since. Here people dumped their rubbish and here the weak sprouts of pale grass fought against the sun and died for lack of water.

On the far side of the bomb-site stood a straggle of terraced houses, leaning one against another as if tired of life and desiring demolition. They were gaunt and reared up against the semicircle of blue sky like an eroded cliff. They had boards nailed over their windows and sheets of corrugated iron over the doors. Their areas were half full of rubbish, their cellars smelt of cats, both alive and dead. The steps of the houses were covered with broken bricks and lumps of plaster; dangerous shards of shattered milk bottles glittered in the sun like silver. The place was a desert of dust and it smelt of excrement and trouble.

It was typical of a Borrible hideout. Borribles are obliged to live where they can and they prefer these abandoned and decaying buildings which are rarely, if ever, in short supply. If a house is already occupied they will sometimes use its cellar; they also camp overnight in schools, especially during the holidays when the buildings are left empty and unused for long periods.

In the middle of the bomb-site Twilight halted. 'I was out looking for you,' he said, 'because we found somebody who said she'd come to see you.'

'See me?'

'Yeah, we came across this girl wandering about on the other side of Spitalfields. White girl, come all the way across London, so she reckons. We checked her ears; she's Borrible all right. We brought her home and then went out to look for you.'

'What's her name?'

'Something funny,' said Twilight, 'but I've forgotten it, something like Harry or Charlie.'

Chalotte drew a breath. 'Was it Sydney?'

'That's it, rings a bell that does, ding-dong.'

'The Great Rumble Hunt,' said Chalotte, 'she was on it too, the Adventure to end all adventures.'

Twilight put a hand on Chalotte's shoulder. 'Let's go and see her then,' he said, and he led the way up the broken and littered stairs of his house.

The front door clanged open, swinging on a loose wooden frame. Inside, half submerged in a litter of bottles, sacks and tattered packages bound with hairy string, lay an old man. His face was unshaven and his shapeless mouth snored. Twilight stepped carefully round the unconscious form and guided Chalotte past a jagged hole in the floorboards.

'I can never understand how he don't fall into the cellar,' said the Bangladeshi, 'but he don't.'

'Who is he?'

'Some meffo,' said Twilight. 'He's harmless, apart from the smell that is.'

The bare wooden stairs were splintered and weak, slippery too with chunks of fallen plaster and slivers of broken windowpanes. At the very top of the house was a small landing with three doors leading from it. Twilight opened one and showed Chalotte into a boxroom which had a sack over the window. On the floor were three old mattresses, darkly stained. A few torn blankets had been thrown across them as well as some newspapers for undersheets and insulation. In a corner, sitting on one of the mattresses, her back against the wall, head in hands, elbows on knees, dressed in worn trousers and a green T-shirt with holes in it, sat Sydney, her eyes closed.

Chalotte crossed the room and crouched to the floor. 'Sydney,' she said. 'Sydney.'

Sydney's eyes flickered once or twice as she tried to come awake. She stared through a heavy glaze of weariness. Chalotte spoke again.

'You haven't walked all the way from Neasden, 'ave yer?'

Sydney yawned and rubbed her face. It was a kind face and Chalotte had always liked it. 'What's up, Sid?' she asked. 'You haven't hiked across London just to say hello, I'll be bound. What's up?'

Sydney looked at Twilight who leant against the door, listening. She hesitated.

'He's all right,' said Chalotte, 'you can speak free.'

'I had a strange message,' said Sydney, 'a Borrible message, passed from hand to hand, you know. I'd never seen the bloke who gave it me, ain't seen him since neither. He said it had come clear across London, but he didn't know where from. Then he ran off.' Sydney reached into a pocket and pulled out a ragged scrap of lined notepaper. She gave it to Chalotte who smoothed it out on her knee and read aloud.

' "Sam is still alive. Last seen in Fulham. Needs help. Signed, A Borrible." ' She whistled. 'Well that's good news . . .' She glanced into Sydney's face. 'Well, isn't it?'

'I dunno, it seems a bit mysterious to me. I'm not sure what to make of it.'

'Who's Sam?' said Twilight.

'Sam's a horse,' said Chalotte. 'He saved all our lives when we were in Rumbledom.'

Sydney shifted on the mattress and hoisted herself upright. 'The horse belonged to a Borrible-snatcher,' she explained. 'We had to kill the man before we could get away. I mean Knocker did.'

'Knocker and Adolf,' said Chalotte.

'We had to leave Sam when we went underground on our way home,' continued Sydney. 'I hated doing that, seeing how much we owed him, and I made a promise that if I ever got out of that Adventure alive I would go back to get him . . . And I meant it, but I've never known where he went or what happened to him. This is the first news I've had.'

'So?' said Chalotte.

'Well,' said the Neasden girl, 'I got this message about two weeks ago and I didn't know what to think . . . The best thing seemed to be to come and see you, so we could talk it over. I mean we owe it to Sam to see him all right if we can. Somebody might be working him to death.'

Chalotte stretched out on a mattress and was silent. What Sydney had said had brought the whole terrifying expedition back to her. What had started as a great Adventure to win names had turned sour and five Borribles had died. Borribles weren't supposed to die, but those five had. Knocker, whom Chalotte had especially liked; Orococco, the black boy from Tooting; Torreycanyon, the square-faced

Borrible from Hoxton, and most dangerous of all, the twice-turned traitor and Wendle warrior, Napoleon Boot. And there had been Adolf too, a four-named Borrible from Hamburg, burnt alive in the halls of Rumbledom. All of them dead. Chalotte sighed. The Great Rumble Hunt had been madness. Never again would she take part in such an expedition.

'I'm sorry about Sam,' she said at length, 'really sorry, but I tell you straight, I'm not marching all the way to Fulham and back on the strength of a dodgy note that's come out of the dark, not a chance.'

'Yes,' said Sydney, 'but I made a promise, a definite promise to Sam.'

Chalotte shrugged her shoulders and quoted from the *Borrible Book of Proverbs*. ' "To keep a bad promise does not make it good",' she said.

Sydney turned her head and stared at the floor. There was silence.

Twilight waited but the girls did not continue the conversation. He unfolded his arms and pushed himself away from the wall. 'Look,' he said, 'Sydney must be very tired, she ought to rest this afternoon, really, and while she's asleep I'll go back to the market with some of my mates. When she wakes up there'll be a feast ready for her.'

'And me too?' asked Chalotte.

'Of course,' said Twilight. 'I'm very good at stealing specialities.' He went to the window and raised the sacking to look out over a jumble of collapsing houses and sloping slate roofs. The whole vista trembled in a heat haze. 'I tell you one thing, Sydney,' he said. 'Chalotte may have had enough adventures, but I haven't. If you ever decide to go looking for your horse, I'll come with you.'

Sydney looked at Chalotte and smiled. 'Thank you, Twilight,' she said, and rolling a blanket to make a pillow she curled her body on the mattress and in a few seconds was fast asleep.

'And so,' said Chalotte, 'eight Borribles were chosen, the best runners and fighters and catapult artists in all London.'

Twilight ladled some curry into Chalotte's soup plate and she leant back against the wall. She and Sydney were sitting side by side on two metal milk crates. Twilight and six of his Bangladeshi friends squatted round a large black saucepan. They had come to eat and to hear the story of the Great Rumble Hunt.

Twilight had been as good as his word. While Sydney had slept and Chalotte had waited he had revisited the market. In less than an hour he'd returned with everything he needed to prepare a rich and highly flavoured curry. Cooking it had been no problem; most Borribles are good electrical engineers and Twilight was no exception. In the damp basement of his house was an old electric stove and the Bangladeshis had long ago mended it and tapped into the nearest supply to provide themselves with power. They had all the electricity they wanted.

'Where did they come from,' said Twilight, his mouth crammed, 'these eight Borribles?'

'From all over,' Chalotte went on. She talked slowly, between spoonfuls. The curry was hot; her eyebrows perspired, her forehead shone. Sydney was so busy eating that she hardly bothered to join in the story telling, but she nodded vigorously every now and then.

'There was a Humper from Hoxton, a Totter from Tooting; Sydney is a Nudger from Neasden, there was me and there was a Wendle from Wandsworth. They live underground they do, vicious and sly Wendles are.'

'I've heard about them,' said Twilight, 'never seen one.'

'You ain't missed much,' said Chalotte. 'Anyway, we all met up in Battersea and Knocker trained us. He came along in the end although he shouldn't have done because he had already earned his name, which we hadn't. Spiff wangled that . . . he's double crafty is Spiff.'

Sydney moved her head up and down as fast as she could.

'Spiff?' said Twilight.

'Yeah,' said Chalotte, 'Spiff. A Battersea Borrible and sharp enough to cut yer nails with. I don't like him. Anyway, we nicked a boat and went up the River Thames in it . . . Then we went underground with the Wendles, they're greeny-faced and not a bit friendly. The one we had with us, Napoleon Boot, well we didn't know if we could trust him or not, so we didn't. Later on, when we came out on the other side of Wendle territory we were captured by a Borrible-snatcher and his son. Diabolical that was, he starved us and made us steal for money. We only escaped by killing him. We we left we took Dewdrop's horse and cart, that's how we took Sam to Rumbledom and lucky we did too. There was a terrific battle at the end and we were surrounded by hundreds of Rumbles and we would have died for certain but Sam saved us. Rumbles can't stand horses, you see, horses eat Rumbles, find 'em tasty, reminds 'em of hay and that. But Adolf was killed there; it was a mess all right with Rumbles shouting and waving their spears. We were all wounded and this big entrance came crashing down and Adolf couldn't get out of the way. Great bloke he was . . . We never saw him again, dead, incinerated. Orococco was on fire and Knocker had deep burns across the palms of his hands.'

'That's his second name,' added Sydney, 'Burnthand.'

Chalotte went on. 'We got away and you might have thought that was the end of it, but it wasn't. We were in bad shape and Sam took us down to Wandsworth but Napoleon and Knocker quarrelled and we were betrayed by Napoleon and the Wendles locked us up. They have a leader, not like ordinary Borribles, called Flinthead, greedy and hard. He's the worst Wendle of all the Wendles, and that's saying something. He would have killed us for sure if Napoleon hadn't changed his mind and helped us escape. But we didn't get off lightly, I can tell you. Four of us didn't come back—Knocker, Napoleon Boot, Orococco and Torreycanyon. They stayed behind to guard a tunnel so that we could have time to get away. We never saw them again either, slaughtered by Flinthead they were. You know, I've never wanted to kill anyone but I would him. So only five of us survived to tell the tale: Sydney and me, Bingo from Battersea, Stonks from Peckham and Vulge from just down the road here in Stepney. Afterwards, Borribles called it the Adventure to end all Adventures but I call it madness. We lost five good friends, if you count Napoleon, and nothing's worth that, not the greatest Adventure in the world, not even the best name you could ever earn.'

'I like your story,' said Twilight. 'I have never heard the truth of it before but the rumours say something else, something about a great treasure, a box of Rumble money.'

Chalotte spooned some more curry into her plate and put the lid back on the black saucepan, then she looked at Twilight and her eyes narrowed to a thin line of hardness.

'That was the cause of all the trouble,' she said. 'If it hadn't been for the treasure Adolf wouldn't have been killed, Napoleon wouldn't have betrayed us and Flinthead would have let us pass through the underground citadel of the Wendles without bothering us one bit. Without the money no one would have died, except Rumbles.'

'So Flinthead got the treasure,' said Twilight.

'No, he didn't,' said Sydney. She finished eating and put the empty dish down beside the saucepan.

Chalotte allowed herself an ironic smile. 'We were taking it out in the boat. How we agreed to take the money I don't know; we wanted to get our own back on Flinthead, I suppose. We were crossing the great mudflats of the River Wandle, just after it goes underground. Hundreds of Wendle warriors came at us, frightening they are, carrying Rumble-sticks, catapults, dressed in rubber waders and little orange jackets they nick off the roadmen; they got the treasure away from us. Stonks, the strongest Borrible I've ever seen, he got it back, but in the struggle the box slipped overboard and the money went down into the mud, a quarter of a mile deep it is there, so they say; not even Flinthead can get it out now. The mud is the best place for it, too. Borribles shouldn't have money, they never have had.' Chalotte looked up and quoted her favourite proverb, ' "Fruit of the barrow is enough for a Borrible." '

Twilight wiped his mouth with the back of his hand. 'This Vulge,' he said, 'he's a survivor, according to you, and he lives in Stepney. Well, that's not far. Why don't we go and see him tomorrow? You could ask him what he thinks about the horse, about the message.'

Chalotte was silent but Sydney looked her straight in the eye. 'I'd be willing to do that, and anyway it'd be nice to see him again. He was badly wounded in the leg, limps now.'

'What's he like?' asked Twilight.

Sydney laughed. 'Vulge is a bit special. He's small, mousy hair, got a pointed chin; he wags his head sideways, like he knows everything. He looks like he wouldn't say boo to a goose, but he's as tough as nails and never gives in. It was Vulge who killed the Rumble chieftain in his bath . . . and a score or two more. Oh yes, you'll like Vulge.'

2

The next day was just as hot, and the heatwave, which had begun two months earlier in the middle of May, showed no signs of breaking. Twilight woke the two girls early and as they sat up he gave them an orange each.

'Eat these,' he said, 'they're lovely.'

That was breakfast and ten minutes later the three Borribles left the house and made their way towards Whitechapel where they discovered the main road full of the din and uproar of a Monday morning rush hour. Pedestrians hastened along the pavements, running towards work with faces anxious and miserable, as if they had been unhappy and insecure away from their offices and workshops. The tramp of their feet was heavy, raising the dust, and although it was not yet nine o'clock, the sun beat down on the grey macadam of the road and melted it. Each car tyre that passed sounded like a zip unzipping.

Chalotte glanced to right and left, on the lookout for policemen. She saw none. 'Vulge lives down on the Limehouse Fields Estate,' she said, 'I don't know where exactly.'

'It's round the back of the canal,' said Twilight. 'The best thing we can do is go along that way and ask a Borrible.'

They crossed the main road, dodging the traffic, and went away from the noise and exhaust fumes into Fieldgate Street and on down Stepney Way. After walking for a quarter of an hour they came to a large housing estate built in brick of brown and black. Scores of children were already out in the courtyard, loafing in the shade, imprisoned by the rising heat.

'I like the school holidays,' said Sydney, 'there's so many normal kids about the Woollies haven't a chance of spotting us.'

'Don't be so sure,' answered Twilight. He went into the yard of the estate and the girls followed. 'There's got to be a Borrible hiding among all this lot,' he said. 'What about that one in the corner, sitting on the bottom step?'

Chalotte and Sydney looked. The boy on the bottom step was wearing half a mauve stocking on his head, well down over his ears.

'Got to be,' said Sydney, 'no one but a Borrible would wear a hat like that on a day like this.'

'Let's see,' said Twilight, 'but take it easy or he'll run off.'

They crossed the yard and above them faces peered over the balcony walls and someone spat, but the aim was bad and no one was hit. Chalotte saw the gob explode on the ground and without looking upwards she raised two fingers in the air.

The gesture attracted the attention of the mauve-hatted Borrible, who reached behind and pulled a catapult from his back pocket. Borribles are never friendly straight off, even with their own kind. They quarrel frequently, often they fight and they never trust strangers. Quickly and calmly the Borrible loaded a stone, then he gave a piercing whistle between his teeth and the head and hands of a colleague appeared on the first balcony. He too held a catapult.

A yard or two away from the steps Twilight stopped and, his movements deliberate, showed his own catapult and then returned it to his pocket.

What Twilight had done was important. The catapult is the Borribles' traditional weapon and they have used it for generations because of its simplicity and deadliness. It can be made anywhere, and long ago in the nineteenth century, when Borribles endured great hardships, it had become their favourite method of defence. By showing his catapult Twilight had indicated that he was a Borrible and by putting it away he had made it obvious that he came in peace.

'I'm Borrible,' said Twilight, 'and me and these two are looking for a Borrible called Vulge; he lives round here. These girls were on the Great Rumble Hunt with him.'

The Stepney Borrible put his catapult away. He waved a hand and his friend on the balcony disappeared. 'Show us an ear,' he said.

Chalotte lifted her long hair slightly. The Borrible nodded, satisfied.

'Great Rumble Hunt, those two? Don't look as if they could cross the road on their own. Still I'll take your word for it, thousands wouldn't . . . Tell me what Vulge looks like, if you're a friend of his.'

Chalotte described him as Sydney had. 'And he's got a limp now,' she added, 'where he was wounded in Rumbledom.'

The Stepney Borrible nodded. 'All right, go round the back of here, over Halley Street, up by the canal towards Oceans Estate, and opposite the recreation ground you'll see some abandoned houses. The third one down is the one you want . . . I dunno, girls.'

Chalotte glared at him. 'I could take your ear off with my catapult from a hundred yards,' she said.

'And I could put a stone up your nostril from the same distance,' said Sydney.

The Stepney Borrible laughed, a cold sound in the baking square of the black courtyard. 'I heard the story from Vulge,' he said. 'You must be the one who drowned the Rumble in the soup.'

'That's right,' said Chalotte, 'I did.'

'Well it's hard to believe and you can tell Vulge so when you see him.'

'What's your name, then?' asked Twilight.

'Hatrack,' said the Borrible, 'what's your'n?'

'Twilight,' said Twilight.

'Bleedin'-well suits yer,' said Hatrack. It was obvious that he did not like Bangladeshis and he said no more. Twilight forced himself to make a compliment.

'Hatrack is a good name,' he said. 'I would like to hear the story of it, one day.' And then he turned and walked out of the estate with Chalotte and Sydney beside him.

They soon found Vulge's house and, making sure they were unobserved, the three Borribles slipped along an alley to the back of the building. There was no sound and the terrace seemed deserted;

there was no glass in the windows either and not a door standing. The rubbish from the streets had drifted high into the houses and for the most part the ceilings had collapsed as well; debris was ankle deep and everything smelt of decay.

'I'll go first,' said Chalotte. Cautiously she led the others up a flight of stairs, stairs which shifted a little under the weight of three people. As she went Chalotte whistled, hoping that Vulge, if he was there, would recognize the sound as the signal they had used on the Great Rumble Hunt.

She stopped. Somewhere above them a door opened and a voice said, 'Clear off, you're in the wrong house.'

Chalotte glanced upwards but could see no one.

'I've come to see Vulge,' she said, 'it's Chalotte and Sydney.'

'Well I'll be clipped,' said Vulge, as he moved into view on the landing above. 'Get on up here and let's have a look at yer.'

The two girls ran up the remaining stairs and threw their arms round Vulge's shoulders.

'Gerroff,' he said. 'Come in my room 'ere, and have a cuppa, bring that friend of yours too, if he is a friend.'

In his room Vulge sat everyone down and brought out a teapot and a packet of tea. Then he switched on an electric kettle. 'I always keep it full,' he explained, 'I drinks a lot of tea.'

Chalotte looked round the room. It was like most other Borrible rooms she'd seen, including her own. The window was covered with an old blanket, there was one bare electric light bulb, a mattress, a few orange boxes for cupboards and a couple of small barrels, upended, to sit on.

Vulge squatted by the kettle and waited for it to boil.

'This is Twilight,' said Sydney.

'A good name,' said Vulge.

'If it hadn't been for Twilight,' explained Chalotte, 'I'd 'ave been clipped by now.' She told the story of her rescue and Sydney's arrival.

Vulge squinted at the Bangladeshi. 'Anyone who saves a friend of mine is a friend of mine,' he said. Then the kettle boiled and he made the tea, pouring it, when ready, into four jam jars, stirring in the sugar with a knife. He limped across the room to distribute them.

'How's the leg?' asked Chalotte.

'Better than nothing,' said Vulge, and he touched the old wound and grinned. 'I don't have too much trouble getting about. I can still run though I looks like a three-legged dog when I do. Still, I stays out of bother. I don't want no more adventures, that Rumble hunt was enough.' Vulge suddenly screwed up his face and a look of suspicion came into his eyes. 'You're a long way from home, Sydney, what you up to?'

'Tell him,' said Chalotte.

Sydney took the scrap of paper from her pocket and handed it to Vulge. 'What do you think of that?' she asked.

Vulge read the message aloud. ' "Sam is still alive. Last seen in Fulham. Needs help. Signed, A Borrible." ' He handed the paper back and was silent for a moment or two. His face darkened. 'It could be a trap,' he said at last.

'A trap!' said Sydney.

Vulge took a slurp from his jam jar. 'Have you heard of the SBG yet,' he said, 'and Inspector Sussworth?'

Chalotte nodded. 'The Woollie who caught me yesterday said something about him. They're trying to catch all of us.'

'They always are,' said Twilight.

'Yes,' said Vulge, 'but this is different. The law got very upset when they found Dewdrop and Erbie, especially when they found 'em dead. They got this Sussworth to form the Special Borrible Group, mainly to find out who killed Dewdrop but also to catch as many Borribles as they could, clip their ears and turn them back into normal kids. They know all about us, got a book of our proverbs, captured a few Borribles and made them talk. They drive about London all the time, day and night, in blue Transit vans with dark windows. If they see a catapult or a woollen hat or a kid near a house like this one, they're out of their van in a second and it's down the nick and never seen again.'

'We know all that,' said Sydney. 'What's that got to do with this note?'

'Like so,' said Vulge. 'If this Sussworth knows about Dewdrop and Erbie then the chances are he knows about the battle of Rumbledom. He might even know that Sam helped us, so all he has to do is drop a few notes like this one about and, if he knows how Borrible messages are passed from hand to hand, then he knows a message like this stands a fair chance of getting to someone who'd actually been on the Rumble hunt. Now if that person were daft enough to go looking for Sam in Fulham, and if Sussworth caught that person, then the SBG would be pretty sure they'd caught someone who'd had something to do with the Southfields murders, wouldn't they?' And Vulge leant back, wagged his head and supped his tea with the air of a Borrible who could read the mind of a policeman from a distance of half a hemisphere.

Sydney's face creased with disappointment and Chalotte felt sad for her. She knew how much Sam the horse meant to the girl from Neasden.

'I hadn't thought of it like that,' said Sydney. 'But it doesn't *have* to be a trap, does it? I mean Borrible messages do cross London this way; it could have come from a Fulham Borrible who'd seen Sam and knew the story. It could be like that, couldn't it?'

'True,' said Vulge, 'but whoever goes looking for Sam better take a telescope with him because there'll be a copper hiding underneath his tail.'

'I would go with her,' said Twilight. 'I am not frightened.'

Vulge turned on his barrel and smiled. His flat brown hair and his pointed chin gave his face a mischievous look. 'It's not a question of being frightened, it's a question of not getting your ears clipped, of survival, like it always is. If you'd seen half of what we saw on the Rumble hunt you'd be quite happy to stay near your market, live in your house and keep away from the Woollies.'

'But that's just it,' said Twilight raising his shoulders, 'I haven't seen half of what you've seen, and I won't unless I do something.'

'What I feel,' said Sydney, 'is that we owe our lives to Sam. I made a promise to go back for him, I've never forgotten that promise and since I got this note I can't stop worrying about it.'

'Well you're not the only one to have thought about Sam,' said Vulge. 'I have too and I daresay the others have. I felt rotten leaving him there on the banks of the Wandle, but travel is dangerous these days and getting more and more dangerous all the time. We shouldn't go charging about London, getting ourselves caught by the SBG. Sam himself wouldn't want that.'

Sydney stared at the piece of paper in her hand. She wanted to believe in it so much and now Vulge had undermined her confidence. 'Well,' she said, 'I know Chalotte doesn't want to come, but I suppose Twilight and me could go, just to have a look I mean.'

Vulge shook his head. 'I don't want to win any more names; I'm not ambitious like Knocker was. He wanted to win more glory than any other Borrible, and where is he now, dead and deep in Wandle mud. How does the proverb go . . . "One good name is enough if the name is good enough"? Well, my name is.'

No one spoke for a long while after that, they concentrated instead on finishing their tea. Vulge even rose from his seat and made some more, and all the while his guests remained silent. Sydney continued to stare at the message and Chalotte could think of nothing to say that might cheer her friend. Twilight kept his own counsel because it was not his business; it was a matter for three old friends, veterans of a wild and perilous experience that he had not shared.

Ten minutes went by. Chalotte could see that Vulge was thinking intently, resting his top teeth on the edge of his jam jar of tea. At last he got to his feet, limped over to an orange box, took out some apples and handed them round.

'This is my idea,' he began. 'It's the school holidays now, safer for us to travel. I'm not in favour of doing anything dangerous, but what we could do is get the other survivors together, there's only Stonksie in Peckham and Bingo in Battersea, then we could all talk about it. We'll find someone who's going Peckham way and send a note to Stonks and get him to meet us at Bingo's house. On our way to Battersea we'll ask any Borrible we see if they've come across any messages about Sam. If they haven't then the message is likely to be genuine, if they've seen a few then it's probably a trap. That way we don't make any decisions about going to Fulham until we've heard what everyone has to say. How's that strike yer, Sydney, is that better?'

Sydney looked up and smiled, her eyes brightened. 'Oh Vulge,' she said, 'that's marvellous, bloody marvellous.'

The four Borribles meant to waste no time and decided to set out the following morning. A message was despatched to Peckham via the Borrible network and Twilight volunteered to make himself responsible for gathering the supplies they would need on the long walk to Battersea. He left Vulge's house that afternoon and promised to return by nightfall.

Vulge checked over his catapult. He also gave Chalotte a spare to replace the one she had lost when captured by the policeman. Later on that day he disappeared for an hour or so, 'To get some good stones,' he said.

That night all four of them slept in Vulge's house and at first light they rose and made a good breakfast.

'We'll get on the streets as soon as it's rush hour,' said Vulge. 'That way we won't be so noticeable. Remember, the slightest sign of trouble and we run. If we get separated we all meet at Bingo's house.'

'This is great,' said Twilight. 'Do you know I've never been out of the East End, let alone across the river.'

'Well,' said Chalotte, 'let's hope it turns out to be just a walk we're going on and nothing more.'

As it happened the walk was a good one. The route lay all along the side of the River Thames and the water glinted and gleamed in the July sunshine. Tugs and barges steamed by on the tide; seagulls swooped down the winding currents of warm air and their long wailing cries made the Embankment sound as exotic as a treasure island. Buses and cars shone and stewed in the heat and the blue smoke of their exhausts floated in a pale stream a yard or so above the bubbling tar of the road surface.

This was central London in summer, and so content were the four Borribles to be a part of their city that they began to sing quietly to themselves as they advanced along the hot pavements, singing a song that told of their way of life and the joy they had in it; one of the most famous Borrible songs ever written:

> *'Who'd be a hurrying, scurrying slave,*
>   *Off to an office, or bound for a bank;*
> *Who'd be a servant from cradle to grave,*
>   *Counting his wages and trying to save;*
> *Who'd be a manager, full of his rank,*
>   *Or the head of the board at a big corporation?*
> *Ask us the question, we'll tell you to stuff it;*
> *Good steady jobs would make all of us snuff it—*
>   *Freedom's a Borrible's one occupation!*
>
> *'Our kind of liberty's fit for a king;*
>   *London's our palace, we reign there supreme.*
> *Broad way and narrow way, what shall we sing—*
>   *Alleys as tangled as knotted-up string,*
> *River that winds through the smoke like a dream—*
>   *What shall we sing in our own celebration?*
> *Ragged-arsed renegades, never respectable,*
> *Under your noses, but rarely detectable—*
>   *Freedom's a Borrible's one occupation!'*

And so they marched along the north bank until they reached Albert Bridge; there they crossed. Once over the water they turned right and went past the bus garages, then into Church Road where a great change awaited them. The high black walls of Morgan's Crucible Works, the tall chimneys that had always stood against the clouds, the acres of sooty windows, had all gone. The factory had been demolished.

'Well, look at that,' said Chalotte, 'ain't it strange?'

They went on, halting for a second by St Mary's church and the Old Swan pub.

'This is where we landed after our escape from the Wendles,' said Sydney, 'and we went into some Borrible houses opposite. They've knocked them down too, everything's going.'

At last they came to their destination, turning into the bottom of Battersea High Street and heading towards the market . . . But they did not go unobserved. As they passed the corner of Granfield Street a Borrible, wearing an old Sinjen's School blazer and tattered grey trousers, stepped in front of them and said, 'What are you lot doing here?'

It was Lightfinger, Knocker's friend, and Chalotte recognized him.

'We're Borrible, you know,' she said. 'Three of us were on the Rumble Hunt.'

Lightfinger was not impressed. 'So what?' he said. 'I still want to know what you are doing here; this ain't your manor.'

'Don't give us any bother,' said Vulge. 'We've come to see Bingo, not you. Why don't you get out of our way?'

Lightfinger took a step towards Vulge. 'Long as you haven't come to start some dopey adventure like the last one. Where's Knocker now eh, where's my friend? Dead, ain't he?' Lightfinger clenched his fists and squared his shoulders, ready to take them all on, one against four.

'Oh, don't be daft,' said Chalotte. 'We've come for a chat with Bingo, that's all.'

'I'll tell him,' said Lightfinger. 'As for you lot, you'd better go and see Spiff.' With that he spun on his heel and ran off. The four travellers watched him go.

'Friendly little feller, ain't he?' said Twilight. 'Hides it well.'

'He liked Knocker,' said Chalotte, 'so he can't be too bad. Perhaps he hates us because we came back and Knocker didn't.'

'What about Spiff?' Sydney wanted to know. 'It's funny but not one of us had thought about going to see him, had we?'

'What's he got to do with it?' asked Twilight.

'He has the Borrible house where Knocker used to live,' explained Chalotte. 'It was him really who talked everyone into going on the Rumble Hunt. It was him who gave Knocker the secret job of getting the Rumble treasure and bringing it back. If you ask me the money was all he was interested in.'

'We don't know that,' said Vulge, wagging his head.

'No, we don't,' agreed Chalotte, 'but I reckon that Spiff's so crooked you could use him to unblock a sink. Still, if we don't want trouble I suppose we'd better tell him we're here.'

Spiff's house stood halfway up the High Street. It was tall, wide and derelict, all its windows boarded and a heavy sheet of corrugated iron over the main doorway. The front of the building was painted in grimy grey and in black letters along the front was written, 'Bunham's Patent Locks Ltd. Locksmiths to the trade.'

The four Borribles loitered outside for a while and waited until their stretch of street was empty of pedestrians; no Borrible likes to be seen entering an abandoned house. When the coast was clear they went down steep steps into a basement area where they found an open door through which they entered a room that was damp and green and devoid of furniture. Plaster in large quantities had fallen from the ceiling and lay everywhere in lumps.

Vulge looked at the walls and sniffed. 'We left from here,' he said to Twilight, 'this very room, eight of us; Spiff lives upstairs, come on.'

On the first landing Vulge stopped at a paintless door and gave the Borrible knock: one long, two short, one long. The door opened immediately and Lightfinger appeared. He jerked a thumb over his shoulder as he pushed past.

'He knows you're 'ere,' he said, 'I told him.' Levering his shoulders backwards and forwards as he walked he went down the stairs.

'He's not so bad as he seems,' said a voice. Spiff stood in the doorway.

Chalotte regarded him closely. The little bugger hasn't changed a bit, she said to herself, not a bit. It was his face she remembered: clear and bright like a twelve-year-old's, with eyes that always shone, dark with a fire of deep cunning, a craftiness that might have been ages old. He wore the same orange dressing gown and the same red hat of knitted wool.

'You'd better come in, all of yer,' he said, beckoning them across his threshold.

Inside the room Spiff lowered himself into his old armchair. In spite of the summer's heat his paraffin stove was burning low, and bubbling on top was a large brown enamel teapot. Spiff set four cups on an orange box and poured out a liquid that tasted like gun-powder and needed spoonfuls of sugar to make it drinkable.

'Well, well,' he said after the first sip, 'it really is nice of you to come all this way to say hello. Sydney, Vulge and Chalotte, isn't it? Must be six or seven months since I saw you. Who's this black lad? Don't know him, do I?'

'My name's Twilight,' said the Bangladeshi with some pride.

'That is an unusual name,' said Spiff. 'I hope that while you are here you will find time to tell me your story.'

Spiff then suggested that the four Borribles should take their cups and sit on the barrels arranged along one wall of his room. They did as they were asked and relaxed and drank and perspired in the overheated atmosphere, though they said nothing. This silence was embarrassing and Chalotte wondered if Spiff had been nudged off balance by their arrival. It was always difficult to assess his reactions exactly. There were great echoing corridors of artfulness in that small hard skull.

'Lightfinger said you'd come to see Bingo,' he said eventually across the top of his teacup. The steam strayed upwards over his face and dimmed the light of his eyes. He waited and smiled as if suspecting his guests of knowing something he didn't want them to know and yet wishing, without giving anything away himself, to discover the full extent of their knowledge.

Sydney looked at her three companions, wiped some sweat from her eyebrows, coughed and said, 'We . . . that is me . . . I went to see Chalotte because I was worried about Sam.'

'Sam?' said Spiff, and his brow furrowed as if he didn't know the name. Chalotte tightened her mouth in scorn. She was certain that Spiff remembered every detail of the Rumble expedition and, what was more, spent a great deal of his time thinking about the Rumble Hunt, what had happened on it and what might still happen because of it.

'Sam,' she said, allowing the sarcasm to show, 'was the horse.'

'Oh yes,' said Spiff, 'the horse, of course.' He smiled at the rhyme.

'Well,' continued Sydney, 'I made him a promise that I'd go back for him . . . then the other day I received this.' Sydney handed the message to Spiff, who read it very carefully, examining the piece of paper on both sides.

'Mmm,' he said when his perusal was concluded. 'Fulham; are you going to go?'

Vulge leant forward and settled his elbows on his knees, holding his cup between clasped hands. 'The point is, Spiff, I think the message is a come-on, I think it might be something set up by the SBG.'

Spiff looked at the note again. 'That's a thought,' he said. 'Those Woollies of Sussworth's have become a real pain. I've had this house searched twice, only just got away the second time. We've got Borribles watching each end of the street now. As soon as one of those blue vans arrives, matey, we're off.'

Vulge nodded. 'It would have been dead easy, you know, for the SBG to send that note . . . though I must admit we spoke to a lot of Borribles on the way down here and none of them had seen a message about Sam, so I daresay it's straight. On the other hand, if we do decide it's a trap then we ought to forget about the horse altogether.'

'I should cocoa,' said Spiff. If he had been nervous earlier he was now visibly relaxing. 'What do you think, Chalotte?'

'I don't think anything. I came along for the walk and to see Bingo and Stonks. Sydney made a promise but I didn't.' She shrugged her shoulders.

Twilight interrupted. 'I would go to Fulham like a shot.'

Spiff laughed. 'He's like Knocker, he is.'

'Yeah,' said Chalotte, 'and Knocker's dead and that was your fault. You're so crafty you don't know whether you've been or gone. I say that to your face.'

Spiff's expression darkened. 'I only wanted to share the money out.'

'Borribles should stay away from money,' said Vulge.

Spiff grimaced. 'Well, money certainly stays away from Borribles.' He looked straight into Chalotte's eyes. 'You never liked me, Chalotte, even before Knocker died, but you can't deny that we haven't had a peep out of the Rumbles since we attacked them, not a peep.'

'That's right,' said Chalotte, 'now we've got the SBG instead.'

'The world don't do us no favours,' said Spiff, and then he quoted from the *Borrible Book of Proverbs*. ' "The only gift given to a Borrible is the one he takes." ' He studied his visitors for a moment. 'What are you going to do?'

'Talk it over with Bingo,' said Vulge, 'and Stonks.'

'Fine,' said Spiff. 'I think you ought to find out where the horse is. If it really is in Fulham and you come to the conclusion that it isn't a trap then we could just wander over there and take a look.'

'We?' exclaimed Sydney.

'Yes, why not me as well? I haven't been on a trip for ages. Don't want to sit here all the time. Besides, it would do me good to get out.'

Sydney and the three others stared at each other. This was a turn of events that flabbergasted them completely. They had never known Spiff leave his room for any length of time.

'I wouldn't walk down the street with you,' said Chalotte.

Spiff raised his eyebrows. 'It doesn't matter, you said you wouldn't be going anyway. Sydney, Twilight and me could manage on our own, even if Bingo and Stonks don't want to come.'

'Wait a minute,' said Vulge, reddening. 'I wouldn't be against going as long as I felt sure that it wasn't an SBG set-up.'

Spiff leant forward. 'It's no good us deciding anything till we get more information. I've got a few friends in Fulham; I'll try to find out if there's any truth in the message.'

Chalotte banged her empty cup on the floor. 'Have you ever had any news out of Wendle country?' she asked.

A gleam of hatred glowed at the back of Spiff's eyes. 'Nah,' he said, 'only rumours, but then not much news comes out of Wendle country at the best of times.'

Chalotte pointed a finger at him. 'You don't even care what happened to Knocker,' she said.

Spiff poured himself another cup of tea. 'I've been a Borrible for years,' he said, 'more years than the rest of you put together. You just watch your lip, Chalotte, or I'll thump you into the middle of next week.'

'Not while I'm here,' said Vulge quietly.

'Nor me,' said Sydney.

'Or even me,' added Twilight.

Spiff raised his cup and bent his head in mockery. 'All right,' he said. 'The top room is empty. There's the market every day of the week; help yourselves, just stay out of trouble and don't upset any Battersea Borribles while you're here.'

'Thanks very much,' said Chalotte, and she went quickly from the room. The others filed after her, only Vulge stopped on the way out.

'Go easy on Chalotte,' he said. 'It upsets her when she remembers the Adventure, Knocker and all that. She thinks it's not right for Borribles to go looking for trouble.'

Spiff smiled his craftiest smile. 'Who has to look for trouble?' he said. 'Trouble knows its way to everyone's house, the trick is to be out when it gets there.' And he threw back his head and his smile broke into pieces and became harsh laughter. Vulge said no more but turned and went away, closing the door quietly behind him before following his friends upstairs.

Upstairs was Bingo. 'I saw old misery-guts Lightfinger in the market,' he said, and clapped Vulge on the back. 'Hello, you old cripple, how's the limping, getting better?'

Bingo was slightly built, even for a Borrible. He was about the same size as Twilight but thinner. His skin looked healthy and he had blue eyes that moved all the time though never furtively. His hair was dark and tightly curled, like wire wool. When he talked he smiled; it took a lot of trouble to get him down.

'The limping's very good,' said Vulge, and pushed his mate gently in the face with the palm of his hand.

'Who's the spade?' asked Bingo.

'My name's Twilight,' said the Bangladeshi, drawing himself up to his full height and looking Bingo straight in the eye.

Bingo shouted in delight, 'Twilight is a great and magnificent name. O Borrible from beyond the water, tell me its story.'

'Beyond the water,' said Twilight, becoming angry, 'don't be bloody stupid, this is the first time I've been out of Whitechapel.'

Bingo winked. 'Ah, but you had to cross the river to get here, didn't you?'

'He's having you on, Twilight,' said Chalotte. 'Leave him alone, Bingo. Twilight saved me from a Woollie the other day.'

Bingo went serious for a second. 'Anyone who saves my friend,' he said, 'is my friend,' and he slapped Twilight on the shoulder.

The Bangladeshi was so pleased with this reception that a lump rose in his throat. He found no words to say but just nodded and smiled.

'At any rate,' Bingo continued, 'I won't have you all staying here, it's rotten. I have an empty cellar next door to a supermarket on Lavender Hill. I took a few bricks out of the wall so food is no longer a problem. I offer you a feast and there are mattresses galore. How about it?'

The decision was easily made and the five Borribles clattered down the wooden stairs, halting just for a moment on the ground floor so that Vulge could tell Spiff where they were going and also to leave a message for Stonks.

'All right,' said Spiff, 'I'll tell him and if I hear anything about the horse I'll send a runner. Be careful now, and don't get caught.'

'No,' said Vulge, 'we won't,' and he limped away.

The period of waiting passed enjoyably. As Bingo had promised there was a ready supply of food in his cellar and most days the five Borribles wandered together round the busy streets of Clapham Junction, talking to other Borribles and joining in the games of ordinary children. Twilight told the story of his name and in return Bingo gave him yet another version of the Great Rumble Hunt, telling of his fight in the library against the best warrior of Rumbledom, a fight to the death with the Rumble-stick, and he told how Napoleon Boot had killed scores of Rumbles and had set fire to the great library.

'That Napoleon Boot,' said Bingo, shaking his head as if he couldn't believe that he had met such a person, 'what a scrapper he was, loved it, he did. I know it was him got us into a mess with the Wendles but I liked him, and you have to remember that it was him that got us out of it in the end. No one else could have, not even Knocker . . . and nobody else could have tricked Flint-head.'

'What was he like, Flinthead?'

'The chief of the Wendles! He's the toughest, coldest, nastiest, cruellest Borrible git in creation,' said Bingo. 'If you ever have the bad luck to meet him, turn and run like hell. Don't try to be brave or anything stupid like that, just run. Flinthead is the kind of person that likes sticking pins in worms and watching 'em wriggle.'

Early one morning, after a week of idling and talking, a message, scrawled on a piece of paper, arrived from Spiff. 'Stonks is here,' it read. That was sufficient, Spiff knew, to get the five Borribles down to Battersea High Street in a hurry, and he was right. They left Lavender Hill at a trot and kept it up all the way. They found Stonks waiting for them at the top end of the market, leaning against a traffic light.

Stonks was big for a Borrible, strong-looking with dark heavy eyebrows and a red face which was slow to register his feelings. Stonks never minced his words; he wasn't witty but he was dogged, persistent and dependable. A good friend to have beside you when things turned nasty.

'I've been waiting ages for you bunch of layabouts,' he said, and although he tried to look stern, pleasure forced its way into his expression. 'It's miles from here to Peckham.'

'Shuddup,' said Bingo, 'or I'll let Chalotte push yer face in.'

When these greetings had been exchanged the six friends passed into the market, took some food as they went, and continued along the High Street until they reached an open area of dusty ground between the railway embankment and a scrapyard where the wrecked bodies of old cars were piled four or five high, slung precariously one on top of another. There the Borribles sat themselves down on the stony dirt in the shade of a plank fence, the hot sky stretched tightly above them. Every ten minutes or so a dark blue electric train rattled by, the noise turning hollow as the wheels clanked over Battersea railway bridge. The Borribles were safe in that spot and they liked it. They ate the fruit they'd stolen and they talked.

'I don't give a monkey's about the SBG,' said Stonks. 'I mean they don't know we're worried about Sam, or that Sydney made a

promise. I think we owe that horse at least a try at finding him . . .
I've always felt rotten about leaving him behind.'

'That makes four of us,' said Twilight, 'me, Sydney, Bingo and
now Stonks.'

'Five, if you count Spiff,' said Chalotte.

At that moment the conversation was interrupted by a scrab-
bling sound and Spiff himself sprang through a hole in the fence.
No longer the tea-swilling Borrible wrapped in an orange dressing gown, but dressed for the road, he looked hard and ready for
anything.

'Don't see you out often,' said Bingo.

'I'm out now,' answered Spiff, and he pushed into the group,
squatted down and, without any preamble, began to talk, as if continuing the discussion of a week earlier.

'I just heard from a Borrible along York Road; he told me that
when Dewdrop was killed there was a bit in the paper about it . . .
how the Woollies found all the stolen gear in the house and how
they think Borribles did the stealing and then killed Dewdrop in a
quarrel over the sharing out. This newspaper also said how the
horse was found, cut and bleeding, in King George's Park. It was
recognized as belonging to Dewdrop but nobody claimed it. It
seems that Dewdrop didn't have any relations except his son and
he wasn't much use, seeing as he was dead too, so the horse was
given to the RSPCA.'

'That was six months ago,' said Sydney. 'Where's the horse
now, I wonder?'

'Well,' said Spiff, 'I looked in a phone book and the RSPCA
have got an office in Battersea Bridge Road, by the traffic lights.
What I reckon is that a couple of you ought to go down there and
say you're distant relatives of Dewdrop. You know, kid them
you've just heard about the horse and would like to see it, make
sure it's all right. Bingo's good at that kind of thing, with that in-
nocent face of his.'

Bingo, lying full length on his stomach, scratched a pattern in
the dirt. 'I wouldn't mind a little run down the road,' he said. 'I
could be there and back in half an hour.'

'I'll come with yer, if yer like,' said Stonks.

'And me,' added Twilight.

'OK,' agreed Bingo, 'the rest of you can wait here.' He pushed himself to his feet and Stonks and Twilight did the same.

'You be careful,' said Chalotte, 'we don't want any complications.'

'Don't worry,' said Twilight, 'I move very fast; they call me the black mamba of Whitechapel Road, you know.'

Battersea Bridge Road was scorching underfoot, wide and cluttered with hot traffic. The heatwave hung over the city like blue enamel and breathing was like drowning in warm water.

'Strewth,' said Twilight, 'I'm glad I don't live in one of those tropical places abroad.' He backhanded the sweat out of his eyes.

Stonks gazed into the distance. 'You can bet your life,' he said, 'that if you want a number in a road that has a lot of numbers then the number you want is always the number at the other end of the road.'

'Yes, Stonks's Law,' said Bingo.

They trudged on and on for what seemed miles until at last they came to a row of shops by the traffic lights at the corner of Westbridge Road. Here they found, among others, a dull shopfront with its plate glass smeared over with bilious green paint. Above the window was written, in dim yellow letters: RSPCA, Local Office.

'Well, here we are,' said Bingo, 'and in I go. You two better stay out here, in case there's trouble.'

'Trouble, what trouble?' said Twilight. 'They ain't interested in kids, ain't got the time, it's all "puss-puss" and "down Rover" with them.'

Bingo looked at Stonks, who said, 'There's enough of us, we should be all right.'

Bingo opened the door and the three Borribles found themselves in a bleak office furnished only with a cheap desk and a few chairs. There was a typewriter, a telephone, a lady in a brown cardigan and a thick-set man dressed in a shiny black suit. The strange light from the painted window made everything a ghostly green, especially the two adults. They looked like they'd been recently dug up in some damp and mouldy cemetery.

The lady raised her head from the papers on her desk and smiled like a dentist. The man, his buttocks overflowing the small perimeter of his chair, smiled too. Bingo didn't like either of the smiles.

'Yes,' said the lady, 'and how can we help you three nice little boys?' She patted the crust of lacquer on her lifeless hair and her eyes glinted. The man rolled his lips around and said nothing. Inside his heavy suit his body was cooking like a chicken in a microwave and sweat gleamed and trickled across the acres of his pale skin. Bingo looked to the floor expecting to see a puddle of perspiration—he was disappointed. He looked back at the lady, confused. 'Is this the NSPCC?' he asked.

The lady's laugh jangled about the room like an armful of brass bracelets. 'Oh no, my dear,' she said, 'this is the RSPCA. We're the ones with the Royals in front. We look after animals and the ones without the Royals do the children.'

'That's what I meant,' said Bingo. 'I always get them mixed up. My parents sent me . . . to ask about a horse.'

'A horse,' said the man suddenly, 'what kind of horse?'

'Well,' explained Bingo, 'there was this horse found, in King George's Park, about six months ago, and my mum and dad, they are related to the person who owned that horse. Do you know what I mean?'

The lady nodded. 'Of course we do, boys,' she said, purring like an untrustworthy cat.

Bingo went on, 'You see my mum's mad about horses, and I was coming over this way, to visit my friends 'ere, and she said I was to ask you what had happened to the horse, that's if you knew, like.'

'And where do you live, sonny?' asked the man, pushing kindness into his face as hard as he could.

'Clapham Common, South Side,' said Bingo. 'We looked you up in the phone book.'

'I see,' said the man, 'how very enterprising.'

The lady tittered like a toy piano and pulled open a drawer. 'It's not really our part of London,' she said, and her hand appeared holding an address book, 'but I'll phone up Central Records for you, they'll be bound to know something.'

Bingo nodded and shifted his feet. There was something about these two adults he didn't like. Twilight stepped nearer the door, staring at the lady while she composed the telephone number. Her expression went vacant as she put the receiver to her ear and her eyes spun inside out to show only blank whites, though when someone spoke at the other end of the line her face lit up in a series of flashes so that she looked like a fruit machine.

'Ah, hello, Central Records . . . of course you are. This is Battersea here, Battersea. I have three lovely little boys in my office who are very worried about a horse, yes. It was lost in King George's Park about six months ago . . . Yes, certainly.' Her eyelids fluttered and found Bingo. 'They've gone to get the file,' she said, 'we'll have to wait,' and she pursed her lips in a gesture of affection, making her mouth hard and unlovely like a chicken's arse.

'I don't reckon this,' whispered Stonks, 'there's a cop shop just up the road from here, what if that old biddy has tipped 'em the wink?'

'Hello,' said the lady, smiling fiercely into the telephone as if the person at the other end might be improved by it. 'Yes, name, Samson, found in King George's Park, badly cut, now in good health and working for the park keepers on Eel Brook Common . . . Splendid, thank you so much. I'll do my best, bye-bye.'

'I hope you had nothing to do with that poor defenceless creature being wounded,' said the man, still trying to look kind but unable to keep the vicious tone out of his voice. 'I'd horsewhip any child I found hurting a horse.'

'I love animals,' said Bingo, 'and so does my mum, she'll be ever so pleased it's all right. We'll be able to go and visit the horse now, won't we?'

'Of course,' the lady screeched, and then she giggled like a lunatic baby-strangler.

'We'd better get going,' said Stonks, 'we'll be late for our tea.' The Peckham Borrible tugged at Bingo's sleeve and nodded towards the door where Twilight hovered, ready for flight.

'Oh, don't go yet,' cooed the lady. 'I've got some sweeties here somewhere, and I've got more to tell you about the horse.'

'Yes,' snarled the man, 'you wait a minute.' He sprang to his feet and the stiff smile fell from his face like a shutter falling from a shop window. 'I want your addresses,' he said, and, suddenly agile, he took one long stride and folded the flesh of his damp right hand round Bingo's neck and began to squeeze.

Twilight threw open the door and sunshine flooded in. Stonks hesitated, anguished. How could he leave Bingo, but what could he do?

The man squeezed harder at the muscles of Bingo's neck and the Borrible's feet left the floor.

'Run, Stonks,' he yelled in pain, 'run as fast as you can.'

Still Stonks hesitated. The lady began to stand up, still smiling. Stonks charged towards the desk and pushed it at her.

'Oooer,' she said, falling back into her chair, 'you little horror, I'll spank you.'

At that moment a door at the rear of the office opened and a uniformed policeman burst into the room; there was a chequered band circling his hat and SBG in letters of silver on his shoulder.

'Run,' gasped Bingo. 'Run.' The air was scarcely passing through his throat and his limbs were no longer moving. His face was purple.

Stonks hesitated no more. There were three adults already in the office and perhaps more policemen at the back of the building. He shoved Twilight through the doorway and leapt with him onto the pavement. They made as if to turn to their right but the wailing of a police siren stopped them. Three hundred yards away and bearing down in their direction, its blue light whirring round and round like an evil and disembodied eye, was a blue Transit van, a van of the SBG.

'Cripes,' said Twilight, 'time for a touch of the opposite directions.' And he and Stonks turned and ran like they'd never run before, pumping their arms and legs as fast as their hearts could stand, away round the corner and into Westbridge Road.

'We've got a couple of minutes before that van catches up with us,' panted Stonks. 'We've got to get off the street and out of sight, otherwise we've had it for good and proper.'

Vulge saw them first and he didn't like the way they were running, fast and panicky. He was sitting by the hole in the fence, on watch; the others were playing fivestones behind him and Spiff was winning. Vulge's face showed worry. 'Oh no,' he said.

The Borribles dropped the stones and got to their feet just as Stonks and Twilight came through the fence. Chalotte was the first to speak and she was angry.

'Where's Bingo,' she snapped, 'what the hell's happened?'

Stonks looked at the ground.

'He's been caught,' said Twilight. 'there was a big RSPCA man there, and a lady, and a Woollie. We only just got away . . . They must have had it set up with the SBG.'

'We couldn't do anything,' said Stonks. 'A van arrived and we had to run for it. We hid in the Somerset Estate.'

'This is terrible,' said Vulge. 'Bingo caught . . . bloody RSPC-bloody-A.'

'Will they clip his ears?' said Twilight in a small voice.

'What else will they damn-well do?' said Spiff, clenching his fists in anger. 'That is they will if we don't get to him quick enough.'

'What do you mean?' asked Vulge. 'Rescue him?'

'We've got to do something,' said Spiff. He looked as unhappy as anyone had ever seen him. Lines of anxiety pulled at his face.

Chalotte rounded on Sydney. 'I told you the horse was a bad idea, now we've gone and lost another Borrible, one of the best too.'

'All right,' cried Sydney, 'so it's my fault, say what yer like, but arguing don't help. We've got to save him if we can.'

'Of course we have,' said Spiff. 'There's no question of adventures or horses now. It's Bingo, Bingo alone, and the sooner the better. Anyone who doesn't want to help should say so.' He looked straight at Chalotte.

'I didn't want any trouble,' she said, 'but this is different. Bingo is Bingo. I'm in.'

'All right,' said Spiff. 'Now this is what I say, anyone who thinks they've got a better plan can say so afterwards . . . Did they tell you where the horse was?'

'They said something about Eel Brook Common,' said Stonks, 'working for the park keepers.'

'Right,' continued Spiff. 'I've got some good catapults indoors, some of those steel ones left over from the Rumble Hunt, one each. Stones we want, food we want, good running shoes. We'll get into Sinjen's School tonight and get a blazer each so we look like proper kids. If we get stopped on the road we'll pretend we're out on some holiday project. We'll leave tonight, as soon as it's dark. We'll break into the RSPCA office on the way, see if we can find out anything about what's happened to Bingo. Failing that we go on to Eel Brook Common, I know where it is, over Fulham way. You see I reckon they'll take Bingo there as soon as they can, show him to the horse and see how the horse reacts. If that horse recognizes him the SBG will know they've caught someone involved in the Southfields murders, and they'll soon make him talk and they'll be on to us in no time. We've got to get there before the law does. A rescue is the last thing they'll be expecting. Anyone got a better idea?'

'No,' said Vulge, 'only get a telescope.'

'A telescope,' said Spiff, 'all right. Get down the market the lot of yer and take what we need before it closes. I'll go back to my house and look out the catapults and see what else I've got. Meet yer back there and we'll rest and eat before we go. And for Pete's sake don't get caught, one rescue a day is enough.'

At ten thirty that night a window at the back of Sinjen's School slid open and Spiff's leg came out of it, followed, a second later, by his face. 'It's all right,' he whispered, 'no one about.' He pulled his body across the window ledge, twisted and then dropped to the ground. The others came after, one by one, all of them clothed in stolen blazers and grey flannels, even the two girls. On their feet were trainers, excellent for running. In their pockets were torches, high-grade steel catapults and enough stones to see off an army of coppers. They weren't the best equipped of expeditions but for a trip to Fulham and back they were more than adequately provided for.

Spiff led his five companions into the blackness of the play-ground and then out into the yellow light of the streets. The Borribles spread out in single file, three yards between each, ready to disperse at the first sign of danger. It was getting late and traffic was heavy; people were driving home from cinemas and bingo halls, the pubs were turning their customers out on to the pavements and everywhere there were drunks stumbling home, lifting their feet high over imaginary kerbstones, tottering backwards down non-existent slopes. Police cars lurked in the dark side roads too, lying low in the gutters like feral cats waiting for carrion.

Resolute and vigilant the Borribles tramped and jogged along and when, after about a quarter of an hour, they reached the traffic lights at Westbridge Road, Spiff slid into the dark entrance of the RSPCA office and tried the door. It was firmly locked. He stepped back and looked at the plate glass window and then up at the two smaller windows on the first floor.

'I won't have any bother getting in here,' he said. 'You others get over to that bus stop and pretend you're in the queue. If you see anything suspicious give a whistle.'

The bus stop was in fact only twenty yards from the office but by the time the Borribles had reached it Spiff had disappeared.

'Look at that,' said Vulge, 'he's inside already. He must be one of the best Borrible burglars ever.'

'The stories say he's got at least twenty names, you know,' said Stonks. 'I've even heard tell that he's been a Borrible for a hundred years, but I find that hard to believe.'

'There's certainly more to Spiff than meets anyone's eye,' agreed Chalotte, 'but nobody knows what it is. I wouldn't trust him further than I could spit upwards. He's got enough neck to look up his own ear'ole, he has.'

'Steady,' said Twilight, 'here he comes now.'

Spiff joined them at the bus stop. 'Not a lot in there,' he said, 'but it looks like an SBG set-up all right. I found a notepad on the desk with Sussworth's address and telephone number written on it. There was also tomorrow's date, and it said Eel Brook Common, nine o'clock.'

'Well,' said Sydney, 'when Sam sees Bingo he's bound to recognize him, and then he's had it.'

'And we'll have had it too,' said Spiff.

'In other words,' said Stonks, 'even if we didn't want to rescue Bingo, which we do, we'd have to try anyway, to save ourselves.'

'Dead bleedin' right,' said Spiff, 'either that or we'd all have to move a long way away from where we live now.'

'It's Hobson's,' said Twilight. 'Hobson's as usual.'

'We'd better get going,' said Spiff looking round. 'It wouldn't be a bad idea to be hidden somewhere near Eel Brook Common before the Woollies arrive tomorrow morning. That way if it looks like a trap we can stay hidden and keep quiet.'

And the Borribles moved on from the bus stop and began to trek up the long slope towards the crest of Battersea Bridge. Once over the bridge they would be in unfamiliar territory and danger would be all around them. They each knew this but they marched on with spirit and determination; they knew very well that they had to rescue Bingo—what they didn't know was that the second great Borrible Adventure had begun.

3

The headquarters of the SBG were not located in a police station and they were not easy to find, which was exactly how Inspector Sussworth liked it. His aim was to pass through life unnoticed by the general public; that was where his strength lay. He wanted to work quietly and secretly. Only the men who took orders from the inspector knew where to find him and their orders were to tell no one.

With concealment as their main objective the SBG had taken over a house in the crumbling hinterland behind Fulham Broadway, an unobtrusive place in Micklethwaite Road, a road that led nowhere. From the outside it looked dilapidated, a ramshackle establishment with varnish peeling from the front door and cracked windows hidden under white paint so that no one could see in and no one could see out. But inside it was different; it was antiseptic, it was smart and it was systematic, Inspector Sussworth saw to that. He liked things to be polished and properly arranged.

Behind the front door, and adorned with thick sick-green linoleum, was a narrow hallway leading to a narrow staircase which climbed steeply to three landings. On each landing were two rooms; each room had a desk, a telephone and a couple of deep, plastic-covered armchairs. At the rear of the ground floor was an enormous stainless-steel kitchen and dining room combined where the men of the SBG cooked meals and made their tea. In the garden a large sports room had been constructed; it contained showers, ludo boards, ping-pong tables and chest expanders. Inspector Sussworth insisted that the constables who formed his group were fit, keen and spotless.

On the first floor the two rooms were occupied by the inspector and his assistant and helpmate, Sergeant Hanks. The inspector had a larger desk than anyone else, a wooden desk that had been varnished and polished so often that its surface shone like a black mirror. He had the softest armchair too, and a colour television. Behind the television, in the corner furthest from the door, was the entrance to the inspector's private lavatory, his pride and joy which he washed and disinfected every day, allowing no other person to use it. The lavatory's every wall was tiled in six-inch squares of white porcelain, so was the ceiling. On the floor was a green carpet of cord and the toilet seat itself was padded and plush-covered; 'just like they are for the Royals,' Sussworth always said, proud and smug. Under an ever-open window, and within arm's reach of the velvet throne, stood a small bamboo table which always carried a pile of tough, water-resistant lavatory paper and several copies of the *Police Gazette*. This was Sussworth's inner sanctum, this was where he retired to think.

In the sergeant's room there was only a small desk but it did have three telephones as well as a radio receiver and transmitter. Hanks did not have a television of his own but he frequently watched programmes with the inspector. In fact, considering how totally different they were, it was amazing how well the two policemen got on. Some people said that Sussworth only kept Hanks in the group to remind himself and his men how gross and unpleasant the world really was. Others, more cruel perhaps, said that the sergeant only maintained his place in the SBG because he knew how to flatter Sussworth to the limit and how to do his bidding, even before it was bidden. Whatever the truth of the matter, they relied on each other a hundred per cent.

On the day of Bingo's capture, and not many hours after that event, Inspector Sussworth sat at his desk in the house in Micklethwaite Road and doodled on a piece of paper, his face lowering in deep concentration while in front of him the vapour rose from a cup of tea: no milk, no sugar, and very strong. The inspector dressed well and his uniform was as splendid as any grenadier's; it was neatly pressed and its buttons shone like stars against the deep blue serge of the material. Sergeant Hanks, always servile, always unctuous, relaxed in an armchair and waited for his leader to speak.

'So,' said the inspector when he had gathered his thoughts, 'we've caught a suspicious Borrible at last, but that's only one, Hanks. This is only the beginning; we've got to do better, much better.'

'We have indeed, sir,' said Hanks, bobbing his head up and down several times, 'and we will, I feel sure.'

The inspector picked up his cup of tea between two delicate fingers and sipped. The beverage was exactly how he liked it and he smiled. He had a strange thin face, made stranger by this smile, and in the face every feature took the wrong direction. His chin, which was sharp, did not go the way it should have gone. His nose bent itself in the middle and tried to aim the end sideways, while his ears threw themselves forward with energy instead of lying back with decorum. Sussworth's face was like a three-fingered signpost, turned by mischievous hands so that everything pointed down the wrong road.

His forehead was narrow, his eyebrows dark and well marked. His hair was lank and oiled and fell over his forehead in a solid lump. His eyes skulked deep in their sockets and, when they could be seen, were the colour of used washing-up water left overnight and found greasy-grey in the morning. Under his nose lived a small black moustache about the size of a jubilee postage stamp; it led a life of its own, that moustache, and twitched whenever it thought it would. Sussworth was only five feet six inches tall, with a slender body. Whether he sat or stood his feet always moved with nervous energy. He kicked the ground when he was annoyed, he did a little three-step dance when he was pleased. He was stubborn and he was proud; his blood bubbled with a lunatic zeal, he was an evangelist for rectitude and decorum, an enforcer of law and order.

By comparison Sergeant Hanks was an enormous man with broad shoulders and hands so big that when he clasped them it looked like he was carrying six pounds of raw pork sausages, unwrapped. His arms were as muscular as other people's thighs and covered all over with curly ginger hair, stiff as wire. He had a belly that surged frontwards; it began just below his neck, it ended just above his knees, but there was nothing flabby about it. It was a powerful belly, and sinew rippled across it all the time and made his uniform move as if he had a large python living underneath his jumper.

His jacket had egg stains down it from collar to hem and from shoulder to shoulder, like the medals on a general's tunic. There was only one thing that Hanks liked more than regular meals and that was the meals in between. His favourite food was four eggs and ten rashers of bacon with as much fried bread as could be stacked on a plate: what he called a 'double-greasy'. His fleshy round face lit up when he smelt such a feast and heard the hot fat sizzling in the frying pan. At such times his pastel blue eyes would shine and glint with greed, but his silver buttons were always dull.

The inspector sipped his tea prudently, like a tea taster. 'Tomorrow morning,' he said, 'we'll take that little malefactor to Eel Brook Common and see what the horse makes of him.'

'We will,' said Hanks, 'indeed we will.'

'And those two little blighters who got away, they'll have run off and told their mates what happened, won't they?'

Sergeant Hanks rolled his head.

'And we know what Borribles do when one of their mates gets caught, don't we?'

'Why,' said Hanks, 'they tries to get their friend uncaught before we clips his ears.'

'Right, Hanks, right. So you can bet your next double-greasy that tomorrow we'll be seeing quite a few Borribles at Eel Brook Common. They'll be there . . . but so will we.' Sussworth jumped to his feet, tipped the remainder of his tea into his mouth and then perched himself neatly on the edge of his desk like a paperweight. 'Get the men down here,' he ordered. 'I want to give them their instructions.'

Sergeant Hanks pressed a button and all round the house bells rang. A moment later there was the sound of heavy boots in the rooms above and in the kitchen below. The noise moved on to the stairs and the door to Sussworth's office opened. Twelve men in blue came to stand in front of their commander, not at attention but relaxed and confident.

'I'm glad to see you section leaders ready,' began Sussworth. 'Now we were lucky today, we caught one. Tomorrow, when we take him to see the horse, I expect a rescue attempt to be mounted. We must be prepared.' He leant forward and stamped twice on the floor. 'During the night I want men from vans two, five and eleven to take over the area surrounding the common. I want some of you to get into the houses, some others up on the roofs. Men from vans three, six and nine will guard all escape roads. You let anyone who looks like a Borrible in, but you don't let anyone who looks even remotely like a Borrible out. At exactly eight thirty I will arrive in van number one with the prisoner. This is an ambush that must work. You will be in position by midnight tonight. I don't want anyone even to suspect that you are there . . . I have made arrangements for the vans to be hidden in lock-up garages until they are needed. Are there any questions?'

There were none.

'Right, men,' continued Sussworth, 'it only remains for me to commend the work you've done in the past and hope for even better in the future. Remember this is our finest hour. This little blighter we've nobbled knows what we want to know and I'll sweat it out of him just as soon as we've captured his mates.' The inspector slipped from his desk and stretched out both his arms. 'I have only one ambition and I know you men share it with me . . . to rid this city of Borribles. They are a threat to any normal way of life. They say they don't want much and I say that's too much. They say they want to live their way and I say they ought to live the way everyone else does.'

Sussworth's eyes swivelled in his face and he dropped his arms to his side. He stood straight and stiff and he gazed up at his men. 'Go and prepare yourselves,' he said. 'That is all.'

The policemen saluted their officer, nodded at Sergeant Hanks and left the room, shuffling down the stairs one after the other. When they had gone Sussworth fell back into his chair, exhausted by the effort of his speech. He groped for his cup and held it out, at arm's length, to the sergeant. He needed a refill.

'Oh, sir,' said Hanks, taking the cup like it might have been a holy chalice, 'you certainly know how to inspire men. You stir their blood, sir, make their hearts beat the faster. I see it as clear as day.'

The inspector stared dreamily at the surface of his desk. 'It is only because I always tell them the truth,' he said, 'and the truth is what men want to hear.'

It was a languid dawn that rose over Eel Brook Common and the Borribles were early awake in it. The night had been warm and sleep difficult. The travellers had arrived in the middle of darkness and hidden themselves in the tiny front garden of a house that faced the common, screened from view by a low wall of brick and a scraggy privet hedge. All night the windows in the street had hung open and gross adults in their beds had snored and blasted their way through sleep, grunting and shouting in their dreams.

'Blimey,' said Twilight, 'if only we could harness all that energy and gas we could obliterate the SBG in five minutes.'

Slowly the sky over London paled and became purple. Traffic started to growl in the main roads like an old monster, the stars glittered one last time and front doors slammed as bus drivers left home for work. Bedroom lights came on brightly and then faded as the day grew stronger; the grunting and snoring softened to nothing. The Borribles rubbed their eyes, sat up and peered through the hedge across the empty yellowness of the flat common.

'Bloody parks,' said Spiff, 'draughty old dumps. Just look at it, nothing to steal for miles. I don't know how anybody can like them.'

It was true that there was little to be seen except, on the far side of the field, a few small wooden huts behind a hedge and an iron railing. It was the sort of place in which park keepers store their tools and eat their sandwiches.

'I bet that's where they keep the horse,' said Sydney.

'Finding the horse,' said Vulge, 'is easy; it's getting it away from keepers and keeping it away from keepers that's tricky.'

'It's difficult to disguise a horse,' said Twilight. 'I mean you can't stick it on wheels and shove it down the street like it was a toy, can you? It might drop a load just as a copper came round the corner.'

'Quiet,' whispered Spiff. 'SBG.'

The others looked where he pointed and they saw a blue Transit van emerge from Wandsworth Bridge Road and come to a halt on the southern side of the common.

'It's full of John Law,' said Stonks.

Spiff shoved a hand in his pocket and pulled out a small collapsible telescope.

'Well I never,' said Vulge, 'you got one.'

'Found it in Sinjen's School,' said Spiff. 'Like you said, very handy.' He raised the telescope and poked it between the leaves of the hedge. He put his eye to it and studied the van. Two policemen emerged.

Spiff grunted. 'Two out, but I reckon there's about eight more inside. Can't see too clearly, they've got mesh across the windows.'

'Look at their shoulders,' said Chalotte. 'What rank are they?'

'Strike a light,' said Spiff, 'that's an inspector, that little squirt. It must be Sussworth 'imself, ugly sod, have a butcher's.' Spiff passed the telescope over to Vulge who stared through it while his companions stared at him.

'Cripes,' he said after a while, 'he's horrid all right, frighten Frankenstein rigid he could, and the sergeant with him ain't a work of art either, strong though, crack yer philbert open as soon as look at yer.' Vulge returned the telescope to Spiff.

The two police officers stood by the side of the van for a minute or two until they were joined by a park keeper wearing a brown uniform and a brown hat. After shaking hands the three officials walked away from the road, heading across the common in the direction of the wooden huts. When they got there the keeper took a key from his pocket, undid a padlock on the iron gate and disappeared behind the hedge. The policemen did not have long to wait. Within minutes the keeper returned leading a small horse behind him, a dingy horse with its head hanging at the rein and its feet dragging over the grass. An unhappy horse.

'Is it Sam?' asked Sydney. 'I can't see from this distance.'

Spiff passed her the telescope. 'Have a look,' he said. 'I wouldn't know your horse from a ham sandwich.'

Sydney raised the instrument to her eye. 'Oh,' she gasped, her face bright with joy, 'it is, it's Sam. The horse who saved our lives.'

'He didn't save my life,' said Spiff.

Chalotte sneered. 'Nor would anyone with any sense,' she said.

'Knock it on the head,' said Stonks, 'something's happening.'

While the Borribles had been talking the keeper had manhandled a small rubbish cart from one of the huts and was buckling Sam into it. At the same time a side door to the Transit van slid open and two more policemen appeared. Between them they held, by the arms, the small and dispirited figure of Bingo Borrible. His hat was gone, his ears were revealed.

Spiff snatched the telescope from Sydney. 'He's still got his ears,' he said, 'there's still a chance.'

'They're taking him over to the horse,' said Chalotte.

The six Borribles crouched behind their hedge and watched. The traffic was thick round the common now and people were striding this way and that towards bus stops and Underground stations. Meanwhile the sun was mounting steeply into the sky, ready to scorch the city for another day.

Bingo was shoved across the common. He did not struggle, neither did he go willingly. His head was down and his feet scuffed over the dry turf. Nearer and nearer to Sam he was dragged, made small and pitiful by the size of the men who escorted him, vulnerable in the middle of that great open space.

'If only he knew we were here,' said Chalotte.

But Bingo did not know. He was hauled up to the horse and made to stand in front of it.

'Don't do anything, Sam,' whispered Sydney, 'don't do anything.'

It was no good. Sam had been lonely and maltreated when he'd toiled for Dewdrop and Erbie and he'd known no love until the Borribles had freed him. He'd never forgotten the great Adventure and he'd not forgotten the face or scent of any one of the Adventurers. He'd dreamed of them many a sad night over the months and months since they'd been obliged to abandon him. Now he raised his head and his nostrils flared and quivered. He saw the uniforms and swung his neck away for he did not like uniforms; then he caught the smell of Bingo and swung his head back. He saw the Borrible—he shook his head and stamped his feet hard into the ground. A huge neighing of happiness burst from him and he strained forward, pulling the cart along with him.

Bingo tried to step backwards, averting his face, but the two big-boned policemen were holding him and they stood firm in their massive boots. Sam came close to Bingo and licked his face and nudged his shoulder, and though the Battersea Borrible tried desperately not to show the slightest emotion it was obvious that the horse knew him and knew him well. In the end Bingo gave up all pretence and threw his arms round the horse's neck. Even though this action placed him in great peril he remembered Sam with gratitude and knew that he owed his life to the horse. He knew also that friendship is never more valuable than when expressed in the deepest danger. Besides, he thought, why should the Woollies make him behave in a manner that was unnatural, in a way that was not like him.

'Sam,' said Bingo to Sam alone, 'there are others who will rescue you. Whatever happens we haven't forgotten our promise.'

From their hiding-place the Adventurers watched as Inspector Sussworth separated Bingo from the horse and they saw too how the police escort seized the captive and frogmarched him away. Sussworth and Hanks shook hands with the park keeper once more and left him. The doors of the Transit van opened and six more policemen came out of the vehicle. They stretched their arms to the sky and smiled.

As soon as Bingo arrived back at the van he was thrown into it and the doors were locked. His white face came to the window immediately and he peered through the grille at Sam who was now obliged to begin his day's work, pacing round the fringes of the common, stopping and starting on command while the keeper loaded the cart with all the litter he could find.

The policemen now stood in an untidy group, congratulating their chief. Sussworth's face became contorted with smiles, his

moustache jerked to right and left and his feet stabbed the ground
with pleasure. Sergeant Hanks was content too; cradling his magnificent belly in both hands he jiggled it up and down so that he
could laugh more easily.

It took some while for the policemen's mirth to subside but
when it had the sergeant pointed across the main road to where a
man in a dirty white overall was taking down the shutters from the
front of a small transport café. The policemen crossed the road in
a bunch and the man in the white overall opened the café door and
ushered them in. The SBG were going to celebrate success with
eggs and bacon and mugs of tea.

'Bingo's alone in the van,' said Sydney. 'Can't we do something now?'

'It looks bloody dangerous,' said Chalotte.

Spiff pushed his telescope through the hedge and peered carefully round the common. 'Of course it's bloody dangerous,' he said,
'and what makes it worse is that I can't see anything the slightest bit
suspicious out there, which probably means the opposite.'

'We won't get another chance like this,' said Stonks. 'We've got
to have a go, we've got to.'

'Hang about,' interrupted Spiff, 'there's no need for us all to
rush over there. Vulge better stay here because of his limp, Sydney too, and Twilight. Chalotte and Stonks come with me. Now, if
we get Bingo out we'll head into the back streets between here and
the river. I'll open the van on this side, away from the caff, that
means you three here will have to watch the park keeper. If he
looks up he'll spot us. If he tries to warn the Woollies you'll just
have to run out there and clobber 'im. If that happens nick the
horse and cart and drive like the clappers, away up the common,
make as much noise as you can, create a diversion. After that
you'll have to run into the side streets and split up, hide, get into a
house, anything.' Spiff drew a deep breath and looked at the circle
of frightened faces around him. 'I know it's not much of a plan,'
he added, 'but it's all we got.'

'How are you going to pick the lock?' asked Stonks.

Spiff smiled. 'How do you think I did the RSPCA office?' he
said, and he drew a small bundle of stiff wire from one pocket and

a bunch of filed-down car keys from another. 'I'm a little boy scout,' he explained, 'always prepared.' Spiff smirked then and looked at Twilight from under his eyebrows. 'You'd better take the telescope, and don't look down the wrong end. If you see something you don't like, whistle.' And Spiff thrust his hands into his pockets and sauntered, tough and truculent, out from the garden and on to the pavement. Stonks went too and Chalotte, after grimacing fearfully at Sydney, did the same.

Twilight raised the telescope and studied the keeper for a minute or two. Nothing out of the ordinary there. Next he turned his attention to the café, but the windows were thick with the dirt thrown up by passing juggernauts and the Bangladeshi could see nothing through them. He surveyed the houses opposite, the gardens, the roofs. Everything seemed normal.

Spiff reached the van. Chalotte knelt by its front wheel and watched the café and Stonks stood near the back doors and scanned the common. Spiff, the most casual and courageous burglar in the world, leant on the SBG vehicle and attacked the sliding door with his set of keys. He was a good workman; he didn't rush and he didn't panic, not even when Bingo's face appeared close to his own, separated from it only by half an inch of soundproof security glass. The prisoner moved his mouth but Spiff heard nothing above a murmur. He bent his head and went on with his work, saying, 'Don't worry, Bingo, don't worry, nearly got it.'

'All quiet on the common,' said Stonks, his voice tense.

'All quiet in the caff,' said Chalotte, 'but get a move on.'

Two minutes went by, three. Chalotte continued to keep a sharp eye on the café door, willing it to stay shut. She heard Spiff swear but refused to turn her head, then came the sound of the lock clicking, the door slid open. Bingo was free.

She half rose from her crouching position and turned to see Bingo, pale and bedraggled, leap from the van and into Spiff's arms, shouting, 'You fools, you damn fools, it's a trap, the common's lousy with coppers.'

Chalotte glanced across the road and her mouth dried and her blood congealed into a ball of stone that stuck in her heart. The door of the café had been flung open and the policemen were spreading along the pavement, pushing pedestrians out of their way, cutting off any Borrible escape into the streets that led to the Thames.

'It's coming down harder, now,' said Spiff. 'We'll have to try and get across the common.'

Back behind the hedge Twilight jumped to his feet, dropping the telescope. 'The Woollies are coming out of the caff,' he shouted. 'Sydney, Vulge, come on. It's the cart before the horse now.'

Loading their catapults the three of them ran from their hiding place into the open, making as much noise as they could. The keeper saw them coming and turned to face them, squaring his shoulders as if for an attack he had always expected.

Vulge faltered. 'He knows,' he said, 'he knows.'

'I don't care how much he knows,' shouted Twilight, 'all the knowledge in the world won't stop a catapult.' The Bangladeshi knelt and let fly a stone which flew straight at the keeper and struck him cleanly on the elbow, drawing blood.

'Come on, Sam,' yelled Sydney. 'It's me, Sam, it's me.'

Sam needed no telling. He was a veteran of the Great Rumble Hunt and he could smell danger just as well as he could smell the scent of his Borrible friends. He neighed like a warhorse, eager for battle, swished his tail and ran in the direction of his beloved Sydney, his lips curling back over his teeth in ferocious glee.

There was no time for greeting, not then, not in the middle of such a hue and cry. Sydney sprang on to the cart and seized the reins; Vulge and Twilight leapt up beside her, catapults ready.

'I came back for you, Sam,' cried Sydney breathlessly. 'I told you I would.'

Spiff and his band ran diagonally across a corner of the common. They ran fast and in a fair race would have soon outdistanced their pursuers, but the trap had been well laid. Sweat ran into Spiff's eyes.

'Make for that street over there,' he panted, 'we'll leave 'em behind in no time.' But even as he spoke a blue Transit van skidded round the corner of the road he had indicated. All its doors burst open and another dozen Woollies jumped into the fray. 'Hell,' said

Spiff, 'we've been set up.' He swerved in his tracks, the others followed and they ran up the side of the green towards the next street. Another blue van appeared and the Borribles were forced to run on.

'What about the other side of the common?' asked Chalotte.

'Take a look,' said Stonks. Chalotte saw and heard three vans screech into view. They did not stop at the kerbside either, those vans, but drove and bumped and swayed out on to the yellow grass.

'Shit,' said Spiff, 'they're really coming for us today.'

'It was nice to escape,' said Bingo, 'even if it was only for a minute.'

Sydney spied her friends and directed the cart towards them.

'Sam,' she wailed as the horse ran, 'this is not how we meant it to be. Now we're caught for good, now they'll clip us and we'll grow up and hell and dammit.'

The policemen began to advance from three sides, both on foot and in their vans, but Sam's blood came afire with the urge to help his friends and he galloped like he had on Rumbledom. He swerved and slid the cart in front of Spiff and the others and they threw themselves aboard and Sam was away again, heading for the top of the common where the field narrowed to a point and there were no blue vans to be seen.

The seven Borribles, united now, aimed and shot their catapults as rapidly as they could and the policemen on foot fell back under the onslaught of those deadly missiles, but four vans drew alongside the cart and kept pace with the gallant horse.

'Aim at the windscreens,' called Spiff, but it was not that easy. The SBG vans had thicker glass than ordinary cars and the stones rebounded harmlessly into the air.

Sam galloped on, sheering this way and that, trying to reach the streets. More vans drove on to the common, fast at first, then they slowed and circled the cart, drawing closer and closer, forcing Sam away from the edge of the field, into the centre.

Sam wheeled again and looked for a way of escape. There was none. The blue vans slithered to a halt on the dry grass, the doors banged open and scores of policemen rushed into the sunlight—

Sussworth's men, his pride and his joy, in full riot gear. They held shields in front of their bodies and on their heads black helmets reflected only a black sunshine. In front of the men's faces were see-behind visors, in the men's hands, long truncheons. The SBG marched towards the cart; the world was theirs and the Borribles were hostages for it.

Sam swerved but he was hemmed in completely and the end soon came. A policeman leapt up and grabbed at Sam's bridle. The horse reared and lifted the man from his feet but he held on. Another policeman ran forward, then another. The Borribles fired stones at their knees, their ankles; many men fell but others ran round them, protecting the injured with their shields. It was a fierce battle but the SBG would not be intimidated and they did not fall back. Sam reared again and the cart crashed into one of the stationary vans. The horse whinnied piteously as he struggled to be free. He bucked, he kicked.

'Leave him alone,' shouted Sydney, and fired a stone at the constable who was punching Sam on the nose.

The cart pitched and tipped and Spiff, drawing back the rubber of his catapult, was thrown to the ground badly stunned. He groaned and rolled on to his back. Chalotte was seized by an ankle and dragged from her feet. Her back cracked against the side of the cart, she was grabbed and chucked from one policeman to another. Someone cuffed her and dropped her down beside the unconscious Spiff. She screamed and covered her ears with her hands.

'Don't clip me,' she yelled, 'don't clip me.'

Stonks was strong. He was held by the leg. He kicked out and the hand let go. He jumped over the edge of the cart and butted someone in the stomach. A way was clear before him, he moved for it but a truncheon struck him across the back and all the wind went from him, sucked from his lungs. He fell to his knees and that was the end of his battle.

Sydney had not thought of fighting. In her heart she was weeping because it had been her idea to look for Sam in the first place and now that idea had brought them all to this defeat. Never had there been such a thing in the whole of Borrible history. Never had so many been caught in one fell swoop.

Vulge sprang from the cart but he was caught in midair by two policemen and they grasped him by the legs and wrists and his skinny body writhed in the air between them. Twilight was on the ground, so was Bingo. Everyone had been taken.

With her heart breaking Sydney jumped on to Sam's back, fell on his neck and clung tightly to him. 'Oh, Sam,' she cried, 'this was all for you and it's all gone wrong, you'll never see us Borribles again.' But there was no time to say more. She was plucked from the horse by brutal hands and flung to the ground.

Spiritless she gazed at the sky. It was blue still and burnt the world. Her body ached and sweat ran over it. The earth was hard in her back and she could feel it spinning, faster and faster. All around her, staring down, was a ring of helmeted heads, moving and motionless, like the rim of a gyroscope. Blank masks: no eyes, no noses, no mouths. Nothing.

Suddenly a section of the circle fell away and into the gap stepped a short man in officer's uniform. He had twisted features and a black moustache. Beside him stood a fat policeman with a shiny face made uneven and bumpy by glowing pearls of perspiration. It was Inspector Sussworth and Sergeant Hanks.

The inspector jeered and clapped his hands and looked at the faceless faces of his men. Sydney saw him do a little jig of happiness, pirouetting from one foot to the other. The sergeant stared lovingly at the prostrate captives and licked his lips as if he were contemplating his favourite food.

'Well, well,' said Sussworth when his dance was over and a smile set crooked on his ugly mouth. 'What a lovely batch of Borribles I've got. Welcome home you little brats, welcome back to the straight and narrow.'

After their capture the Borribles were handcuffed together in a long line and locked into one of the Transit vans. Eel Brook Common looked like a no man's land. Two vans had crashed and one of them lay on its side, dented and demolished. Police equipment was strewn over an immense area and many of the SBG, exhausted by the heat of the day and the exertion of the chase, lay where they had fallen, like corpses on a battlefield. On the main road loitered little knots of people, gazing without understanding at the aftermath of the conflict. Some of them questioned the policemen about the cause of the affray but received no answer. They went to leave but halted to witness one last flurry of excitement.

Sam the horse had not finished yet; his body shook all over and his legs trembled, there was froth on his lips. He stood dejected in the shafts of the rubbish cart, his head touching the grass in sorrow, and the park keeper, one elbow bandaged, came up to the horse and caught him violently by the reins.

'Come on, animal,' he said, 'it's back to work for you, and no mistake.'

It is difficult to know what goes on in a horse's mind but something snapped in Sam's. He had tasted freedom for a few minutes, he had seen his friends for a while, knew he was loved, but at the end everything had been taken from him. It was more than he could bear. He lunged and he reared, snorting out a challenge to the man in brown and all that he stood for. His front legs flailed and the park keeper let go the reins and cowered to the ground, shielding his head with his good arm. In the prison van Sydney pressed her face against the wire-meshed window.

'Look,' she said, 'Sam's escaping.'

Sam kicked his hind legs at the cart that he hated. There was a noise of splintering wood and a shaft broke away. Sam reared once more, high and magnificent, and his valiant neighing rang out across the common, defying anyone to enslave him ever again.

The keeper made a last attempt to seize the flying reins but Sam sprang at him, forcing him back, and the second shaft gave and the traces snapped. Now he was free of the cart altogether; now, unhindered and unfettered, he wheeled like a wild stallion, then he chose his direction and galloped off, his neck stretched and his tail and mane and broken leathers streaming behind him.

The exhausted policemen were ordered to their feet and compelled to link arms and form a human chain across the common. Others raced to their vans, but Sam would not be caught. He launched himself at the SBG line as it advanced towards him; he ran faster and faster, his hooves thundered across the turf and the policemen before him faltered; that horse was insane—it was not going to stop. On and on sped Sam and when only a few yards from the human barricade he soared into the air, as high and as handsome as any hunter, and landed gracefully well beyond the reach of those who sought to bring him down. Across the main road he went then and into the freedom of the back streets, like any Borrible would.

'He got away,' said Sydney. 'Imagine that, he got away.'

Vulge kicked the side of the van. 'Well, we didn't,' he said, 'and what will happen to us now?'

He was not kept in suspense for long. The van groaned on its springs and three policemen climbed into the front seat. One of them switched on the engine and his colleagues turned to keep a close watch on the prisoners. The van drove slowly off the common, bumped over the kerbstones and crawled away in the direction of Fulham Road. It was escorted by another van, and another. There was to be no escaping.

It was not a long drive and within a few minutes, sirens howling, the column of blue vehicles swept into a grey yard surrounded by high brick walls; this was Fulham police station. The vans parked and the SBG men bundled out of them to form up in straight ranks while Inspector Sussworth and his sergeant stood happily before them. Just for a little while there was silence, then the inspector raised his arms and opened his mouth.

'Bloody Nora,' said Vulge who had been watching the policemen through the windows of the Black Maria, 'he's going to sing, like some football supporter whose team's won the cup.'

And sing the inspector did, a fine marching song, a song to rouse the blood, and as Sussworth sang his men saluted and marched and tramped on the spot, and every time their leader completed a verse the constables shouted aloud and sang the chorus with verve and energy: but the song sent a chill into the

bones of the Borribles as they listened, for the words offered
them no hope.

> *'To make a new society*
> *we must reform the human race;*
> *if all the world were just like me*
> *the world would be a better place.*

CHORUS: *'There's law and order in my blood,*
> *and disobedience makes me mad;*
> *I am the friend of all that's good,*
> *I am the foe of all that's bad.*

> *'I hate the fools who won't obey*
> *the rules we set for them to keep;*
> *it's criminal to err and stray—*
> *good citizens behave like sheep!*

> *'Authority must always win,*
> *dissenters are a mortal blight—*
> *I'll straighten them with discipline,*
> *teach them to put their morals right!*

> *'For we know best what's right and wrong;*
> *we make the laws, we know the form—*
> *I'll come down hard, I'll come down strong*
> *on every sod who won't conform—*

> *'Especially these little brats*
> *the Borribles—the lawless shites*
> *with pointed ears and woolly hats;*
> *I'll crucify the parasites!*

CHORUS: *'There's law and order in my blood,*
> *and disobedience makes me mad;*
> *I am the friend of all that's good,*
> *I am the foe of all that's bad.'*

Once the SBG march had been sung no more time was lost. The prisoners were hustled from their van and into the back door of the police station, pushed past some concrete steps leading to the cells, and shoved into the interrogation room. Several policemen went with the Borribles and marshalled them before a large desk. On the desk were piles of paper; behind the desk sat the malignant figure of Inspector Sussworth; beside him, ever subservient, stood Sergeant Hanks.

Inspector Sussworth arranged his papers into squares of neatness and jerked his face into some form of straightness. He cleared his throat. 'I see you're wearing Sinjen's blazers and trousers,' he began, 'some kind of disguise I suppose, pitiful! Well, let's see . . .' He studied a charge sheet. 'I can do you for breaking and entering, damaging police property, resisting arrest, obstructing police officers in the execution of their duty, attacking officers of the law, grievous bodily harm, actual bodily harm, obscene language, horse-stealing—used to be a hanging charge that one, pity—aiding and abetting a prisoner to escape and evade lawful custody . . . I've got enough to put you lot into care until the next millennium, and with your ears clipped I bet you'd grow up into as lovely a bunch of little Lord Fauntleroys as you could wish to see . . . But then I'm not interested in the future, I've got bigger fish to fry.' Sussworth's face twisted and tightened in its anger. 'You lot know something about the Southfields murders; you lot were there and before I've finished with you I'll have you queueing up to tell me about it.'

Spiff looked down the line of prisoners. 'Do you know what he's talking about?' he asked. 'Because I don't.'

Sussworth made a gesture and the policeman standing immediately behind Spiff cuffed the Borrible across the top of the head. Spiff staggered but rode the blow philosophically.

'I've never been to Southfields,' he went on, 'don't even know where it is.'

'I tell you something,' said Sussworth, 'I could clip your ears right now if I wanted to, but I'll give you all a chance. Whosoever gives me the information I want will walk out of here a free Borrible with his, or her, ears unclipped. I can't say fairer than that.'

Vulge stepped forward on the instant. 'I've got something to tell you then,' he cried.

'Yes,' said Sussworth, leaning eagerly over his desk, 'what is it?'

'It's this,' said Vulge, 'I don't know where Southfields is either.'

Inspector Sussworth was not amused. He narrowed his eyes and lengthened his lips. 'A funny man, eh?' he said. 'Well, you won't be laughing long. I'll have your ears done tonight and we'll see how brave you are then.'

Sergeant Hanks propped his belly on the desk and leant into it. 'Perhaps,' he suggested, 'it might be a good idea, sir, if we gave them until tomorrow morning to think it over. They're all a bit full of themselves at the moment but a day and a night in the cells without anything to eat or drink, well, that might help them to see things a bit differently.'

Sussworth's face flared with pleasure. 'Splendid idea, sergeant,' he said. 'You will arrange for the police surgeon to be round here first thing tomorrow morning. We'll soon have these snotty buggers singing a different song.' His eyes moved along the row of Borribles, studying each face, searching for weakness. His scrutiny stopped at Twilight.

'Well, sonny,' said the inspector, 'have you got something you want to tell me? You'd like to save your ears, wouldn't you?'

'Oh, yes,' answered Twilight, 'I would. I wish to announce, categorically, that I am not knowing the whereabouts of Southfields either.'

There was a terrible silence in the room and the tension rose. Under the kneehole desk the Borribles could see the inspector's legs contorting with fury. He drew a breath and held it in his lungs as if to cool his temper. His nose turned in the air like a corkscrew.

'Take 'em down and lock 'em up,' he screamed, 'before I goes berserk. I won't be responsible for my actions if they stays here. I'll see 'em tomorrow; and then, one by one, I'll take their ears off. I'll look forward to that all night.'

The policemen grabbed the Borribles from behind, manhandled them out of the room, and they were taken down a flight of stairs to a corridor along which the cells were situated. A policeman chose one at random and, still handcuffed one to the other, the prisoners were flung inside and the huge steel door clanged shut. A key clattered three times and the SBG men stamped away, their morning's work at last complete.

Left to themselves the Borribles stretched out as best they might on the concrete floor and, for want of pillow or blanket, rested their heads on their nearest friend.

'Well,' said Bingo, 'this is nice. No grub, no hope and after to-morrow, no ears.'

'It stinks of pee down here,' said Vulge.

'Cats?' suggested Twilight.

'No,' said Chalotte, trying to make her head comfortable on Stonks's stomach, 'humans.'

4

The stink came from the prison cubicle next door. Old Ben was in there and Ben was the dirtiest man alive. A retired tramp who no longer tramped, he lived on Feather's Wharf, a huge rubbish dump on the south side of Wandsworth Bridge. He was nightwatchman, rubbish sorter and layabout, and he lived in a ramshackle lean-to in the middle of a wild mountain range of trash. He had only one friend in his life, the stableman at Young's Brewery, and only two occupations, collecting things that other people had thrown away, and drinking beer.

Sometimes Ben drank too much and staggered out of Feather's Wharf and into the streets, weaving along the pavements, rebounding off lamp posts, singing old songs and wagging his finger at everyone who passed. When this happened Ben was arrested and kept in the police cells until he became sober, and that was where he was the day the Borribles were brought in, although he didn't notice their arrival because he was fast asleep, flat on his back on the floor and snoring. The door to his cell was open but then it was always open because no one took Ben seriously enough to lock it. As a general rule the policemen of south London just laughed at Ben and as soon as he had recovered from his bout of drinking they would simply push him on to the streets and tell him to go back to his rubbish dump. 'Keep out of sight,' the coppers told him, 'and you'll keep out of trouble.'

Ben certainly smelt and it was a very special smell: a concoction brewed of body odours, decayed rubbish, dried pee, wood smoke and stagnant Thames water. Ben never washed and the back of his neck was criss-crossed with deep crevices of dirt and pitted with the scars of ancient blackhead volcanoes. Every pore in his body had been clogged with the soot of the smoke that rose from the eternal fires of litter and lumber that he kept burning by the threshold of his shack.

His hair was black and long and gleamed with grease where he had wiped his hands; it had not been cut for years and it grew wild at the ends, tangling into the edges of a huge beard which flourished, abandoned, from one side of his face to the other. Through this hedge stuck an enormous nose, and below, though well hidden, was a large mouth holding prominent brown teeth which had been eroded into wicked shapes by beer and nicotine, saliva and time. Ben's fingernails were jagged too and as broad as shovels, loaded with grime enough, each one, to cultivate potatoes in.

He was tall and gaunt, when he could stand, with hollow shoulders, knobbly hands and eyes tired with wisdom. On his head he always wore a floppy black hat with a wide brim, but he did not wear clothes like other people wore clothes, he inhabited them, layers of them. When his garments became so old or stained that other tramps would have thrown them away, Ben just found another layer and climbed in, discarding nothing. He was like an archaeological dig and somewhere, deep down near his skin, his clothes must have been welded together in an age-old flux of sweat and dust. On top of all his shirts and jackets and trousers Ben wore two or three ancient overcoats, each one of them a labyrinth of tattered linings, poacher's pockets and hidden compartments. In them Ben carried everything he needed: beer, tobacco, bread and matches.

All his belongings came from the rubbish dump where he lived and he wanted for nothing. Ben didn't give a monkey's about the world. He didn't care for work, he didn't care for authority and he didn't care for soap and water. He didn't even care very much for himself.

He had been found the previous night on Wandsworth Bridge, singing 'Shenandoah', his favourite song, and trying to walk along the parapet high above the river. Passers-by had prevented him and had telephoned the police and they had taken him in. Ben didn't mind, he didn't mind anything. 'Might as well do one thing as another,' he used to say. 'All be the same in a hundred years, won't it?'

In his cell Ben groaned, opened his eyes, stopped snoring and sat up. He felt sober and he felt terrible. It was time to go home. He was sure that he had a few bottles of Young's Special Brew hidden away in his shack; just what he needed to put him right.

He attempted to focus his eyes on the door and though at first they dived and swooped, eventually they steadied. The door was open and he knew that if he went quietly along the corridor and up the stairs he would come to the ground floor of the police station. There might be someone in the front office, there might not. It would make no difference, they always let him go.

Ben struggled to his feet and felt in his pockets. All his possessions were there. One advantage of being dirty was that no one wanted to search you, not even coppers. Someone in a Salvation Army hostel had tried to give him a bath once but they'd abandoned the experiment after the first pair of sticky trousers.

Ben went into the corridor and shuffled towards the steps. It felt a little cooler though the air was still heavy and oppressive.

'Must be the middle of the night,' he said. 'Cor, I've been asleep all day; it's a wonder I didn't die of thirst.'

He came to the door of the next cell, grabbed at the grille and looked in. He always liked to see who had been arrested when he was put inside but this time he could hardly believe his eyes. In the light of a single electric bulb he saw seven children lying on the concrete floor, huddled together, not for warmth, but for comfort

'That's not right,' said Ben, adjusting his hat with meticulous care, 'kids in here, wonder what they've done, still . . . none of my business is it? None of my business.'

Ben shuffled on and left the Borribles sleeping; their predicament passed from his mind. He climbed the stairs to the corridor above and went to the back door of the police station.

'Hmm,' said Ben. He stared out. It was dark, the darkest part of the night, and a thick white summer mist was rolling up from the River Thames like poisonous gas and lying along the streets like long gobs of cotton waste.

'Hmm,' said Ben once more and leant against the door frame. 'Can't see much, should stay in me cell, really, bound to get lost on my way home . . . Still there's no beer here, leastways not for me there ain't.'

A steady hum of voices and machines came from the busy upper floors of the building. Something stamped in a corner of the yard and Ben tried to look through the soft shreds of mist.

'Can't be,' he said. 'I must be having illuminations.' He looked harder and made out the fuzzy-edged shape of a horse tied to an iron-barred window. 'Well I never, bloody spooky that is, whatever it is.'

He turned immediately and began to slop along the corridor in his broken boots. The door to the interrogation room was open and the front office was also visible. He could see the night sergeant sitting at his desk.

'I'll say goodnight to him,' said the tramp, 'maybe scrounge a couple of bob too. Always good for a touch, he is.'

As Ben advanced the policeman's telephone rang; he picked it up, listened for an instant and then got to his feet. When Ben reached the room it was empty; only the swinging door showed that the sergeant had gone upstairs.

'Hm,' said Ben, 'I'll wait a bit.' He went over to the desk and gazed down at it in wonder; it was not often that he saw such tidiness. Cleanliness and order never failed to bewilder him.

'Ain't they marvellous,' he reflected, 'all that writing things in books, squaring things off, adding things up, underlining things in red . . . Funny way to spend your time.' His eyes wandered to the shelves behind the desk; they carried rows of files and baskets of statements. Ben shook his head. 'And they calls me mad,' he said.

It was then that he saw the keys, hanging on a hook screwed into the side of one of the shelves. He rolled his head on his shoulders, first left, then right; he was alone and there was no sound of alarm from upstairs. Ben's face broke open with pleasure and a big brown smile forced a way through his beard.

'Well,' he said, 'the keys, eh, all numbered and neat, cells and handcuffs, my my. 'Course, it's nothing to do with me, but then nothing is so it won't matter, and even if it did it wouldn't would it? Anyway, it's about time I did something for a lark, haven't had a lark for years, the change will do me good.' Ben raised his right hand and unhooked two lots of keys. 'Don't you jangle now,' he said to them, 'don't you dare jangle.'

He shoved the keys into one of his overcoat pockets so that they would not rattle and retraced his steps as quietly as loose boots and no socks would allow. When he reached the Borribles' cell he peered through the grille for the second time.

'Still there look, it don't seem right, do it? Nice little kids like that.' Ben smacked his lips together, took the keys from his pocket, selected the one that bore the same number as the door and slipped it into the lock. Then he turned it till it would turn no more and the door clicked open, swinging silently on oiled hinges.

Ben entered the cell and began to undo the handcuffs that pinched the skin on the sleeping Borribles' wrists. 'Look at them red marks,' he said when he'd finished, 'terrible really. They'll have to run like the clappers when they get out of here, though. John Law won't like this a smitherin'.'

Chalotte opened her eyes and raised her head, puzzled. She couldn't remember where she was. Slowly her nose wrinkled and her lips tightened into a figure of eight. 'Cripes,' she swore, 'you don't 'arf niff.'

Ben smiled, showed his gothic teeth and held up a fistful of handcuffs. 'Don't mock that smell,' he said theatrically, like an explorer naming a new continent, 'that smell is the smell of freedom.'

Chalotte raised her unshackled hands and stared at them. Then she noticed the open door. 'Who are you?' she asked.

'I'm Ben,' said Ben, 'and I'm on my way home. Coming?'

Chalotte jumped to her feet and shook her friends awake. 'We're getting out,' she whispered. 'Don't ask me how it happened but it has.'

'Who's this bundle of rags?' said Spiff, rubbing his eyes.

'It's Ben,' said Ben again. 'Follow me.'

The old tramp led the Borribles out of the cell and along the corridor. 'Wait here,' he said, 'there may be a copper up above.' Ben climbed the stairs until his eyes were level with the ground floor, then he poked his head round the banister and saw that the office was still empty. He waved a hand behind his back. 'Come on up,' he said.

One by one the runaways crept towards the back door while Ben kept watch for the sergeant.

'What about you?' said Chalotte, who was the last to appear from below. 'Will you be all right?'

'Don't worry about me,' said Ben, 'Those coppers think I'm half drunk all the time; what they don't realize is that I'm only all drunk half the time.'

'Thanks for getting us out, Ben,' said Chalotte. 'I've never known a grown-up do anything like that for a Borrible before.'

'Borribles, eh,' said the tramp, raising his bushy eyebrows, 'I met a few when I lived on the streets, always treated me right they did . . . Why don't you come down to Feather's Wharf, I've got a lovely place down there, plenty of room.'

Chalotte's blood ran cold. She'd been through Feather's Wharf on the Great Rumble Hunt and for her it was just a square mile of desolation where the River Wandle meandered through a moonscape of rubbish before vanishing underground into the sewers—down into the mud of Wendle territory.

'Yes, Ben,' she said, 'we might, one of these days. Right now we'd better run like hell. Goodbye, and thanks.' She left the tramp and went to join her companions in the yard behind the police station.

Outside, but only for a second or two, the Borribles were rooted to the spot in astonishment. There was mist everywhere, damp and warm and clinging to everything it touched, filling the whole world with the smell of the decaying river. Here was a mist that curled and swirled, climbing up into sinister cliffs of dirty white cloud which, as they slowly altered shape, created great canyons of deep darkness below them.

'This'll help us get away from the Woollies,' whispered Chalotte, 'won't it?'

'It won't if we can't find our way home,' said Spiff.

Suddenly Sydney saw the horse on the far side of the yard. 'Look,' she said in great excitement, 'it's Sam; they must have caught him and brought him here.'

'We haven't got the time for that now,' Spiff said. 'We've got to get as far away from Fulham as we can, and you can't do that with a horse.'

'You do what you like,' said Sydney. 'I'm not going to miss a chance like this. I'm not asking any of you to help me. I'd rather you didn't, come to that, then if anything goes wrong you won't be able to blame me if you get caught.' And Sydney tossed her hair, walked over to Sam and began to undo the rope that tied him to the window.

'Let's run while we've got the chance,' said Vulge. 'We'll have to get the horse some other time . . .'

Vulge's comments were cut short by the appearance of Ben, a silhouette in the oblong of light that shone from the back door of the police station.

'You kids ought to buzz off,' he called, 'don't want them coppers running you in twice in a day . . . Shove off home.'

Then things began to happen. It was at this moment that the duty sergeant, returning from his errand, entered the front office. He heard Ben talking and, intrigued by the tramp's behaviour, directed his steps towards the back door to find out what was going on. As he neared the tramp the sergeant heard a horse being led across the yard, then the sound of scampering feet and whispering, and finally Ben's voice chanting, 'Watch out, watch out, there's a Woollie about.'

With a roar of rage the sergeant sprang at Ben and heaved him from the doorway with all his strength. The old man spun on one heel, lost a boot and teetered at high speed along the corridor until he crashed against the iron railing of the banister and slipped slowly to the floor. Ben stared at his bare foot and waggled his grimy toes. 'Me bleedin' boot's come off,' he said.

The sergeant peered into the mist. He saw a child on a horse at the precise moment she saw him. The horse bared its teeth and neighed like some flesh-eating monster; there was a flash of steel-tipped hooves and the animal clattered away through the yard gates, then echoing back from the hollow streets of Fulham came the dull rumble of fast-moving hoofbeats and the triumphant noise of children liberated.

'Strewth,' said the sergeant, 'it's the prisoners,' and he ran back into the building and down the stairs to the cells. He saw the open doors, he saw the pile of handcuffs. 'Oh, my God,' he said, 'Sussworth will have my guts for garters,' and he dashed to the first floor to tell his colleagues of the catastrophe that had befallen.

Left to himself, Ben replaced his boot and slouched back to the office, his hands thrust deep into two of his many pockets. He felt the metal of the keys rap against his knuckles.

'Oh, dear,' he said, 'they'll need those,' and he took out the keys and replaced them on their proper hooks. 'There,' he pronounced with a certain amount of pleasure, 'look at that, nice and tidy, just how they likes it. I'll go home now, all this shennanigans is nothing to do with me.' Staggering slightly, Ben aimed himself with great care across the room, through the main door, down the steps, and into the gloom of Fulham Road, singing as he went his own special song:

> 'Wot's the point of workin' 'ard?
> Wot's the good of gainin' riches?
> Money's mean and banks are bitches;
> Profit's just a prison yard.

> 'Sling yer 'ook, an' sling it stealthy;
> Gob some grub an' swig some booze,
> Find a place ter kip and snooze—
> Now you're 'ealthy, wise an' wealthy!

> 'Let the world roll round an' round,
> Wiv its hard-worked folk in fetters:
> All 'oo think themselves yer betters,
> Money-mad and dooty-bound.

> 'Make yer choice, there ain't so many,
> No ambition's worth a fart;
> Freedom is a work of art—
> Take yer stand with Uncle Benny!'

Not two seconds after the tramp had left the police station the duty sergeant ran down from the first floor and went straight to the telephone.

'Quick,' he said into the receiver, 'this is a general alarm. Alert the SBG and every patrol car in the area, every man on the beat. The Borribles have escaped, every last one of them, yes. How do I know? They're not here, that's all, but I do know we'd better catch 'em. Sussworth will go bananas else.'

The sergeant banged the telephone down and looked at the shelf where the keys were hanging. He refocused his eyes and stared. Was it his imagination or were those keys swinging on the hook? He glanced at the door; there wasn't a breath of air nor a whisper of draught. In spite of the summer's heat he felt a shiver of fear trickle down his spine.

'There's something cock-eyed going on here,' he said, 'something definitely cock-eyed.'

Ben sauntered along the Fulham Road and London was silent, just how he liked it; murky and deserted, with no cars and no human beings. Even so he could sense the millions of people all round him, twitching under the weight of bad dreams, their warm toes sticking straight up from beneath wrinkled sheets, groping for the cool air of the night. Ben sighed happily. It was a real luxury, having a city to yourself.

He rubbed his big nose with the back of his hand. Under the street lamps the paving stones gleamed dank and dark yellow and the mist surged across the black tarmac of the road in huge rolling banks. Beyond and between the feeble pools of electric light were deep corridors of gloom that could have led anywhere.

Ben stopped and listened to the quiet. He spat. 'Nah,' he said, 'they don't have those old fogs like they used to, real pea-soupers where you couldn't see your hand in front of your face, people hacking and coughing, dropping dead at bus stops, undertakers working 'emselves to death. Lovely that was.'

As the old tramp went to move on the mist meandered and thinned for a moment and he realized that he was on a corner. At the same time a nameplate showed itself. 'Rumbold Road,' read Ben, 'that'll do nicely, I'll go through there.'

Once he had left the lamps of the main thoroughfare behind him Ben could see nothing and he was obliged to feel his way forward by limping along the gutter, one foot down, one foot up, his body rising and falling as he plodded on. His progress was slow but he persevered until he eventually entered the maze of narrow streets that lie on the north side of the River Thames near Fulham Power Station, there where the great metal containers of the oil depots loom solid and high, like giants petrified.

As Ben approached the river so the mist curdled and its smell became more noxious. Past the Stephendale Works he went, by Pearscroft Court and Parnell House, using instinct to find a way, talking to himself and swearing hard whenever he found that he had strayed into a dead end he did not know.

Finally, after wandering for an hour or more, Ben emerged into Townmead Road, a wide and ghostly place with a dull brick wall that soared into invisibility on the southern side, a brick wall that was pierced with iron gates giving access to the ugly oil wharves. The whole hemisphere seemed asleep and Ben halted yet again to cock an ear. He could hear something. Across the night and down the graveyard streets came the sound of a shod horse walking, hesitant, lost in the river's fog.

The old tramp felt his skin prickle, he had completely forgotten about the animal he'd seen back at the police station. His matted hair shifted on his scalp and some strands of it separated, one from the other.

'Strewth,' he said aloud, 'an 'orse. Is this the ghost of Dewdrop and Erbie, still roaming the streets, looking for lumber?'

Ben raised his hands to his throat and gathered the loose collars about his neck. He had never met the rag-and-bone man from Southfields but he had heard the story of Dewdrop's murder and the tales that told of his restless spirit questing through the streets of south London by night, searching on and on for more and more wealth.

Another wave of mist rolled in from the river and broke in

silent slow motion against a row of terraced houses. Ben shivered and shuffled on. 'This is creepy, this is,' he said, 'double creepy.'

The hoofbeats came nearer, insistent, not to be denied. Whichever way Ben turned the noise seemed to be waiting for him. Louder and louder came the sound until, at the place where Townmead Road meets Kilkie Street, a wall of mist rose into the air and without warning Ben came face to face with one of the children he had released earlier. She looked pale and scared and in her hand she held a rope which floated away behind her.

Ben jumped back in surprise, so suddenly that his feet left both his boots behind on the pavement.

'Oh my 'eart,' he cried. 'What the dickens are you doing, creeping about like an evil wish, where'd you spring from?'

'I'm lost,' said Sydney, just as terrified as Ben was. 'I'm not from this part of London, am I? This could be the backside of the moon for all I know about it.'

Ben was on the point of answering when he heard a large beast snort down its nostrils and, though he could not see it, the creature sounded very close.

'My gawd,' he said, 'it's the 'eadless 'orseman, ain't it? The devilish Dewdrop.'

'Don't be daft,' said Sydney, 'that's only Sam, he's with me.' Hearing his name Sam came into sight and gave Ben a friendly nudge in the chest.

The tramp was reassured by this gesture, and flexing his shoulders bravely he slipped his bare feet back into his boots.

'Swipe me,' he said, 'that is a relief. I thought it was one of them bovver beasts what eats 'umans. When you get the dt's as often as I do you never know what yer going to meet.'

'Ain't you the bloke that got us out of the cells?' asked Sydney.

'I am indeed,' said Ben, patting Sam on the neck, 'though I would deny it if called upon.'

'Is there any chance of you getting me across the river?' said Sydney. 'I must be out of sight before daybreak, and I need to find somewhere to hide the horse. Seems like I've been wandering around for hours.'

Ben now laid a hand on Sam's back and although the horse curled a lip at the smell that hovered about the tramp he did not back away.

'If you could just hop me up on to this animal,' said Ben, 'we could travel in style. Our objectives obviously lie in the same direction.'

Sydney did not hesitate; far away on the main roads she could hear the sound of police sirens under the low night sky, and if she did not hurry, her escape route would be blocked and dawn would find her still out on the streets, an easy catch for the SBG.

She backed Sam over to a brick coping about two feet high and helped Ben to climb on to it. Then she shoved and heaved him from behind until he was astride the horse with the reins in his hands.

'Here,' she said, 'hold those, though you won't really need 'em. Sam understands every word you say. Do you think you'll be all right up there?'

'Most certainly,' said Ben proudly. 'I have been a fine horseman in my time,' and as he raised a hand to emphasize the point he swayed alarmingly from the hips, only saving himself from a nasty fall by clutching at Sam's mane. 'Whoa,' cried the tramp fiercely, though the horse had not budged an inch, 'bugger me, but this animal is a lively lad and no mistake.'

Sydney had serious doubts about Ben's ability to find his way out of the back streets at all but she sprang up behind him, drew a deep breath against the dreadful smell and tapped the horse's flanks with her heels. That slight touch was enough and, taking his orders from Ben, Sam set off at a stately pace in the direction of Wandsworth Bridge.

The old tramp was supremely happy, indeed rarely had he been happier. He sat on Sam's back with his arms loose and his long legs rigid, while his boots hung precariously from his hooked toes and his tattered overcoats floated gently out into the mist like a highwayman's cloak. But, as the outcasts rode along, there came again, and from not so far away, the sound of a police car tearing through the night.

'Sod the law,' said Sydney, 'I hope the others are getting on all right.'

* * *

The others were not getting on all right. They were trudging, hopeless and lost, through the same muddle of faceless streets as Sydney and Sam, only they did not have Ben to show them the way. They had stuck together and they were following Spiff, mainly because he had assured everyone that he knew the way to Battersea like the back of his hand, but, as time went on, it seemed less and less likely that he did. The Borribles had turned a hundred corners and retraced a thousand steps; now they no longer had any idea where they were. They were tired, dispirited and almost ready to give up.

A siren howled strangely in the night and an SBG van passed nearby. The Borribles ducked behind a low wall but there was no real need. Down there by the river the mist was too dense for light to penetrate. Nothing the police had, neither revolving blue beam nor yellow headlamp, showed up at more than a yard or two. When the van had driven into the distance the runaways resumed their march, and as they did another sound came out of the huge cavern of darkness that surrounded them—the eerie footfalls of an invisible horse stalking along the roadway.

'It must be Sydney,' said Chalotte, 'with Sam. Let's give 'em a whistle.'

She lifted her fingers to her lips but Spiff raised a hand of his own and clasped it over the girl's mouth, jerking her head round roughly so that he could glare into her eyes.

'You bloody fool,' he hissed. 'And it might be a mounted Woollie, and it might be a trap. You whistle and we could be back inside just as sure as eggs is fried. Keep quiet, everyone. Even if it is Sid and Sam the last thing I want is a bleedin' 'orse clip-clopping along behind me telling every copper in London where I am.'

Chalotte struggled but she could not break free of Spiff's grasp and none of the others made a move to interfere. As far as they were concerned Spiff was right. It could be Sam out there but it could be the police too and nobody wanted to be captured a second time. So the Borribles stood without moving, held their breath and listened to the ghostly hoofbeats passing by.

'We'll wait here,' said Spiff, 'till everything's nice and quiet.'

* * *

Ben was enjoying himself. Sydney was not. Ben sang snatches of his song to while away the time. Sydney was trying to live without breathing. She liked the tramp well enough of course and was grateful to him for the part he had played in her rescue and escape, but riding behind him, arms round his waist and nose bumping into the small of his back, was not a pleasure. Ben's odour, especially at close range, was mature and strong. No one in the history of the world had ever smelt like Ben and he not only carried this smell with him, he added to the strength of it every few seconds, with a great deal of noise.

'I can't help it,' he explained, 'it must be all that beer I drinks.'

Sydney was a brave girl. 'How much further?' she gasped.

Ben glanced to his right and then to his left. He could see nothing. 'Looks like Demorgan Road,' he said, 'we'll be round the corner soon and on to Wandsworth Bridge.'

'Wandsworth Bridge!' Sydney felt frightened. Wandsworth Bridge was right on the eastern frontier of Wendle territory. Beyond it lay the River Wandle and the deep sewers where the most violent and untrustworthy of all Borrible tribes lived: the Wendles.

'Couldn't you take me to Battersea Bridge?' said Sydney. 'Any bridge except Wandsworth.'

Ben twisted round so that he could look at his companion. 'See 'ere, sunshine,' he said, 'you wanted me to bring you to the river, and that's what I'm doing. I'm going to where I knows best, ain't I? I have to; it's pitch dark, see, and I ain't got no radar in me pocket.'

'It's not that,' said Sydney, embarrassed at appearing ungrateful, 'but the Wendles live round here and they don't like us.'

Ben spat and a solid oyster of gob spun once in the air and went splat in the darkness. 'Them Wendles is only bits of kids like you, Borribles, ain't they? I sees one or two of 'em from time to time, on Feather's Wharf. They won't hurt yer, long as you're with me.'

'I hope not,' said Sydney, 'but I don't like it down here.'

Ben took no more notice and faced about. 'Come on, horse,' he said, 'down 'ere a bit and then left.'

Sam stepped out earnestly, thrusting his head into a mist which now grew thicker and warmer at every step, a mist that became so impenetrable by the river that the two riders did not realize they were on a bridge until they felt the ground rising steeply beneath them.

'This is it,' said Ben, 'soon be over the water.'

Up and up went the roadway and Sam stamped his hooves hard upon the tarmac, pacing forward till he reached the high point at the middle of the bridge and there, where the slope began to fall steeply away on the southern side, he stopped for a moment.

All about him was silence, except for the careless slap of a wave or two far below as the black river rolled seawards, forcing itself between the great stone pillars that held the bridge steady in the air. Sydney could see nothing. For a split second she felt that she was soaring, hovering above a sleeping city that was pinned down powerless by the muscular weight of the warm night.

Ben had no such thoughts. 'Come on, Sam,' he urged, 'I'm thirsty, I am. Was born thirsty, wasn't I?'

The horse moved forward once more and soon, though they couldn't see it, Ben and Sydney came to the great modern roundabout which is set at the beginning of the Wandsworth one-way system.

'We'll go right here,' said Ben. 'Wrong side of the road, of course, but us night-riders don't have to worry about rules and regulations.'

On they went, under the railway bridge and past a pub or two but not a car overtook them, not a window shone and the street lamps were blind. Only the wail of a police siren occasionally arced through the blackness, faintly and from far, far away across the wide waters. Sam did not falter for an instant; off Armoury Way he strode, right by the splendid entrance of Wandsworth Town Hall and along the High Street, coming at last to the great crossroads at Garratt Lane where the Spread Eagle pub stood locked and silent on the corner.

'Whoa,' said Ben and he swung a leg over Sam's neck and slid his feet to the ground. 'You just sit tight, girl,' he said to Sydney. 'I'll show you somethin', got to hide this 'orse, ain't we?'

In spite of the man's fearful smell Sydney felt her heart go out to him. 'Do you know, Ben,' she said, 'you're almost like a Borrible, but grown-up somehow, and that's impossible.'

'So's most things, sunshine,' said Ben, and he walked on, leading the horse.

At the far side of the road junction Ben came to a high wall of glazed brick; it was dripping with mist. He turned left there and waddled along for a few yards until he reached two enormous wooden gates. Sydney followed him, her mouth open, amazed by the size and magnificence of what she saw; it was like standing before the ceremonial portals of some ancient and fortified city.

Ben's fingers patted at a buttress of the wall until they found a bell-push. He winked at Sydney, then pressed the button, and beyond the gates and on the remoter side of courtyards and warehouses, the bell rang and the sound of it echoed along a river bank and told Sydney where she was. She caught her breath and remembered; she was outside Young's Brewery on the banks of the River Wandle, right in the middle of Wendle territory.

'Dammit,' she exclaimed, leaping from Sam's back to lean against the wall and stare into the darkness. 'Ben,' she asked, 'why have we come here?' She sounded very frightened.

'Come to get a drink, ain't I?' said Ben. 'Young's Brewery this is. Lovely drop of stuff they make here, but over and above that they uses horses to deliver their beer, don't they? And to have horses you have to have stables and to have stables you have to have someone as can look after them, someone who likes horses, and it so happens that the person I means is a mate of mine. On the road together we was in the old days, walking and talking and scrounging, just like the aristocracy. That's the way to live, sunshine, when you're young enough. Sam will be safe here, you'll see, safe as houses, and there's not a copper in Christendom will think of looking for him in a stable, is there?'

While Ben was talking the sound of studded boots started to clang across the uneven stones of a cobbled yard. Nearer and nearer banged the boots until at last they stopped quite close and a dead voice came from nowhere suddenly and the words it spoke suspended themselves in the darkness, like damp tea towels left overnight on a washing line.

'Who is it that wants me at this unearthly hour?'

Sydney shivered as the words touched her, but Ben was unworried. 'It's Ben,' he said, 'and he needs help.'

The voice did not answer but Sydney heard two iron bolts rasp and a small door set into the main gates creaked open and a man's face appeared, floating on its own in the night. It was a face that glowed pale under flat spiky hair. On either side of a hard bony nose two sombre eyes angled up and down. Under the nose grew a moustache.

Sydney pressed her body tight into the warm sweat of the brick wall. The man blinked at Ben as if he'd never seen him before, then he swung his head round to take in Sydney. The expression did not change at first but as the eyes slid beyond the Borrible and saw Sam the face broke into a smile that warmed and transformed the whole countenance. The man spoke through the smile and his tone was no longer loathsome, but friendly and welcoming.

'Well, Ben,' he said, 'and where did you get such an 'orse from, eh? What a beauty. Tired out though, ain't he? Been ill-treated, I'd say.'

Ben wagged his beard. 'He has been, Knibbs, he has been. Name of Sam, this girl's 'orse. Her name is . . . ?'

'Sydney,' said Sydney.

'It's like this,' said Ben, 'we got here by way of escaping from police custody and we needs to hide the 'orse while we goes to ground, like.'

Knibbs studied Sydney closely, his eyes keen. 'I'll look after the 'orse,' he began, 'I like 'orses. Can't hide you two though; they'd spot you. Might call the law in, then they'd notice me. Got a bit of form, I have, but they'll never even see an extra 'orse in a stable full of 'orses. Best place to hide church lead is on another church roof, I always say.'

'Ta, Knibbsie,' said Ben, and he went to hand Sam's leading rope to the stableman, but the horse wrenched its head away and sidestepped, frightened by the tall gates and the overhanging walls.

'Now then, come on,' said Knibbs in his kind voice, 'you'll be all right here with me.' Another bolt slid and slowly the big gates opened until there was a gap large enough for Sam to walk through.

Sydney put her arms round the horse's neck. 'You have to hide, Sam,' she said, 'just for a day or two. I'll come back as soon as I can, and I'll never leave you again, honest.'

Knibbs clicked his teeth and stroked Sam gently on the nose. 'It's the life of Riley in here, old son,' he said. 'It's a five-star stable and no mistake.' At last encouraged, the horse stepped through the gap and into the brewery yard.

Once Sam was safely inside Knibbs closed the great gates but the little door he left open. Ben held out his arms, there was a clink of glass against glass and Sydney heard, rather than saw, three pint bottles pass between the two friends.

Ben tucked the beer into the layers of his clothing. 'Ah, thanks, Knibbsie,' he said, licking his lips, 'thirsty work, staying alive, thirsty work.'

Knibbs nodded. 'I'll take care of the 'orse,' he said, shutting the door finally, though they could still hear his voice, 'but in future make sure you come the back way.' And that was all except for the sound of Sam being led away across the cobbles.

'Let's be off,' said Ben, and he began to trudge away into the fog; Sydney walked by his side.

'Are you quite sure that Sam will be all right?' she asked, anxious now that her horse had really gone.

Ben fumbled in his overcoat and brought out one of his bottles and an opener. ' 'Course I am,' he said. 'Knibbs likes nothing more than an 'orse. He'll look after 'im like a babby, so fat and pampered he'll be, you won't recognize him.'

Ben took the top off his beer and looked at the bottle as if he'd never seen one before. 'My God,' he said, 'I've been waiting a lifetime for this.' He raised the drink to his lips and Sydney watched while he took a deep swig. From miles away over the river came the rise and fall of a police siren, howling through the night like a banshee.

Ben lowered the bottle and expelled a sigh of satisfaction from the middle of his beard. 'That's the stuff,' he said. 'It puts hair on your chest, marrow up your bones and lead in your pencil.'

'Are we going somewhere now?' asked Sydney.

'Somewhere, I say we are,' answered Ben, 'we're going to my

place. You can bet yer boots that the Woollies are pounding the streets for you and they won't be full of joy and goodwill if they finds yer, neither.'

Ben laughed at his own joke, tipped the bottle to his mouth again, and still walking, drained it dry. When the beer was finished he gave a fruity belch. 'By gum,' he said, 'I needed that, felt weak and trembly I did.'

'Do you think my mates are all right,' said Sydney, keeping close to the tramp so as not to lose sight of him. 'I hope they all got away.'

Ben looked down at the small Borrible from somewhere beneath the bushes of his eyebrows. 'Them friends of yourn,' he said, 'are alive or dead, free or caught, and all we can do right now is look out for number one.' And with that he plodded off at a fast rate and Sydney kept up with him as best she might, having no wish to be left alone and lost in the middle of dangerous Wendle country.

5

Spiff tiptoed into the garage forecourt. All about him the big petrol pumps, their computer faces half hidden in the shadows, stood like Martians come down to earth. The Borrible halted and looked carefully to right and left. Nothing. Underfoot the oil-stained concrete gleamed in the light that fell from some half a dozen overhead fluorescent tubes; a strange mauvish light it was and one that diffused itself over a million particles of mist and hung in the air like dirty raindrops on a dusty spider's web. It was not yet dawn and the sky beyond the garage was dark and unbroken.

Spiff looked round once more, satisfying himself that the garage was well and truly closed for the night, then he whistled the Borrible whistle and, one by one, his companions stepped out of the blackness.

'Where are we?' asked Vulge.

'Dunno,' answered Spiff, 'but wherever we are we ain't far from the river. Smell.'

Everyone sniffed and the strange odour of the Thames in London, a mixture of varnish and vinegar, was drawn into their nostrils.

'Well,' said Bingo, 'where there's a river there's a bridge and we'd better get across it. If we ain't off the streets by daylight we might as well clip our own ears and save Sussworth the trouble.' He groped his way over to the far side of the forecourt, the rest of the group following.

'Look,' said Twilight, 'ain't that a main road there, anybody know it?'

There was no answer, but after a moment Spiff, who had been

staring hard at the ground, said, 'I reckon it's straight on, see how the road rises slightly in that direction, like it was going towards a bridge.'

'Well come on,' said Stonks, 'we don't want to hang about. There's nowhere to hide on a bridge; let's get over before the mist goes.'

But the mist showed no signs at all of going and as the Borribles moved forward it continued to steam up from beneath their feet, growing strangely heavier as it rose, swirling and turning, making it impossible for the runaways to see where they were or where they were walking.

Suddenly Spiff, who was leading, raised a hand and stopped. They had arrived at the highest point on the bridge, where the road began to slant downwards and out of sight as if it had come to an abrupt end on the edge of the world.

'Well, it's definitely a bridge,' said Spiff. 'Look, it goes down this side, over the hump.'

'Yeah,' agreed Stonks, 'but which bridge? I don't recognize it.'

'It ain't Battersea Bridge,' said Bingo.

'And it ain't Albert Bridge or Chelsea Bridge,' said Vulge.

'And it's not Westminster, Lambeth or Vauxhall Bridge,' said Stonks.

'Or Hammersmith Bridge or Putney Bridge,' said Twilight.

Chalotte pushed through the group and put her face, tight with anger, close to Spiff's. 'You know which one it is, don't yer, Spiff?' she said. 'It's the only one it can be . . . You knew you were bringing us here all the time. Go on, tell them.'

Spiff laughed. 'It don't matter which bridge it is,' he said, 'long as we get across it, does it? So it's Wandsworth Bridge, so what?'

'So what,' Chalotte sneered, 'because Wandsworth is Wendle territory. Last time we were here we nearly got killed and four of our mates did. You're up to something, Spiff, and I wish to hell I knew what it was. What's your game?'

'My game,' said Spiff, screwing his face right back at Chalotte's, 'is getting back 'ome with me ears still on.'

As the two of them glared at each other the hoo-ha, hoo-ha of a siren came from somewhere near at hand and there was no more time for argument. All six Borribles ran down the southern slope of the bridge just as fast as they could. If they could make it to the great roundabout they would be able to bear left into York Road and head straight for Battersea; with luck, and in a little while, they would be safe at home, hidden and protected by friends.

It was not to be that easy. Two indistinct and menacing figures, one large and one small, grew out of the mist in the path of the speeding Borribles. Spiff skidded to a halt and the others bumped into him.

'Sussworth and Hanks,' said Spiff, 'and not a catapult between us.'

'A Borrible,' said a voice.

'Cripes,' said Vulge, 'it's Wendles, which is worse.'

'Don't be daft,' said the voice again. 'It's Sydney, and I've got Ben with me; you know, the bloke who got us out of the nick.'

'Oh, it's me all right,' said the tramp, and there was the clink of a bottle in his clothes. 'Small world, ain't it?'

'Wait a minute,' said Spiff suspiciously, 'have you got that bloody horse with yer? We don't want him following us about, clip-clop, clip-clop.'

'Don't you worry,' said the tramp, pulling a bottle of beer from a pocket, 'he's in a safe place.'

'None of that matters now,' said Twilight. 'Look behind you.'

The Borribles did and there, just a little beyond the rim of the bridge, they saw a halo of harsh whiteness reflected on the underneath of the dark sky. It was the beam of a car's headlamps as it got into position on the north side of the bridge, the side the runaways had left only moments before.

As they watched there was more noise behind them: tyres screeching, car doors slamming, men shouting. They turned again; once more a brightness glowed and another arc of silver light clamped itself against the low-lying mist, this time on the southern shore of the Thames and only three hundred yards from where the Borribles stood.

'It's that bloody Sussworth,' said Spiff. 'I bet he's blocked every bridge between Richmond and the sea.'

'We're caught in the open too,' said Bingo. 'Once daylight comes we've had it.'

Ben leant against the balustrade of the bridge and drank from the second of the bottles that Knibbs had given him. 'Well,' he said as soon as the bottle was empty, 'I think you kids better come home with me.'

'Oh, yeah,' said Spiff, 'and what do you think the coppers will do, help us on our way?'

Ben scratched inside his coat and ignored Spiff's sarcasm. 'Behind me,' he said, 'as I stand here, though you can't see it, is the end of the bridge. Behind that is a narrow roadway, next to the river here, and down there is a pub, stands all on its own that pub, in empty ground, called the Ship it is. Behind that pub, about eight feet high and with only a little barbed wire on top is a wall; behind that wall is Feather's Wharf rubbish dump. In the middle of that rubbish dump is my 'ome, a palace with room for everyone.'

'And what's beyond your palace?' asked Spiff.

'The River Wandle,' said Ben, 'where the cranes load the barges with trash before they sails away to export.'

'It's where the Wandle meets the Thames,' said Sydney, 'don't you remember, it's awful.'

'It could be ten times awful,' said Spiff, 'but it's the only way we're getting off this bridge.'

'One thing's certain,' said Chalotte, 'we're getting deeper and deeper into Wendle territory . . . It's almost like someone wanted us to go there.'

Spiff smiled mysteriously. 'Don't blame me,' he said. 'We've got no choice now.'

They did not have far to go. A few paces beyond where they had been standing they came to a slope that dropped steeply away from the bridge; this slope soon became a road and after following it for about a hundred yards, leaving the Ship Inn on their left, they came to a solid brick wall, and as Ben had said, the top of it was looped along with barbed wire.

'We're right on the river now,' explained the tramp, 'so if you climb up this little embankment wall here you can reach round the end of the big wall and you'll feel an iron ring on the other side.

Hang on to that, throw your legs out over the water and, lo and be'old, you'll find yourself on Feather's Wharf.'

'And if we falls in the river . . . ?' asked Vulge.

Ben snorted. 'I've done it hundreds of times drunk, so I'm sure you bits of kids can do it sober. 'Ere, watch this.' The old man hauled himself on to the low parapet of the embankment, grasped something that was out of sight, kicked his feet, threw himself into space and disappeared. After this exploit there was a second or two of silence, just time enough for the Borribles to look at each other anxiously, then they heard the crash of a body hitting solid earth.

'I hope he's all right,' said Sydney, but at that moment Ben's voice resounded loudly through the night.

'Ouch, ooer, it's me back, bugger it! Come on over, you lot. I'll catch yer this side.'

'I don't want to fall in,' said Twilight, 'I can't swim.'

'Tough,' said Spiff. 'I'm going anyway. I'd rather fall into the Thames than fall into the hands of the SBG.' He sprang on to the wall and leant sideways, an expression of concentration on his face. 'I can reach the ring,' he called down. 'You have to push yourself round here and hang on tight. Like this.' And with that Spiff disappeared as well.

Stonks was next up and he followed Ben and Spiff without the slightest hesitation. Then Sydney went, then the others. Chalotte waited to be last and as she swung her legs out above the rolling darkness of the river she glanced upwards and saw that the sky was becoming pale; she could even see one or two weak stars. The mist was going and dawn was on the way—it was time for the Borribles to be under cover.

Down on the ground there was no light. When Chalotte had pivoted through the air and landed on a patch of hard and dusty dirt she found that the faint glimmer she had seen in the heavens did not penetrate the murk of Feather's Wharf.

Ben's voice came to her from somewhere in the dead atmosphere beside the brick wall. 'Ah . . . what'll we do? Ah yes, best follow me in single file, you lot, and don't take the wrong path, 'cos you'll end up in the rubbish crusher if you do.'

Having given them this warning the old tramp set off into a vast and lightless terrain. This was the wasteland that stretched between Wandsworth Bridge and the River Wandle, an abandoned country which rose in crumbling hillocks and fell in deep valleys of brown and black earth. It was a place of desolation where nothing was visible in the dark but where the Borribles could sense the danger of an emptiness somewhere near, like an unseen cliff beneath their feet.

Silently they trudged, keeping close behind Ben as he went along a narrow track whose surface had been packed firm over many a month and year by the slow scufflings of his broken boots. The path wound this way and that across the land; through wide depressions in which half-squashed tins and rotten cartons were knee-deep, and over hills so precipitous that the Borribles were forced to climb them on all fours, just like the rats that scampered and squealed all around.

There were fearsome smells too, making the air thick as soup as it floated in from the Thames; a foul stench compounded of rancid sewage, mouldering cardboard and the rotting flesh of dead seabirds. The odours pricked at Chalotte's nostrils and as she walked she remembered, from her previous visit, the grotesque ugliness of this strange landscape: a square mile of dullness strewn with the white rectangles of rusty washing machines and gutted gas stoves; a maggoty place.

Chalotte gritted her teeth and followed the shape in front of her, up and down, left and right. Finally the shape and the shapes in front of it stopped, and she heard Ben's voice come from the head of the column.

'We're here,' he said, ' 'ome, sweet 'ome.'

Staring into the gloom Chalotte could just make out an oblong of shadow that could have been a small building. Ben's tall form merged with it and there was the scraping noise of bone dry hinges grinding on rust. Slowly the Borribles edged through a doorway, step by step, until they stood, seeing nothing, in the unknown space of Ben's hideout, and there they waited, hardly daring to breathe.

For a while they listened to Ben fumbling and swearing in the dark, then they heard the scratch of a match, then another, and a tiny flame sputtered into life. Ben brought the candle to the flame and the light flickered up for a moment, fastening on to the wick and finally growing large and steady. The tramp was strangely silent. He put the candle down and, still without speaking, he went round the room until he had lit every other candle he possessed. When that was done he brought three larger oil lamps from a shelf and lit them too. And now the golden light filled the whole shack and the Borribles gasped and gazed around in wonder. They were in the most remarkable residence they had ever seen; it was a palace, just as Ben had said it would be, but a palace in his own style. Nobody but Ben could have made such a house.

The tramp laughed at the amazement on the faces of the Adventurers and fell into a chair at the head of the long table which occupied the centre of the room. Then he groped under his seat and began to pull bottles of Special Brew into sight, lining them up, one beside the other, until there was enough for everybody.

'Here you are then, mates. You'd better have one of these, celebrate your arrival at Ben's gaff, like.' He looked round the room until he could contain his pride no longer. 'Well,' he asked, 'what do you think of her, eh? I tells yer straight, even ole Queenie ain't got nothing like this; she wouldn't know what to do with it even if she had.'

The Borribles nodded. There was a lot in what Ben said.

They were standing in a large room which had been made by banging tarred planks into the ground and then nailing sheets of corrugated iron across them to form a roof. It was a rickety building and one that seemed liable to collapse at any moment, but it was not the shack itself which astounded the Borribles so much as its contents.

The table, at the head of which Ben now sat drinking his ale like a Viking chieftain, had elegant bulging legs and a chenille tablecloth of a deep burgundy colour. All Ben's candles burned in graceful twirly candlesticks from which the silver plate had worn away to leave the brass gleaming through, brighter than gold.

At one end of the room was an enamelled wood-burning stove with a pot belly and three feet made like lion's claws. Its doors must have fallen off at some time in the past but they had since been re-hung on hinges improvised from the thick wire of a coat hanger. The hut's earthen floor was covered with several layers of carpet, warm and luxurious to the feel of the foot. There was no shortage of armchairs either, all of them threadbare, shapeless and comfortable. Against one of the longer walls leant a huge dresser overloaded with brightly glazed cups and plates; they were chipped and cracked but remained, for the most part, quite serviceable.

Ben had plenty of food too, though it looked as second-hand as the furniture and cascaded out of the front of a large kitchen cabinet: torn packets of cornflakes, broken boxes of dried milk, bags of biscuit pieces, tins of steak and kidney pudding and loaves of sliced bread, mouldy at the edges and spilling out of their waxed paper like grimy playing cards, spreading across the floor, trodden into the carpets.

But that was only a beginning. All round the room at every height were planks of rough wood, loosely bracketed to the walls and sloping precariously. These were Ben's shelves and on them he stacked the things he called useful, the things he had discovered in the mounds of rubbish on Feather's Wharf: old-fashioned valve radios, magazines, knives and forks, sardine cans filled with nuts and bolts and spring washers, bicycle chains, torches, spanners, screwdrivers. The Borribles gazed and gazed. There was even a beer crate under the table stuffed to the brim with dozens of pairs of old shoes and, on a worm-eaten chest of drawers, an ancient wind-up gramophone with a pile of old seventy-eights beside it. Such was Ben's shanty.

The tramp wagged his beard in contentment, pleased at the surprise on the faces around him. He scratched an armpit and opened another bottle of beer.

'I've got something of everything,' he said. 'It's diabolical what people throw away; and that ain't the half of it, just have a look at this.' Ben pulled himself to his feet, seized an oil lamp and went to a curtain that was draped across a corner of the room.

'You see,' he explained, 'this shack we're in now was here when I came so all I had to do was furnish it, but there was so much good rubbish going to waste that I had nowhere to put it all, so I kept adding other shacks to this one. You can come and see if yer like.'

Ben drew the curtain aside, held his lamp high and stepped through a narrow doorway with the Borribles following. Once again they gasped. They were in a lean-to in which pile upon pile of second-hand clothes rose in towers to the roof. There were clothes of all kinds: trousers, coats, shirts, sweaters, cloth caps. There was hardly space enough to move.

'I don't know what to do with it all,' said Ben. 'I swaps some from time to time, just for grub and beer, but people throws their stuff away quicker than I can pick it up . . . There's a damn sight more than this too.'

And there was. Ben had added at least six or seven sheds on to the original one and each construction leant weakly back upon its neighbour for support, looking ready, so it seemed, to fall over at the first puff of wind. It was all dangerously ramshackle but Ben had been obliged to make his house out of the materials that had come to hand: splintered doors, squares of asbestos, bits of broken window, sheets of enamelled iron bearing advertisements, the timber from shattered packing cases, everything nailed and wired together to form a warren of rooms and corridors, and not one of them at right angles to another but sprawled about all higgledy-piggledy, making haphazard corners inside and triangular yards outside, shapes that were ideal for storing the thousands of things that Ben had collected over the years.

In the third room were countless bottles of all colours, stacked row upon row, smelling of stale alcohol and covered in dust and thick black cobwebs: wine bottles, beer bottles, cider bottles and lemonade bottles.

The next lean-to was where Ben kept bits and pieces of hundreds of oil lamps, antique and modern, and between the slanting shelves there were brass hooks and from each one hung a coloured mug or flowered chamber pot. The fifth room had its walls concealed by thousands of tin cans, cleaned and flattened with a hammer and then nailed in position, making the place glitter like a pub at Christmas. Here too were beds and sofas with coverlets, blankets and eiderdowns, enough to sleep an army.

'This is where I snoozes,' said Ben, and he held his lamp up to show a huge brass bedstead adorned with five or six interior-sprung mattresses, making the bed so tall that the tramp needed a stepladder to get into it.

The sixth room was stacked to the height of a man with bundles of newspapers, magazines and books. The seventh was a kind of workshop where Ben stored tools and kept a few deckchairs and sun loungers.

'I like to watch the barges and tugs going by in the summer,' he said, 'and the people rushing over the bridge in their cars on the way to work. It makes you think, that do, all that galloping about so they can throw this stuff away so as I can sit 'ere and watch 'em.' And he shook his hairy head and fell silent, puzzled by this great mystery of life.

When the tour was ended Ben shepherded the Borribles back to the main shanty, sat them down, poured them a mug of beer each and set about making a meal. He began by lighting his stove from a pile of kindling that he kept near the door, and as soon as his fire was burning well he unhooked an iron frying pan, encrusted with grease, and filled it with the ingredients that came to hand.

There was dried milk, dried egg, tinned tomatoes, cornflakes and some cans of beans, all of which the tramp mixed together in a kind of swill and cooked piping hot. When it was ready he laid white soup plates on the table, put out some spoons, and while everyone gathered round he rummaged in the food cabinet and found a couple of sliced loaves that were not too green at the edges.

'You'd better tuck in,' he advised the Borribles. 'In this world you cannot tell what's going to happen tomorrow and you never know where your next meal's coming from.'

The Adventurers did not need to be persuaded of this philosophy and they attacked the food with an appetite. Ben leant his chair against the wall, propped his feet on the table, and watched his guests with pleasure, tipping a bottle of beer into his mouth every time he felt the need. 'Bloody marvellous,' he kept saying, 'bloody marvellous! I ain't never 'ad anyone visit me before.'

In next to no time the plates were empty and the Borribles began to stretch their limbs and relax, forgetting for a moment the dangers that surrounded them. All of them that is except Spiff. He wiped his plate with a slice of bread, licked his fingers clean, left his seat and without a word to anyone went outside.

'Where's he gone?' asked Ben.

Chalotte closed one eye. 'Always on the lookout is our Spiff. Don't trust no one and never leaves anything to chance.'

'Well, he's right, isn't he?' said Vulge. 'If Borribles don't look alive, they're very soon dead.'

Twilight grinned and folded his arms. 'I could live here for ever,' he said. 'This is the best house I've been in . . . All we need now is about twenty-four hours' sleep and we'll be as right as rain.'

'There's enough beds here for yer,' began Ben. 'If you like to go in the other room you can—' but he was interrupted by Spiff who suddenly reappeared, slamming the shack door behind him.

'There'll be no sleeping now,' he said urgently, 'we've got to get out of here, as quick as we can, if we can.'

'How d'yer mean?' asked Stonks.

'The Woollies,' said Spiff. 'It's light outside and I saw them, through the mist, looking over the wall. I had a look the other way too; there's a couple of police cars near the unloading wharf, lights flashing. We're outnumbered and we're surrounded.'

The Borribles stared at each other; the food congealed in their stomachs and went hard like golf balls. Ben hiccuped, took his feet from the table and lowered the front legs of his chair to the floor.

'Let's take a look,' said Vulge. 'There's got to be some way out.'

The Borribles hastened to the door, dropped to their hands and knees and crawled outside to crouch behind the nearest pile of rubbish. It was a silent landscape they saw; not a car could be heard on the streets and no tug hooted on the river. The night had risen halfway into the sky and, though the air was still black on its highest edge, the ground was clearly visible save where the mist formed large pools in the hollows and where white shreds of it twirled upwards like will-o'-the-wisps eager to evaporate.

Spiff pointed to the barrier that divided Feather's Wharf from the Ship Inn. 'Look,' he said, 'along the top of the wall, they must be standing on the roofs of their cars; you can see the heads of about twenty Woollies, just watching.'

'Do you reckon they know we're here?' asked Twilight.

'Could do, easy,' said Bingo. 'They might have been near us in the mist, heard us talking when we came over the bridge.'

'Come round the other side of the shack,' said Spiff, 'it's worse.'

Slowly, so as to make no noise and to attract no notice, the Borribles crept to the other side of Ben's shanty and peered cautiously across no man's land. There was no mistaking the line of sombre figures waiting for the dawn to establish itself along the banks of the Wandle. The police officers stood like shadows, magnified in the last drifts of the early morning haze; behind them were three or four police cars, their whirling blue lights casting a cold and unlovely hue over the whole landscape; it was a colour that drained the life from every living thing. There would be no escape in that direction.

'Let's get under cover,' said Spiff, 'before it gets any lighter.'

Inside the shack there was desperation.

'There's only one way,' said Spiff, 'and that's a run to the river, and the chances are that Sussworth's got boats on it. We might be able to get up the Wandle . . .'

'That bloody Sussworth,' said Chalotte.

'Who's Sussworth?' said Ben, opening another bottle of Special Brew. 'What's he got against yer?'

The Borribles explained.

'Oh,' said Ben, waving his drink in the air. 'SBG eh, don't worry about them. Any friend of mine is a friend of mine.' Ben was getting drunk and once he was on the way he went very quickly.

Bingo called from the door where he had been keeping watch. 'They're coming over the wall. I can see Sergeant Hanks, now Sussworth and . . . blimey, they're handing a bleedin' great Alsatian dog over.'

Ben swayed upwards out of his chair. He blew into his beard and banged his bottle on the table like a declaration of war. 'That does it,' he snarled. 'I don't often do anything but when I do I do. Dogs, is it? I'll shove so many dogs up this Sussworth's nostril he won't know if he's a Pekinese or a poodle.'

With that the old man fell forward on to his hands and knees and began to pull at the edge of his carpets.

Sydney rushed to him anxiously, thinking that he was overcome by emotion and perhaps dying of a heart attack. 'Are you all right, Ben?' she asked.

Ben turned his head to the light; his red-veined eyes shone with anger. 'Course I'm all right, sunshine, and so will you be in a jiffo. Give a hand here, roll back these carpets.'

When Sydney heard this she bent to the floor and peeled back several layers of carpet to reveal the studded metal cover of a manhole. It was rusty but the words embossed on the edge of it were quite legible: Wandsworth Borough Council.

Spiff chuckled and tapped the cover with his foot. 'The sewers,' he said. 'Well, the Woollies won't follow us down there, that's for sure.' He looked at Bingo. 'What are they doing now?'

'They're waiting for everyone to get over,' answered Bingo. 'There's about ten of them on this side of the wall now, the others are coming. It won't be long before they're in here with us.'

Spiff took a sharp poker from the fireplace and handed it to Stonks. 'Right,' he said, 'let's get it open.'

Stonks forced the point of the poker into the slight crack which ran round the lip of the cover. Spiff knelt by his side and levered upwards with a table knife. They shoved and twisted with all their strength until Spiff made a gap and managed to ram the knife in as far as it would go; then Stonks prodded with the poker and pushed the handle downwards and the great cast iron disc gaped away from the floor. Spiff, with a ready courage, dropped the knife and grabbed at the manhole with his fingers, taking the whole weight of it while Stonks altered his grip and came to Spiff's assistance. Twilight and Vulge took a hand too and on Spiff's word of command the four Borribles heaved together and the lid pivoted upright on two stiff hinges to disclose a large and dangerous-looking hole.

'The Woollies are coming this way,' said Bingo, 'and searching every bit of ground. They're spread out, torches, truncheons, dogs sniffing. Hurry up for Pete's sake.'

Stonks surveyed the steaming blackness at his feet. He wrinkled his nose and then raised a worried face to his companions. 'I recognize that smell, don't you?'

'Not half,' said Vulge. 'It's the stink of Wendles and mud and blood.' As he spoke the smell became noticeably stronger, rising from the depths on a visible curl of green air. The Borribles stared at it, mesmerized with fear until Spiff broke the silence.

'Yeah,' he said, 'and out here it smells of coppers and ear-clippin'. I'm going down. I ain't scared of a few Wendles.'

'You know what Flinthead will do if he catches us,' said Chalotte.

'Then he mustn't catch us,' retorted Spiff. 'Wendle country's big enough, we'll have to hide down there and keep out of the way.'

Ben laughed and his head rolled loosely on his shoulders. He had drunk a lot of beer now. 'You'll be all right, just go down the hole, only don't go far. As soon as the coppers have been and gone I'll let you out again, easy, see.'

'Ben's right,' said Spiff. 'We may only have to stay there half an hour.' He went towards the door and looked over Bingo's shoulder so that he could see what was happening.

Everything had changed outside. The dawn had struggled to the top of the sky and was brightening from grey to blue. The mist had lifted and the line of policemen was plainly to be seen as they walked steadily across the dump, poking at the ground with rods and shining their torches into the dark places. A dog barked, then another. Spiff recognized the small figure of Inspector Sussworth with his long overcoat flapping at his heels; next to him was Sergeant Hanks.

'We'll have to go anyway,' he said between clenched teeth, 'the Woollies will find us in a minute.'

Ben waved his bottle. 'You'd better bugger off, all right; what's the good of me telling this Sussworth feller I don't know you if he walks right in and sees you standing there? Won't look reasonable, will it?'

Spiff elbowed his way past his companions and went to the

edge of the black pit. 'Thanks, Ben,' was all he said and then he stepped on to the broad rung of the iron ladder that was built into the side of the manhole and, without sparing a glance for anyone, he climbed rapidly down into the rising steam. In a moment he was gone.

'When I got home from the Rumble hunt,' said Vulge, 'I swore I'd never go within ten miles of a Wendle again . . . Well here we are. I'll be lucky if I'm limping on both legs after this.' And with a sideways jerk of the head he too went down into the stinking vapour.

Just then a police whistle shrilled outside and shouts were heard, the loudest coming from Sergeant Hanks. 'We know you're in there; you'd better come out with your hands on your heads.'

The remaining Borribles waited no longer. Twilight flung himself down the ladder; Sydney followed, so did Bingo and Stonks. Chalotte went last, easing her feet on to the second or third rung so that her head was level with the ground. She looked at Ben. He was sinking lower and lower in his chair. In a few moments he would fall asleep but if he didn't close the manhole behind her it would be obvious to the police where the runaways had gone.

There was another roar: 'You'd better come out, you kids; it'll be the worse for you if you don't.'

Chalotte stretched an arm and grabbed Ben by the ankle and shook his leg. The tramp swung his eyes open with a lurch of the face and stared down at Chalotte. For him she was a disembodied head rolling about on the floor and yet still speaking.

'My God,' said Ben, and he leant forward, his elbows on his knees, 'bloody good stuff this Special Brew.'

'Oh, Ben,' pleaded Chalotte, 'don't be daft, it's me. There's coppers outside. They'll be in here in a twinkling and your only chance is to say you haven't seen us. You've got to close this manhole, roll back the carpet and then move the table over a bit. Do it now Ben, otherwise Sussworth will skin you like a banana. Hurry.'

Ben blinked. The talking head had gone but it had shocked him sober enough to do what was required. He dropped his beer bottle and fell to the carpets, landing on all fours. He took a deep breath to gather strength, and crawled round and round until he got himself behind the manhole cover. Once there he pushed it hard with his shoulder several times, grunting and swearing until it pivoted past its centre of gravity, slamming shut with a muffled thump that echoed through the sewers below but was almost silent above.

Ben was the only person in the world who could move on hands and knees and still stagger. He did it now, wobbling backwards and pulling the carpets after him, smoothing them down as he went. Another shout came from the police cordon. There was a banging of truncheons on the walls of the hut. Ben made one last effort, grabbed hold of a table leg and dragged it towards him. When this was done he smiled and groped for the bottle he had dropped earlier. As soon as he found it he rolled over and gazed at the roof, enjoying the support of the ground in his back.

'I'm weary,' he said, and fell fast asleep.

Sergeant Hanks was the first officer into the shack bashing his way through the door like a fifty-ton tank, his truncheon swinging. Tramping on his heels came half a dozen policemen, heavy and tall, their arms held stiffly by their sides.

'You'd better come quietly,' shouted Hanks, 'the place is surrounded. You can't get away and if you try we'll split yer heads open.'

'There's no one here,' said a policeman after looking carefully into every corner of the room.

Hanks smashed the table with his truncheon. 'Well investigate the other rooms,' he cried, 'they can't get away.'

The sergeant moved round the table and stumbled over Ben's body. 'Here's one,' he said, and while his men searched the lean-tos he sat on a beer crate and gazed into the tramp's dirty face.

More and more policemen stormed into the hut and prodded and stamped their way everywhere. At last Inspector Sussworth came and he stood near the door, lifting himself up on his toes every now and then, stretching his neck like a cockerel. Hanks removed his right index finger from his left nostril and wiped a yellow bogey on to the leg of Ben's table. Then he saluted.

'There's no one here, sir,' he said, 'except this specimen on the floor.' And he kicked Ben in the ribs to show Sussworth where the tramp lay.

The inspector squared his shoulders and sniffed and his little moustache danced under his nose as he tried to identify the various odours imprisoned in the shack.

'There's a malodorous pong in here,' he said, 'a very nasty pong. I suspect it emanates from this recumbent malefactor, alleged.' Sussworth clasped his hands behind his back like royalty and squeezed his fingers till they hurt. He was looking very smart in his flowing overcoat and chequered cap. He took a delicate step round the table and looked at Ben, who still slept contentedly on the floor. 'Wake him up,' said the inspector, 'and ascertain if he can help with enquiries.'

Hanks smiled. This was the kind of job he liked. He grabbed the tramp by the lapels, pulled him into a sitting position and began to shake him vigorously, like a pillow he was knocking the lumps out of. After a few moments of this treatment Ben's eyes blinked, then they opened.

'Oooer,' he said, 'I feel a bit sick.'

Sussworth bent over, tipped the tramp's hat off and seized a fistful of hair, twisting it tight until the tears welled up in Ben's eyes.

'I want to know the present whereabouts of those children you aided and abetted,' cried the inspector. 'Where are those Borribles?'

'Bobbirols,' said Ben, 'whazzem when they's at home? Bobbirols.'

Sussworth pulled Ben's hair tighter and struck him in the face with his free hand. 'Borribles,' was all he said.

'Them kids you saw at Fulham police station,' said Hanks, 'you know who we mean.'

'Oh, them,' said Ben, trying to sniff up his tears, 'them's Bobbirols, are they? Well, I heard 'em in the fog, followed me along they did. I could hear them moving about. Scared stiff, wasn't I? I thought they was going to mug me, you know what kids are like today. Where was the law and order then, I asked myself. I could have been duffed up by them hooligans. I'm an old man, I need protection at my age.'

Sussworth struck Ben once more. 'You will do,' he said.

'I come over the bridge on me way home,' explained the tramp, 'and they went on towards Battersea, I think, down York Road.'

'You're lying,' screamed Hanks, and he jabbed his truncheon deep into Ben's stomach. All the breath he possessed shot out of Ben's lungs and his face was drained of blood in an instant. 'You liar,' shouted Hanks again, 'we had the bridge closed off by then. Our men heard you chatting; don't chat to yourself, do you?'

'Of course I bloody well does,' retorted Ben, trying to look indignant at the same time as having no breath. 'Who the Saint Fairy bleedin' Anne would I talk to else? There ain't no one, is there?'

'For the last time,' said Sussworth quietly, 'those children have absconded from police custody and have stolen government property; item, one horse belonging to the Greater London Council Parks Division. Where are they?' At each word the policeman tried to twist Ben's head from his shoulders, yanking it round and round as if he were unscrewing it.

'Aaagh,' screamed Ben in pain, 'leave off, can't yer? I'd tell yer if I knew, wouldn't I? Can't stand kids, can I?'

The inspector released his grip on Ben's hair and stood up. He stamped his feet angrily on the floor, his body jerking in a spasm of bad temper. 'We're getting nowhere with this imbecile, Hanks,' said Sussworth. 'Those children can't have disappeared, nor the horse. They can't be on the river, they aren't north of us and they can't have got through the cordon back to Battersea. There's only one place they can be, the one place we can't go without getting our noses bloodied.'

Hanks scrambled to his feet in consternation, releasing Ben's lapels with such abruptness that the tramp, who hardly knew what he was doing anyway, fell backwards to the ground, rapping his head so sharply that he rendered himself unconscious.

'You don't mean they've gone below?' the sergeant said.

The inspector looked carefully at his men who, having searched the seven rooms of the shanty, now awaited further orders. 'They'll have dumped the horse and gone down to Wendle country,' he pronounced with finality. 'That much is plain and obvious to the mind of a detective, and if we descended in pursuance of our bounden duty we'd be knee deep in mud and muck, and that I will not tolerate. If the evil vapours did not kill us then there'd be a Wendle behind every corner ready to crack our skulls open with a catapult stone.'

'What are your orders, Inspector?' said Hanks as he crossed his arms and hoisted a fat buttock on to the table to rest it there.

'I know exactly what to do,' said Sussworth twitching his moustache from side to side, delighted with the complication of his own cunning. 'I have a map from the Wandsworth water authority, a map that has every manhole in Wandsworth marked upon it. I'll put a guard on every exit, I'll put a line of men round the whole of this area . . . and then I'll wait. The Wendles won't be able to get out for supplies and will soon conclude and deduce that something amiss is afoot. Wendles are highly averse to strangers; they'll soon find our runaways, and when they do they will boot them straight into our waiting hands.'

At the conclusion of this speech Sussworth stretched his back and made himself as tall as he could. He looked at his men and a black fire burnt in his eyes. He saluted and every officer present returned the salute in a respectful silence which might have lasted quite a long while had not Ben rolled over and farted very loudly in his sleep.

Sussworth blushed and shifted his weight from one foot to the other, embarrassed; his moustache trembled. Hanks touched Ben in the stomach with his boot.

'What shall we do with the prisoner?' he asked.

The inspector narrowed his nostrils against the odours that attacked him from everywhere. 'He's a suspect, he is,' he said, 'accessory after the fact, obstructing a police officer in the pursuance of his duty, drunk and disorderly, carrying an offensive weapon, that bottle for example, obscene behaviour definitely, offending public decency, contravening the health acts, all of them, vagrancy, no fixed abode, squatting, stealing council property . . . My goodness me, there's enough to send him away until the year three thousand and dot. Take him back to Fulham and put him in the cells; only lock him up this time and put him somewhere I can't smell him.'

'Yes sir, certainly sir,' said Hanks, 'but shouldn't we teach him a lesson, sir?'

Sussworth took a step away from the tramp's smell. 'Excellent thinking, Hanks,' he said. 'Get the men to turn the furniture over, break all the bottles, knock down the shelves, rip up the mattresses; let them have a bit of fun, they deserve it after a night like we've had. Next time we ask this slovenly human being for aid and assistance in protecting the *stadium quo* perhaps he'll be a little more disposed to turn Queen's evidence.'

Hanks slipped his bottom from the table and stood firmly planted on his fat legs. He rubbed his hands together with pleasure. 'Oh, yes, sir,' he said, and he gave his orders and two policemen seized the unconscious Ben by the feet and dragged him from his shack. When the tramp's smell had gone Sussworth followed, his legs moving stiffly, his expression cold. As he walked away, along the faint path that wound between the tall piles of rubbish, he heard behind him the sound of falling planks, the crash of crockery and the shouts and laughter of the SBG men. A slow smile crept over the inspector's face. Things were beginning to go well now.

6

The noise of the manhole cover slamming shut sounded terrifyingly loud below ground. Chalotte hung from the iron ladder just under the floor of Ben's palace and listened. She heard a long mumble of voices and she thought she heard someone hitting Ben. Later there came the crashing of furniture and crockery and she felt the earth around her shake with the shock of it. Then there was silence.

Clinging to the ladder still, Chalotte half turned and looked down into the dark. The air was thick about her body and her nose wrinkled at the smell of the sewers. She knew from past experience that it took several days of living underground to get used to it.

'Sounds like they've smashed the place up,' she said, 'pushing Ben about as well.'

'Have they gone?' asked Bingo.

'Seems like,' Chalotte answered.

From further down the tunnel came Spiff's voice: 'Leave it a bit longer.'

They waited a good half-hour, knowing they were near each other but feeling as if miles separated them because they could not see. At last Spiff said, 'Try it now.'

Chalotte placed her ear against the cool metal of the manhole cover. She could hear nothing. She bent her shoulder and pushed, gently at first, then with all her strength. The cover wouldn't budge. Bingo climbed up the ladder and joined his efforts to hers.

'One, two, three,' he said, 'and heave.' They shoved until their eyes bulged white with the effort but the round lump of cast iron would not move. In the end Chalotte made way for Stonks but even he, for all his force and stamina, had no success.

'We need more help,' he said, his breath coming in gasps.

'I know that,' said Bingo, 'but there's only room for two on this top rung.'

Twilight came up then and tried to push Bingo from below in one last despairing attempt but it made no difference. What the runaways did not realize was that Ben's kitchen cabinet, his armchairs and his table lay shattered in a heap over the top of the manhole. There would be no getting out that way. The Borribles were entombed right where they had not wanted to be: in the territory of the Wendles. Slowly Stonks, Bingo and Twilight clambered to the bottom of the ladder and huddled together with their companions in a sad and silent group. They had escaped the men of the SBG, certainly, but they had landed themselves in a predicament that might become far, far worse.

'Oh, hell,' said Sydney, 'I never meant all this to happen.'

'Well it has,' said Vulge, 'and there's no point in moaning. We've got to decide what we're going to do . . . Any ideas?'

'There's nothing we can do, except try to get out some other way,' said Spiff. His voice came from the dark, low and steady. It sounded like he was several yards away in a tunnel. 'The manhole cover is obviously locked or Sussworth has put some effin' great weight on it. We have to go on.'

'Oh, yeah,' said Chalotte, 'and how much food have we got? None. We haven't even got a torch and we don't know where we are. For all we know there are Wendles around us already.'

'That's right,' said Stonks. 'We don't even have a catapult or a Rumble-stick, nothing; our goose is cooked to a cinder.'

After Stonks had spoken there was another long silence as each Borrible considered his fate, but then, when enough time had gone by, Spiff cleared his throat and began to speak, slowly, as if he knew, and had known for a long time, exactly what he was going to say.

'I can get you out of here,' he said, and waited to let the importance of the remark sink in. 'I can see pretty well in the dark,' he added, 'almost like a Wendle.'

'What do you mean?' snapped Chalotte, instantly suspicious. She had never distrusted Spiff more than now and she was convinced that there was a note of triumph in his voice, as if he'd taken a chance on something and it was working out the way he had hoped.

Spiff sighed. 'I have a long, long past,' he said, 'and some of it was here, because, years ago, before any of you were Borribles, I lived here. To cut a long story short, I am a Wendle.'

'I might have known,' said Chalotte, and the words hissed through her teeth. 'I might have known.'

Spiff ignored her. 'I fought against the Rumbles and won more names than I can remember, not many Borribles do that, but I ran away from Wandsworth, ended up in Battersea, been there ever since.'

'Once a Wendle, always a Wendle,' quoted Chalotte.

'The fact remains,' continued Spiff, 'that I can get you out of here easy, if you do as I say. A Wendle never forgets the Wendle ways.'

'That's just what I'm frightened of,' said Chalotte.

'What does it matter?' said Twilight, interrupting the conversation to stop it becoming a quarrel. 'A Wendle's a Borrible after all. If Spiff can get us out then so much the better.'

'Has anyone got any other suggestion?' asked Bingo, 'because I haven't.'

There was no answer, not even from Chalotte.

'Okay,' said Spiff. 'First things first. I reckon Sussworth will block off as many exits from the sewers as he can. We'll have to lie low for twenty-four hours at least, maybe more.'

'But the Wendles will have us,' said Vulge. 'We aren't even dressed like they are.'

'Exactly,' agreed Spiff, 'so the first thing we got to do is find a Wendle storeroom and nick some of their gear, catapults and ammunition too. And we'll need some food.'

'Oh boy, oh boy,' said Twilight, 'this is an adventure at last, just what I wanted.'

'Don't be stupid, Stupid,' said Vulge. 'If I could see you I'd knock your block off.'

'Once we get some Wendle clothes and some weapons,' Spiff went on, 'we'll be able to merge in with the Wendles; they'll never even notice us. We'll watch 'em, see if they go in and out through the various manholes and, if they do, when the time comes we slip out into the streets and back home we go. Does everyone agree?'

'Okay by me,' said Twilight.

'Yes,' said Bingo, 'there's no other way.'

And so the others gave their vote for the plan, even Chalotte, but in her heart she knew that Spiff was up to no good. The triumph in his voice had grown more pronounced, had even developed into a note of pleasure. It seemed to her that Spiff had brought them to Wandsworth Bridge with a purpose, as if he were glad to be back underground where the green slime slid incessantly down the curving walls. She shuddered; there were great dangers ahead. Out there in the darkness some vile horror was uncoiling itself and getting ready to swallow her and her companions one by one. She determined to watch Spiff very closely. He spoke again and she listened.

'Until we get out of here,' he continued, 'you'll have to do as I say, even if it ain't very Borrible. Everyone grab hold of the person in front for now, and don't let go. You get lost down here and the rats'll chew you to nothing, right down to the toenails.'

As they followed Spiff away from the ladder, sightless into the back tunnels, Chalotte found that she was the last in line, clinging on to Bingo's shirt tail. She drew up beside him as she walked.

'I don't like it,' she whispered. 'Spiff's too happy down here. I bet you he's got some scheme up his sleeve. He's so crafty, that one, his right hand's never even seen the left one.'

Spiff suddenly interrupted her, his words curling back along the sewer, brittle with anger. 'Whoever that is, shuddup! Do you want every Wendle in Wandsworth to know where we are? Keep your mouth shut or Flinthead will shut it for you, with mud.'

No one answered Spiff and Chalotte felt her face flush in the gloom. Without another word the little band of Adventurers marched on.

* * *

Spiff led the way with a cheerful confidence. Stonks, who was behind him, said later, when it was all over, that he was sure he'd heard Spiff quietly whistling between his teeth while he walked— as if he were daring the whole world to come and attack him.

Chalotte of course could hear none of this and her thoughts were taken up with wondering what kind of person it was that could remember the tunnels of his early days with such ease. Had Spiff been back to Wandsworth since his escape all those years ago? Did he have a map in Battersea which he studied secretly in his room at night? She could find no satisfactory answer. Spiff was devious and cunning, even for a Wendle.

All at once the marching stopped and Spiff whispered from the front of the column, 'I can see a light, it might just be the first Wendle crossroads, it might be a guard. You lot stay here and I'll creep up and have a look.'

Spiff left them, and as the Borribles waited they heard only the persistent dripping of the slime all around them and the faraway rush of sludge in the main sewers. They stared at the distant light, watching Spiff's silhouette moving between them and it. At last they saw the tiny figure clasp both arms above its head. That was the signal which meant it was safe to go on.

They found Spiff standing in an open space where three corridors met. In the ceiling, in a recess protected by small metal bars, was a pale electric light.

'This is the beginning,' he said. 'From here on you can expect electric lights at almost every junction, so follow me and be twice as careful.' And he spun on his heel and plunged into another tunnel with no hesitation at all.

On and on went the Borribles and as they marched their eyes became more and more accustomed to the gloom in which they moved. Tunnel after tunnel joined theirs and the sound of sluggish waters came from both right and left. The Adventurers were wending their way across a gigantic maze and those who had been on the Great Rumble Hunt recognized none of it. Spiff was taking them by a roundabout route, purposely avoiding the more populated centres of the underground citadel.

Occasionally they heard the distant voices of Wendle patrols calling to one another, and sometimes Spiff halted, cupping his ear with a hand so that he could listen more intently. Once or twice he stopped by mysterious chalk marks that had been scribbled on the brick walls, studying them and moving his lips soundlessly as if he were reading secret messages left by a friend to guide him in the right direction.

Eventually, after tramping for an hour or so, Spiff brought his companions to an open area where five or six large tunnels met. The arches of the ceiling were high and graceful, built in Victorian times. A main culvert passed here, deep and wide with a ledge on each side of it for the sewer men to walk on. In this channel flowed a solid stream of filth, an oily water that looked as thick as molten lava with strange shapes in it that writhed and struggled just below the surface. Grey chiffons of steam escaped from large and lazy bubbles and smell rose through smell. The air felt rotten and crawled over the skin.

Spiff crouched by the bank and picked up half a brick that had fallen from the roof. 'Care for a swim, Twilight,' he said, and threw the bit of brick into the water. There was no splash, no noise. The brick simply disappeared, hypnotized into the mud like a mouse into a snake.

Twilight did not answer but stared at the sewer and swallowed hard. He began to understand what it was to live in Wendle country.

'Enough of jokes,' said Vulge. 'Why have we walked so far only to get here?'

Before Spiff could answer there came the scrape of a foot scuffing over uneven ground. Spiff looked beyond his friends and smiled. Slowly the Borribles turned, their scalps prickling with fear. In the entrance to one of the tunnels stood two Wendles, one armed with a glinting spear or Rumble-stick, the other with a catapult, its elastic stretched, the stone aimed at Stonks's head.

'Don't move anyone,' said the Wendle with the spear. His voice was as friendly as a broken bottle.

In spite of the warning Chalotte glanced at Spiff, still squatting by the bank of the sewer. He was chuckling, an expression of pleasure on his face. Slowly, very slowly, and showing his hands, he rose to his feet and the Wendles saw him.

'Spiff,' said one of them. 'At last.'

Spiff pushed a way through the group of motionless Borribles and stepped towards his Wandsworth brethren.

'What about this lot?' asked the Wendle with the spear. 'Are they armed?'

Spiff stood between the two Wendles and grinned. 'They're all right,' he said, 'and they are not armed.' Then he explained a little: 'These Wendles are old friends of mine. The one with the spear is called Norrarf, the one with the catapult is called Skug; when the time comes they will tell you how they won their names. They have come to help us.'

Norrarf and Skug lowered their weapons but they didn't take their eyes from the Borribles, weighing them in the balance, wondering, in spite of Spiff's assurances, whether to welcome them.

'What's all this about?' said Vulge. 'What's your game?'

'No talking here,' said Skug, his voice rough and mannerless, 'we've got to get you lot out of sight.' Skug had a square chin that was full of aggression and a right shoulder that jerked every few seconds as if he were dying to throw a punch at someone, or even anyone. His eyes looked into the corners of the world all the time and there wasn't the slightest spark of trust within them.

'That's right,' added Norrarf. 'You won't be safe until you're in Wendle clothes. I don't mind helping you, Spiff, but I ain't going to get myself drowned in mud for no one. Your friends is nothing but trouble.'

Norrarf was short and stocky with a face like a squashed lemon, wider than it was high. His mouth was crowded with teeth and he had a greenish tinge to his skin as did all members of his tribe. He was dressed, like Skug and indeed like all Wendle warriors, in thigh waders of rubber, a metal helmet made from an old six-pint beer can, and a chunky woollen jacket covered in orange plastic to keep out the water; the plastic was luminous like the coats worn by the men who work on motorways.

'All right,' said Spiff, 'you lead, we'll follow.'

The two warriors nodded and backed slowly into a tunnel; Spiff went after them as if prepared to leave his companions on their own if they hesitated for one minute, which they did, looking at each other in doubt and puzzlement.

Twilight, new to Wendles and eager for adventure, was not at all perturbed. 'Well, come on you lot,' he said. 'Don't hang about; we don't stand a chance without their help, do we?'

'Yeah,' said Chalotte, 'and I'm not sure what chance we stand with their help, either.' But she, like the rest, had no choice but to follow Spiff into the tunnel.

This time they did not have far to go, only marching for another fifteen or twenty minutes, though they changed direction a great deal and switched from corridor to corridor until, at last, they were taken through a hole in the wall and came into a small guardroom, long since abandoned it seemed by the regular Wendle patrols.

The walls of the room were built of an ancient brick from which the red dust flaked away at the merest touch, and it was furnished with rough chairs and a table. There was a pile of torn blankets too, but most important of all, thrown down in a corner, was a heap of Wendle clothes and weapons: spears, knives, catapults and a score of bandoliers filled with good round stones for use as ammunition. Chalotte drew in a sharp breath and the blood pounded in her temples; everything had been prepared for them.

She sprang on Spiff and seized him by the front of his shirt. 'Why don't you tell us what you're up to, you crafty little bleeder?' she cried. 'These Wendles knew we were coming, didn't they? And that's more than we did ourselves . . . But you knew, didn't you? You twister.' Chalotte was very angry and she raised her free hand to strike the Battersea Borrible across the head.

Norrarf pushed himself away from the wall where he had been leaning and raised his spear but, quick as he was, Spiff was quicker. With a brutal upward movement of his left arm he freed himself from the grip on his shirt and at the same time shoved the flat of his other hand into Chalotte's face so hard and so fast that the girl stumbled backwards and fell into Bingo's arms. Stonks stepped in front of Spiff, disregarding Norrarf's spear.

'Steady on, sonny,' he said. 'You push me if you want to push someone; see if I fall over.'

Vulge sat Chalotte down on a chair and she fingered her reddened nose and wiped the tears of pain from her eyes. There was quiet as her friends watched her, not knowing what to say, tense, ready to fight.

'You'd better tell us what's up,' said Stonks to Spiff after a while. 'We didn't come here to get ourselves killed just to amuse you.'

'That's right,' said Vulge, 'our adventuring days are over.'

Spiff smiled a smile of contempt to himself and began to sort over the Wendle clothing, looking for garments that would fit him. When he had found what he needed he put them on: the tin hat, the waders, the orange jacket. The costume transformed him utterly and the Borribles stared, forgetting their anger, hardly able to believe their eyes. Now Spiff looked every inch the Wendle warrior: violent, cunning and heartless. He smirked as he chose a catapult and swung a bandolier of stones across his shoulder; he was ready for anything and he looked like he didn't have a scruple in the world.

'You wanted us down here,' said Chalotte, 'and now you've got us. I've known that all along. You've got these friends down here, too. You must have had messages in and messages out for months. You know a lot that we don't, like you always do. What I want to know is what is it that you know?'

Spiff shrugged. 'There's nothing to tell,' he said, 'and anyway you wouldn't believe me whatever I said. If you don't like it here why don't you go up the nearest exit and walk right into the hands of Sussworth an' Co?'

'You will, too,' said Norrarf. 'Our patrols have reported that there's a copper standing on every manhole in Wandsworth.'

'Look,' said Spiff, 'all I want to do is get home, but since we're stuck here for a while we'd better make the most of it. Me and the other two will go and look for some food. While we're gone you'd better change into Wendle gear . . . and keep someone on watch.'

'You'll be all right,' said Skug. 'Hardly anyone comes this far out any more.'

'Let's go,' said Spiff, and his voice had a commanding ring to it. He ducked through the hole in the wall and was gone. The two Wendles obeyed him without question, as if he'd always been their leader and had never been away.

Chalotte shivered and remembered Flinthead, the Wendle chieftain. Suddenly Spiff reminded her of him; he had changed from the sly and lazy rogue she had known in Battersea. Now his eyes were cold and hard in his face, like pale blue marbles stuck in a big blob of raw pastry.

Bingo sighed, fitted a helmet on to his head and pulled a Wendle face. 'That Spiff,' he said, 'never does nothing for nothing. This whole thing smells dodgy.'

Chalotte nodded. 'Do you know what I think . . . I think he's come down here to sniff about after the Rumble treasure box. That's why he's been in contact with Norrarf and Skug, that's why he wanted to come with us in the first place.'

Stonks looked up in surprise. 'He couldn't be that stupid,' he said. 'The treasure box got sunk in the deepest part of the River Wandle. You remember, you were there. It must be covered by miles and miles of mud by now.'

'Yeah,' said Vulge, 'the Wendle legends say that the mud goes right down to the centre of the earth just there.'

'I know what the legends say,' cried Chalotte, 'but Spiff has a way of making his own legends.'

'Oh come on,' interrupted Twilight. 'He can't make us do anything we don't want to, can he?'

Chalotte laughed. 'Spiff can make things happen and then make them look as if they just happened,' she said. 'He's very good at it.'

The Borribles waited three hours for Spiff's return and while they waited changed into Wendle uniforms and chose a catapult and a bandolier each. The touch of the weapons reassured them mightily; they felt more confident, more in charge of their own destinies.

It was Bingo who was on guard at the first bend in the tunnel when he heard the noise of footsteps echoing along the brick walls; then there was the trill of the Battersea whistle and a moment later Spiff edged himself into view. He looked tired now and his waders were covered in mud. Over his shoulder was a heavy sack.

'Hello, young feller,' he said. 'Glad someone's on watch.' He went past Bingo and into the guardroom where he dropped his burden on the table. 'Here's some grub,' he said, 'so tuck in.' He upended his bag and stolen food cascaded out loaves, rolls, bacon, pots of jam, beer and boiled sweets.

'Were you seen?' asked Vulge.

Spiff chuckled. 'Course I was, but with a bit of mud across the face and travelling with Skug and Norrarf no one gave me a second look.'

'And are the SBG still on the manholes?'

'According to Norrarf they are. The Wendles have one or two holes that the coppers don't know about but they're guarded by picked warriors and no one goes in or out except on Flinthead's say-so. We'll have to wait till the coppers have gone.'

'I don't care what Spiff wants us to believe,' said Chalotte, 'I think we ought to go and have a look for ourselves.'

Spiff shrugged. 'Suit yerself,' he said, 'but there's one thing you certainly ought to see . . . over the other side of the citadel, over where you lost the treasure . . . You'll never guess what it is.' He ripped a chunk of white bacon fat with his teeth, rolling it into his mouth and chewing it confidently, like he had all the answers to all the questions.

There was silence. Nobody wanted to ask Spiff anything, except perhaps Twilight, and he kept quiet because he realized there was something going on that he didn't understand, that he wasn't part of. Spiff waited and smiled and smiled in the most provoking manner until at last he said, 'Well, all right then. I ain't proud, I'll tell yer. You've got to hand it to that Flinthead, he never gives up. Right out there, in the middle of all that mud and water he's dug a mine shaft, and above it is a contraption like a North Sea oil rigs a platform made of planks, a treadmill, and a chain of buckets to bring up the mud . . . and down below, slaves to do the digging. Fantastic engineering, real Borrible. I tell yer . . . that Flinthead.'

Stonks snorted. 'He's mad, he can't dig up the treasure box, it's too far gone.'

'He's not mad,' argued Spiff, 'persistent he is, he just never gives up.'

Chalotte rose to her feet and stretched out an arm to point at Spiff. 'And nor do you, you rat,' she said, her voice trembling with rage. 'Now we know why you were so happy to get us down here, it was that treasure all along.'

Spiff's face flushed. 'Don't be idiotic,' he said. 'How could I have known for sure that Sam was a trap, how could I have known that Sussworth was waiting on Eel Brook Commen, or that Ben would rescue us? I'm not a magician.'

'Maybe not,' Chalotte went on, looking at her friends for support 'but you didn't care what you did as long as you got us nearer to Wandsworth. You were too scared to come down here on your own so you made damn sure you got us involved.' She jerked her head at Twilight. 'I told you he had a way of making things happen.'

Stonks rolled a rasher of bacon in his fingers and tucked it into his mouth. 'It don't matter a monkey's, that money has caused enough death and treachery. We came to get a horse, that's all; money's out.'

'Right,' said Vulge. 'That money killed Knocker, Napoleon, Orc-cocco, Torreycanyon and Adolf; it very nearly killed me. It smells of death, always has done.'

Spiff gazed slowly round the room, superior and amused, like an adult watching quarrelling children. He snatched a bottle of beer from the table, opened it and took a long swig. 'Ah, lovely,' was all he said.

'A couple of us ought to go and have a look ourselves,' said Chalotte. 'That way we can make sure Spiff's telling us the truth about the manholes. We've got to get out of here before he gets us mixed up in something.'

Spiff raised his bottle in the air. 'Of course, girl,' he said. 'I'll take you to the Wandle mudflats right away, and I'll show you the exits the Wendles are using; I'll even show you the shaft where Flinthead's digging for treasure. And one day, if you outlive me that is, you'll look back and say, "Old Spiff weren't so bad, he knew a thing or two." ' He laughed once more and waved his beer bottle in a circle, embracing everyone in a toast. 'Here's to us,' he said, 'Borribles all.'

As soon as they had eaten it was decided that Chalotte, Stonks and Bingo would go with Spiff to check on some of the exits and entrances of Wendle country. They were to inspect as many as possible and weigh the chances of getting out on to the streets again, the chances of getting home.

Spiff led the three towards the centre of the citadel, warning them to keep close at all times if they didn't want to get lost. Again Chalotte wondered how he remembered his way in such an underground labyrinth. Only years and years as a Wendle could have given Spiff his detailed knowledge of the place. Left here, right there, over this sewer, along that one, now in complete darkness, now in the half-light; it was truly amazing and Chalotte came to realize that the more she knew Spiff the more there was to know.

She also saw that in spite of the summer drought and the heat in the city above, the channels and culverts were deep in filth-laden water. Very often, when there were no pathways, the four Borribles were forced to wade along the middle of the sewers themselves, up to their waists in muck and with green slime dripping heavily on to their helmets from high in the vaulted roofs, while all about them they heard whispering voices and the slosh and slurp of Wendles in waders.

As they journeyed on they began to meet the Wendles themselves, though not all of them were warriors, but Spiff knew the ways of that strange subterranean race and did not baulk at pushing his way through the middle of any group he came across. His three companions, fearful of discovery at first, soon learnt that their best procedure was simply to adopt a surly manner and speak to no one. Spiff made them smear their faces with a little mud too, as if they had been on a long march and had crossed many a stream. In that way, and in the gloom of the underworld, there was no danger of the interlopers being identified as strangers.

Spiff was happy. He nudged Chalotte frequently and his teeth shone when he smiled. Each time he passed beneath a manhole cover he stopped and waited for the others to gather round him so he could point upwards, and there, chalked on the underside of each iron lid, the Borribles saw a circle with a 'X' drawn across it: the Wendle sign for danger.

'There you are,' said Spiff, 'and they're all like that.' He smiled at Chalotte's discomfiture. 'I promise you there's a copper's size thirteen boots standing on the topside of that manhole and there's a size thirteen copper standing in 'em too.'

They marched on at a good pace towards the River Wandle and were not far from their destination when two warriors burst out of a branch corridor and ran off, shouting.

'Come on you lot,' they bawled. 'General meeting, Flinthead's orders, haven't you heard?' Their footsteps died away.

'What do we do now?' asked Bingo, his face pale. 'Hide?'

'Not likely,' said Spiff. 'When Flinthead calls a meeting everyone goes except those who are dead or on guard. If we don't do what everyone else does we'll be spotted and dragged out into the light and he'd recognize us for sure. We'll have to go along, and we'll have to sprint too.'

And sprint they did, speeding towards the great hall, and as they ran they were joined by hundreds of Wendles all scurrying in the same direction. The tunnels grew wider and higher and the number of Wendles increased moment by moment until soon there was a solid host of jostling bodies hastening onwards in obedience to Flinthead.

Spiff and the others, their hearts thumping, were borne along in this violent crush for at least half a mile or so, then the pace of the mob around them slackened to a jog, then to a walk and finally to a shuffle. There were Wendles everywhere now, clamped together, incapable of independent movement. Suddenly they surged forward with a new and frightening power and, caught by an irresistible force, the four Adventurers, their feet no longer touching the ground, were sucked into an immense cavern where the brick roof arched high up and out of sight.

Once, back in the nineteenth century, this hall had been the central chamber for the Wandsworth sewage system until, made obsolete by more modern techniques, it had come under the sway of Flinthead. There he was now, sitting on a tall raised platform, lolling back in a large wooden armchair which served, on all important occasions, as the Wendle chieftain's throne. Beside him was his second-in-command, Tron by name, and within call stood at least fifty members of the bodyguard: hard-fighting warrior Wendles, hand-picked for their loyalty and single-mindedness.

The Adventurers wriggled and pushed through the crowd and made their way to the side of the hall.

'Keep still,' whispered Spiff, 'and don't look up. Whatever happens, don't catch Flinthead's eye; he'll suss you out in no time.'

Chalotte took Spiff's warning seriously and hid herself behind the mass of Wendles who stood between her and the platform, pulling her helmet further down on her head so that she could scrutinize events without fear of being discovered.

Flinthead, she saw, hadn't changed in the slightest since she'd last seen him. Not for him the helmet made from an old beer can; his, and his alone, was fashioned from beaten copper and it had an extra piece that came down the front of his face in order to protect the nose—but that nose was not designed for concealment. It was an evil nose, a big nose, soft and plastic and eager to sniff out anyone who threatened Flinthead or his supremacy. The chieftain's jacket was covered in luminous paint of gold and his waders were soft and of the finest quality, lined with wool to keep his feet warm. But Flinthead's power did not reside in his clothes; it issued from his eyes. They were blank and they did not glint or gleam. Neither did they move unless the head moved; they were opaque and impenetrable, frosted over like smashed windscreens.

Gradually the noise in the great hall died away. Slowly Flinthead raised a hand for silence, but there was no need. The crowd had been stilled by the chieftain's gaze alone. He waited a moment longer before speaking and when he spoke his voice came as a shock. It was a friendly voice and he smiled too, but his mind was a great distance from the smile; his mind was a cold metallic thing, working in silence for its own secret ends.

'Wendles,' began Flinthead, 'I have called you together because there is great danger here. The policemen of the SBG are guarding every exit into Wandsworth . . . I want to know why, I must know why. We have ample provisions of course, but if the blockade goes on too long we will face hardship, starvation even. Why, I ask myself, have we suddenly become the objects of this burst of SBG activity . . . ? You will find out for me. You all know of the work I am doing on the Wandle mudflats, it is important work and it must not be interrupted. I do not want policemen down here, I don't even want them to send the sewer men down here. You will remember the dangers we faced before because of outsiders; we do not want any more. The Wandle is for the Wendles. Be vigilant, you warriors, all of you beware strangers. A time of trial is coming, I smell it. The enemy is all around us. Report anything untoward to me or Tron. Be suspicious, be wary, trust no one. Stand guard at every exit, watch over the mine where the work goes on. I am awake for you day and night, brother Wendles; be watchful for me. Something or someone has penetrated our underground citadel, my nose tells me. Sharpen your knives, carry a spear and a catapult always with you. Wendles beware, there will be blood.'

Abruptly Flinthead rose, and the light from the hand torches that almost every Wendle carried shone against his helmet. He stared at the back of the hall, his shapeless nose twitching. No one moved and no one spoke. Slowly Flinthead turned his face, sweeping his dull eyes across Wendle after Wendle, scaring them, sniffing nervously all the while like a city fox. Spiff, Chalotte, Stonks and Bingo stood without stirring, hardly breathing as Flinthead's rigid gaze came to rest near them. It wavered and the nose tilted upwards and flared long and deep. Chalotte's knees trembled and she was thankful that Spiff had made her disguise herself with those streaks of mud.

'There is much amiss,' called Flinthead, but his eyes moved on and searched elsewhere and he did not trouble to look for much longer. Only a moment more went by and then he raised his hand and dismissed the great assembly with a sign. Tron shouted an order and the special bodyguard surrounded their chieftain with a hedge of spears and escorted him away, chanting a kind of hymn as they did so:

'Glory to Flinthead! Praise our lord,
King of the world below!
*   Sing of his name,*
*   Extol his fame*
From which all blessings flow.

'Glory to Flinthead, great and good,
Wendle without a peer!
*   There are no bold*
*   Heroes of old*
To equal his career!

'Glory to Flinthead, saviour true,
Father and guide and friend!
*   His is the might,*
*   The kindly light*
We'll follow round the bend!'

As soon as the four interlopers were free of the cavern and on their own Spiff halted and spoke roughly to Chalotte. 'Now do you believe me?' he hissed. 'There is a copper on every manhole.'

'I believe you,' answered Chalotte, though her mind was preoccupied with other thoughts—the Wendle hymn haunted her. 'Those bodyguards are mad, aren't they?' she said. 'They really believe in that lunatic leader of theirs; Flinthead could do anything with them.'

'Never mind all that,' said Stonks, his voice strained. 'What about that guardroom where we're hiding, won't they find it now?'

'I dunno,' said Spiff, 'lots of Wendles live in old alcoves like that. I think Skug and Norrarf ought to be able to fob them off. I'm more worried about something else.'

'Something else!' cried Bingo. 'What could be worse than this?'

Spiff rubbed his jaw and reached a decision. 'Come with me,' he said. 'I'll show you something you ought to see.'

Chalotte, Stonks and Bingo studied Spiff's expression for a second. He smiled his superior smile.

'All right,' said Chalotte, 'we'll look, but that's all. Don't you go making things happen.'

Spiff shook his head in reassurance and once more he set off into the dark and sloping side tunnels with his companions following. Once more, also, he directed his steps with confidence and precision and it was not long before the small group of Borribles arrived on the banks of the River Wandle.

'Yes,' said Chalotte, 'I recognize this; it was near here that our boat was moored, and it was over the far side somewhere that we left Knocker and the others so that we could escape with the treasure.' And remembering her friends she contemplated the waters of the river and saw that they were still as thick and as foul as fish glue. The Wandle crawled by her feet with a slow and unstoppable strength, only just covering the rolling banks of mud that shifted and rippled beneath its surface.

Spiff gobbed into the water and the spit made no splash or murmur. 'All very touching,' he said, 'but we'd better get going before some Wendle starts asking us what we're up to.'

They pressed on, following the Wandle in the direction of its current, travelling along a well trodden towpath. From time to time they passed small groups of Wendles roaming this way and that, but they were not too closely scrutinized, nor did they receive more than the usual number of suspicious glances.

As they progressed the vault above their heads flung itself higher and wider until it was almost impossible to see the far side of the river. Now the shoals of mud surged into sight above the water and the stream dawdled and meandered through a vast area of black dunes which gleamed wet in the half-light, pulsating like stranded monsters. These were the treacherous swamps of the Wandle mudflats where a relentless suction threatened the life of any creature that lost its way or of any traveller who put a foot wrong.

There were more and more Wendles round the Adventurers every minute, most of them warriors and all of them taking Flint-head's orders seriously, peering into alcoves and tunnels and inspecting each other's faces. But Spiff was not to be put off by this tactic and did likewise, brandishing his catapult in a warlike manner and approaching each Wendle he passed and staring at him offensively, asking who he was and where he came from and what he was doing. Whatever Spiff's faults, there was no doubting his bravery or his audacity.

Chalotte knew this and was on the point of mentioning it to Bingo when she and the others became aware of harsh and unnatural noises in the distance. She heard first a sharp crack repeated at regular intervals, sometimes followed by a cry; then there was a deep rumbling as of wood on wood together with a grinding and a clanking of metal, and all this strident discord was combined with a slurp, slurp, slurp of water and mud. Chalotte felt a finger of ice prodding at her heart and she reached out to touch Stonk's arm, but the face he turned towards her was just as fearful as her own.

The noises pounded on, clanking, rumbling, slurping; louder and louder, oppressive, terrifying. Suddenly, as the four Borribles rounded a bend in the towpath, the noise swelled to a crescendo and the strangest sight met their eyes. Spiff raised an arm and pointed dramatically.

'There,' he said, pleased with himself, 'ain't that wonderful?'

Far away from the spot on which they stood, in between two vast banks of mud and in the middle of the underground river, was moored a floating platform constructed from huge rough planks of stolen timber. In the centre of the platform was a derrick and at the base of the derrick and spliced on to it with a cumbersome wooden axle was a treadmill, large enough for a Borrible, or even two, to walk in. Some poor mud-covered wretch was already toiling in it and, as Chalotte stared, one of the four Wendle guards on the platform cracked a whip and the great wheel revolved and buckets rattled upwards on a long chain, rising to the top of the derrick. There they rolled over to empty their cargo of sludge into the waters of the River Wandle and begin again their long journey down into the deepest depths of the mine.

Spiff sprawled on the ground at the side of the towpath and beamed; the others squatted near him. 'Marvellous bit of engineering, that is,' he said, 'absolutely marvellous.'

Chalotte glanced along the river bank. There were scores of Wendles doing what Spiff was doing; some were chatting, some were just relaxing, but all of them kept a close eye on the activity in midstream, waiting for something to happen.

Stonks spoke to Bingo. 'This is the exact place we lost the treasure.'

Chalotte swore. 'So it is, dammit.'

'But how can you dig down through a river?' asked Bingo.

'Course you can,' said Spiff. 'They do it all the time, engineers. You start on one of those mudbanks, just above the surface of the water, or you wait till the tide's out, and as your hole goes down so you put planking all round you, nice and tight; tongue and groove is best. How do you think they built bridges in the old days? Just the same.'

'Well, it's bloody clever,' said Bingo. 'You've got to admit that.'

'Invented by Flinthead,' said Spiff. 'And whatever else you can say about him he ain't daft.'

'And who's the poor sod in the treadmill?' said Stonks. 'What's he done to deserve that?'

Spiff let his head fall back and looked up into the roof, making his comrades wait for an answer so that their brains had time to work. 'Well,' he said eventually, 'he did just what we are doing, he got on the wrong side of Flinthead, didn't he? Go and have a closer look, Stonks.' Spiff laughed, as cold as death, his laughter mocking the idea that was just beginning to form in the minds of his companions.

Stonks jumped to his feet and a look of understanding, distant as yet, began to spread across the face of the slow Peckham Borrible. He walked along the bank to a point where the land advanced into the river and brought him nearer to the treadmill. For a long while he stared across at the slave who stumbled forward inside the wheel; he winced every time he heard the whip fall. Then Stonks's head fell on his chest in a great sadness; he retraced his steps and sat once more by the others. The blood had drained from his face and his lips were white with rage. He closed his eyes so that he could not see.

'It's my mate out there,' he said. 'It's Torreycanyon, the poor bleeder, he's still alive, after all this time.' Stonks's voice cracked and it seemed that even the strongest of all the Borribles might break down and weep in front of his friends, openly and without shame.

'It's who?' said Bingo, not believing his own ears.

'Torreycanyon,' cried Chalotte. Her voice rose with emotion and it was fortunate for her that the nearby groups of Wendles were talking loudly themselves and did not notice her. She looked at Spiff with hatred, baffled once again by his duplicity, but all he did was narrow his eyes, his face expressionless.

'Don't do anything silly,' he said. 'If you give the game away Flinthead will have us all down the mine.'

'You knew,' continued Chalotte, and her breath shot out of her lungs like steam under pressure. 'You knew all the time.'

'I wasn't sure until I got here,' said Spiff, his eyes flickering a little. 'I couldn't be certain.'

'And the others?' asked Chalotte, ducking her head to brush away the tears. 'What about Knocker?'

'Ah, your special friend Knocker, yes, he's alive too. He's down the bottom of the shaft with Napoleon, and Orococco goes behind 'em, boarding up the sides of the mine to make sure it don't cave in.'

'How do you know all this?' asked Bingo.

'Norrarf and Skug told me, of course,' said Spiff, 'when we arrived.'

'And don't the prisoners ever come out?' said Stonks, holding down his anger with an immense effort.

'They works there, eats there and sleeps there,' explained Spiff. 'The food is lowered down in a dirty old bucket.'

'The bastards,' said Chalotte, 'and so are you, Spiff. You should have told us they were still alive; we'd have come willingly then.'

Spiff sneered. 'Oh, yeah, you wouldn't have believed me for a second. You'da taken it for a trick. I had to get you here some other way.'

'Just so we could get the treasure for you,' said Chalotte. 'Don't try to kid me that you want to rescue Knocker and the rest, I know you too well.'

'There's nothing to stop us doing both,' said Spiff.

No one could speak for a long while after that. Chalotte could only think of the suffering that the prisoners must have undergone during their long months of captivity, and Bingo and Stonks sat gazing at the treadmill as it went round and round. Torreycanyon had been Stonks's mate; they had fought side by side at the Great Door of Rumbledom, and the more Stonks thought of his friend's imprisonment the more he felt a hatred of Spiff rise up in his throat. But there was nothing he could do or say; he dared not give way to his feelings. He was, after all, surrounded by Wendles, Wendles who were now on the watch for the slightest thing out of the ordinary.

At length Stonks came to a decision and he stood up. 'Let's get back to the guardroom now,' he said. 'I think the others will want to ask Spiff a few questions; they might even want to shove his head through a brick wall.'

The four Borribles walked casually into a side tunnel so as not to attract the attention of any of the watching Wendles. But once out of the sight and hearing of the river bank Stonks raised his arm and caught Spiff a ringing blow across the helmet with his bare hand; the helmet dented under the blow and the sound of it echoed along the damp brick walls. Spiff fell to his knees and shook his head, stunned. A clout from Stonks was no light thing.

Chalotte was excited by the violence; her blood rose and she drew her sharp knife. 'I'm gonna slit his throat,' she said.

'And so could I,' said Stonks, 'but if we do we'll never find our way back . . . It was just that I couldn't resist sloshing him the once.' He stuck the knuckles of his right hand into his mouth and sucked the broken skin.

Bingo helped Spiff to his feet and shoved him forward. 'Come on, Spiff,' he said. 'Take us home and we'll see what the others have to say.'

And so, with his head buzzing from the great swipe he had received, Spiff staggered through the tunnels of Wendle country. Chalotte, Bingo and Stonks followed him, their hearts glad in a way that Knocker and his fellow prisoners were still alive, and yet sad too for the slavery they had endured and the continuing danger of their predicament.

7

Inside the secret house which served as headquarters for the SBG Sergeant Hanks dipped half a bread roll into the pool of egg yolk on his greasy plate and then, when the bread was sufficiently soggy, he folded it into his mouth. The loose flesh on his face wobbled with satisfaction and his blue eyes glinted with pleasure.

'You should eat a bit more, Inspector,' he said, forcing the words through his food so that they sounded moist, 'then you wouldn't worry so much.' Hanks belched fiercely and with an expression of intense concentration began to pick his nose.

Inspector Sussworth lowered his mug of tea to Hanks's desk and set off to the far end of the room. His strides, as always, were nervous and bouncy, like a dancer waiting for his music.

'It's all right for you, Hanks,' he began, 'but mine is the ultimate responsibility. History will look back at this crisis and ask how I handled it. I have the whole of the SBG deployed in Wandsworth you know; my reputation is at stake. The District Assistant Commissioner telephoned me this morning, wanted to know what we were up to.'

'I hope you told him, sir.' Hanks extracted something elastic and green from his nose, examined it closely and stuck it under his chair.

'Of course I did,' said Sussworth, revolving on his right toe like a tin toy. 'I told him that we were on the point of apprehending the dangerous felons whom we suspect of having committed the Southfields murders. "A few more days," I told him, "and the long arm of the SBG would have 'em by the collar.' "

'If only we could go underground,' said Hanks, spreading another large roll with butter and honey.

Sussworth stabbed the floor with his heel. 'I know, but the sewer men have told us time and time again how dangerous it is. They only go down if they have to, you know, and even they daren't go everywhere. I ask you, Hanks, what chance would we have? It's a labyrinth. Every time you lift a manhole cover the noise can be heard ten miles away. Wendles can see in everything but pitch dark, we can't. If we went into those tunnels they'd pick us off with their catapults, one by one. There are times for active discretion and this is one of them, we'll have to starve them out.'

Hanks thought and rubbed his nose. 'Why don't we gas 'em?' he said. 'That would work.'

'I'd love to,' said Sussworth, his moustache quivering happily at the idea, 'but imagine the fuss there'd be from all the do-gooders. We'd be pilloried as monsters.'

Hanks squeezed the bread roll between his teeth and honey oozed from it to form a golden waterfall down the front of his tunic. 'Our hands is tied,' he agreed through his half-masticated mouthful. 'Them Borribles kneecap our best officers with their catapults, they steal, they squat in old houses, all that, yet if we so much as lay a finger on 'em there's an outcry.'

'Don't worry, Hanks,' said Sussworth, placing his hands behind his back and raising his body up on his toes, 'I'll get them. Our men will remain on selfless duty at those manhole covers till kingdom come. When those Wendles are starving they'll soon get rid of those malefactors and then we'll snaffle them, every one.'

The two officers were interrupted by footsteps on the landing; there was a knock at the door and it opened to reveal an SBG constable.

'Excuse me, sir,' he said. 'I've got the prisoner.'

'That's right,' said Hanks. 'Bring him in.'

The door was opened a little wider and Ben shuffled into view. He looked tired and hungry, pale under his layers of dirt, frightened too; his shoulders cringed with fear at the sight of Sussworth and his hands trembled in the steel handcuffs he wore.

As soon as he had entered the room the door was shut behind

him and Ben leant against it. This was behaviour that Sussworth would not countenance.

'You stand to attention, my friend,' he said, 'out in the middle here.'

'How about some food, guv'nor?' said Ben. 'How about some food, or a nice little drink, eh, what about it, Inspector?'

Sussworth ignored the request. 'For the last time,' he said, screwing his finger into Ben's stomach, 'how did those hooligans get out of Fulham police station? And what's more important, where did they go afterwards?'

Hanks swallowed the last of the honey roll and, using his arms more than his legs, yanked himself from behind his desk, then strolled round it until he stood right up beside the prisoner.

'Listen 'ere, you stinkin' lump of scum,' he said, and he started to push the exhausted tramp with his stomach, edging him back towards the door with every nudge. 'Do you know what we've done to your black 'ole of Calcutta, eh? You don't . . . Well, we've had it cleaned up for you, by order of the council.'

'You see,' said Sussworth, peering up into Ben's face like a short tourist looking at a tall monument, 'you're a living health hazard, you are. All those dirty bottles with spiders hiding in them, gone. All those ancient tins of grub, thrown in the river. All those lamps and tin cans, sent for scrap. All that furniture and all those mattresses, burnt.'

Sussworth did a little tap dance to the window and back again, stepping neatly on to Ben's ruined boots on his return.

'We've left you a bed, a chair and a table,' he continued. 'The social services have disinfected everything; it smells like a Jeyes Fluid factory down there now. My, my, aren't you lucky, Ben?' And with this the inspector grabbed Ben's nose and tweaked it until the tears ran down the old man's beard.

'And I'll tell you what else I'm going to do if you don't tell me what I want to know . . . I'm going to get a health department order on your shack. You shouldn't be living there at all really. Feather's Wharf is a rubbish dump, not a holiday camp. How would you like me to get your place bulldozered to the ground, eh? Answer me that.'

Ben shook his head and wrung his hands. 'Oh, guv'nor, don't do that to me; it's me 'ome. Please don't, I'd have nowhere to go.'

'We've thought of that,' said Hanks, and he seized Ben by the beard and dragged him to an open space so that he could begin nudging him with his stomach all over again. 'You see we're going to be really nice to you. Our police doctor is going to tell us how ill you are, when we tell him to, and that way we'll get you really sorted out. You'll be fumigated, incarcerated and renovated. We'll put you into hospital for months. You'll be washed every week, clean clothes you'll have, there'll be nurses everywhere to make sure you get no beer to drink, and to round it all off we'll have you committed to an old folks' home where there'll be a matron with a moustache to tell you what to do all day. You'd like that, wouldn't you, Ben?'

As the sergeant came to the end of his speech he gave a sharp thrust with his belly and Ben, off balance, fell to his knees. The tramp made no attempt to get up but simply raised his hands in supplication.

'Oh, leave off,' he whined. 'Don't send me away. It's none of my business, all this, straight up it ain't. My cell was open like it always is. Them kids was already outside when I got there; they forced me to help 'em, honest.'

'You were heard talking to a girl on Wandsworth roundabout,' said Sussworth, 'and I swear if you don't tell me what you know I'll ram you into that old folks' home so rapid they'll think you arrived by parachute.'

'All right,' said Ben, 'all right. This is what happened. I came out of the cell and they was out in the yard, see. There was a girl . . . she was leading the horse but I tried to walk past 'em, didn't I? I mean it was none of my business, as usual—you know me—but they wouldn't have it. There was about a dozen of 'em too, tough little bleeders. They don't take no for an answer, kids of today, do they?'

Ben looked up but Sussworth said nothing.

'Well, they saw it was foggy like and said if I didn't take 'em down to the river they'd beat me up. Battersea Bridge was what they wanted but I said I only knew the way to Wandsworth, which is true.'

'Why didn't you call out for help?' Sussworth wanted to know. 'There were plenty of policemen within earshot.'

'Call out!' said Ben, amazed. 'Cor, if I'd so much as opened my mouth there'd 'ave been six boots in it. They don't hang about, them Bobbirols.'

Hanks grabbed Ben's beard and banged his head against the wall. 'Where did they go, you stinkin' old goat?'

'How should I know?' said Ben. 'Once we got across the bridge they pushed me to the ground, gave me a kick and ran off into the fog with that horse. They said something about getting to Battersea before the fuzz arrived.'

Sussworth took a turn round the office, hopping and sidestepping as he went. 'Hmm,' he said. 'Battersea, it keeps coming back to that, but I'm not convinced. I'm a detective, I am. It would have made more sense for them to have found a manhole and gone into hiding with the Wendles. They're all Borribles together after all.'

'I heard something,' said Ben. 'I'll tell yer if you don't put me away . . . I couldn't stand that.'

'Well,' said Sussworth, 'what is it?'

'I heard 'em say something about not going to the Wendles, sounded like they'd had some fight with 'em in the past and didn't trust 'em. I don't think they went down there.'

'It could be true,' said Hanks. 'Remember that Borrible we captured once who told us there'd been some kind of war between the Southfields killers and the Wendles.'

Sussworth rubbed his chin. 'I know that, but I've got a feeling and my feelings are always right. You see I've stationed a couple of SBG men, disguised as costers, on a barrow in Battersea market. I've supplied them with descriptions of our villains and they'll report to me as soon as they're seen.'

'Ah,' said Ben, 'but they'd lie low, wouldn't they, very low?'

He leant against the wall and pushed himself to his feet.

Inspector Sussworth went over to the tramp and sniffed. 'My God,' he said, 'but you do smell.' He walked to the end of the room in order to place himself as far away from Ben as he could. 'Look here,' he went on. 'I'll give you one last chance, you can go back to that slum of yours . . .'

Ben smiled.

'. . . but on one condition only. You've got to render us every possible assistance; you've got to keep your eyes open and report to us every day.'

'I want to help, sir,' said Ben, ducking his head once or twice, 'but how can I?'

Sussworth explained: 'You're always out and about, up and down every street and alley in your part of Wandsworth, scrounging and begging; criminal offences both of them, of course. You see a lot of things that we don't. People clear the streets when they see a copper coming, but not when it's a drunken old tramp, they don't.'

'Oh, yes, sir, they trusts me,' said Ben, nodding sagely. 'I knows and sees a lot of things, I do, that aren't really my business.'

'Well you make it your business, you phone me up and tell me, and we'll give you some lovely money for your trouble, we will. I want to see you alert, Ben. Spying round corners, talking to kids, Borribles especially, and then you report everything to us. You do this and I'll see to it that you are left alone. I can make it easy for you Ben, very easy.'

Sussworth made a sign and Sergeant Hanks fished a key from his pocket and undid the tramp's handcuffs. Ben rubbed his wrists.

'You wouldn't have a few bob on yer, would yer, sir?' he asked Sussworth, giving a little bow. 'For the phone calls and such, and I'm ever so hungry, yer see. I won't get any food till I gets back to the wharf and starts sorting the rubbish.'

Inspector Sussworth laughed and felt in his pocket. 'What a scrounger,' he said, and he gave a few silver coins to Hanks who passed them on into Ben's filthy palm.

'There's one more thing,' said Hanks. 'If you give us the information that leads to the capture of the Southfields killers there'll be a special reward in it for you, Ben, lots of reward.'

Ben's face shone. 'Really, sir, that is good news, oh yes, you can count on me. I'd do anything to get me 'ands on a quid or two.'

Hanks threw open the door. 'Right, get out of here, and remember I'll have someone watching you night and day. You try to slip one over on me and I'll hang you up by your feet and have you put through a hot car wash.'

Ben bobbed his head again. 'My Gawd, yessir,' he said. 'Anything I hears, rely on me,' and he sidled into the corridor.

'They make me sick,' said Sussworth when the tramp had gone. 'Sell their grandmothers for a pint of beer. Swine, animals, that's what they are.'

'I agree, sir,' said Hanks, opening a cupboard and taking out a large tablet of chocolate, 'but it is our task to make use of the materials we have. Care for some fruit and nut?'

Inspector Sussworth took a square and absent-mindedly conveyed it to his mouth. 'I suppose you're right, Hanks,' he said. 'Even that dirty old man may be able to help us in our crusade.'

A quarter of an hour later Ben was sticking a fork into a steaming plateful of bangers and mash in a workman's café along the Fulham Road. He sat in a corner, by the window, and talked to himself as he ate.

'He's mad, that inspector,' said the tramp, 'mad. Help him, sunshine? I should cocoa! I wouldn't fart in his face if he was dying of suffocation. Got some money out of him though, didn't I just? Tuck in, Ben, bet you're hungry. I am, yes I am, and that is my business. Wonder 'ow those kids are, wonder 'ow they are? Dying for a drink, ain't I? Don't worry, I'll go and get one in a minute and drink to Sussworth's 'ealth, his bad 'ealth of course.' And laughing, Ben nearly choked on a mouthful of sausage and quickly downed a draught of hot tea to clear his gullet.

Spiff, his hands tied, sat on one of the chairs in the guardroom. Five of his fellow Borribles sat or stood near him, undecided. Skug and Norrarf were still absent on business of their own; Sydney was on guard in the tunnel.

'This'll get you nowhere,' said Spiff. 'Tying me up is stupid. You'll get yourselves caught, that's all.' No one answered.

Spiff tried another tack. 'Skug and Norrarf won't put up with this, you know, they'll put a stop to it right away. They won't give you any more grub if I say so, then what will you do?'

'Just think,' said Vulge, 'our four mates working in that mine all these months and he didn't tell us.'

'I didn't know for sure,' answered Spiff, 'and if I'd told you who would have believed me, eh? You didn't even want to rescue Sydney's horse so what chance did Knocker have?'

'And they could have been killed any time,' said Stonks. 'That mud is only held back by bits of wooden scaffolding, it could collapse easy. We've got to get them out as soon as we can.'

'You can't do it without me,' said Spiff. 'You'll make a mess of it.'

'We did for the Rumbles,' said Chalotte, 'without your help.'

'Rumbles, knickers,' said Spiff with contempt. 'This is different; this is Wendles, and Flinthead.'

'You've no right to be a Borrible,' said Chalotte, tossing her wild hair out of her eyes. She paused a moment and went on to say what she had been thinking all along. 'We should clip your ears ourselves.'

Spiff paled and struggled with his bonds. 'You cow,' he said, 'and you say I'm not Borrible. Can't you understand, all I got in the way of messages from here was rumours. First the treasure was saved, then it was lost; then Knocker was dead, then he was alive. I thought that if we went to Fulham to look for the horse we'd get near enough to Wandsworth to pick up some real news, catch a Wendle maybe, ask him questions. Then there was the battle with the SBG and after that what happened, happened, without my help.'

'We're not cutting any ears, Chalotte,' said Stonks. 'Whatever Spiff might have planned, there's enough clipping in the world without us joining in.'

'Flinthead does it,' said Chalotte defensively. She knew her friends were looking at her strangely.

'That's just it,' said Bingo, 'that's why we don't. We're supposed to stick together, even if we do quarrel.'

'This is getting us nowhere,' said Vulge. 'What's certain is that our four friends are alive. Let's get them out of here, and ourselves as well. We've got a reason for being in Wendle country now, that alone makes me feel better. I'll take on a Wendle or two.'

'That's more like it,' said Bingo, 'and we're going to need everyone who can fight.' He took out his knife and held it ready to release the prisoner. 'What do yer say?'

'I say no,' said Chalotte, but she realized as she said it that the others would be against her.

Stonks looked at the faces of his fellow Adventurers and saw their thoughts. 'Okay,' he said, 'cut him free, but he doesn't give orders any more. It's all down to us now.'

Bingo sliced through the cords that bound Spiff to his chair and put the knife back in his belt. Spiff got to his feet and smirked at Chalotte. 'Right,' he said, 'what's yer plan, because you'll need one, a good one.'

Stonks cleared his throat. 'I saw a lot of Wendle skiffs down on the Wandle mudflats,' he said. 'We'll steal one and get over to the derrick, there's only four guards; we'll knock 'em out and throw 'em down the shaft. Some of us can take their places so as not to arouse suspicion. I'll go down the mine and free the others. Then we get in the boats and row down the Wandle until we come out on the Thames. If we do it at night the coppers on the river won't see us. We'll cross to the other bank and get into the streets before daylight, or we'll row all the way down to Battersea, if the tide's right. I don't see any reason why it shouldn't work.'

Spiff leant against the wall and gave a slow hand-clap. 'Oh, great,' he scoffed, 'really great. And while you're doing all this the Wendles on the bank are lolling back with their hands behind their heads saying, "Oh look, our prisoners are escaping, won't Flinthead be pleased?" Ridiculous. What happens if they sink your boats? What happens if you're forced into the tunnels? Are you going to carry Knocker and the others over your shoulders? You saw how weak Torreycanyon was; the other three will be the same, worse even. They won't be able to walk, let alone fight. It won't work.'

'So what would you do?' asked Stonks.

'What would I do? I'd wait till the treasure's found, and then, when the excitement is high and the Wendles are celebrating, I'd move in and take the prisoners. You'd be halfway home before Flinthead realized you'd been here.'

'Oh, no,' cried Chalotte. 'I can see him coming a mile off. He wants to wait till the treasure's found so that he can try and take it with him, and get us to help him fight his way out. Not a chance.'

'Chalotte's right,' said Vulge. 'We got all messed up by the treasure in Rumbledom, let's not do it again.'

'That settles it,' said Stonks. 'We'll attack tomorrow night. We'll row out to the platform as if we were taking a message or changing the guard. I'll try to entice the sentries into the shaft on some pretext and deal with them there. When I come out with the prisoners we'll have to get the boats moving downstream as fast as we can and hope the Wendles on the bank don't notice anything until we run. Vulge, Bingo and Sydney can come with me to the platform. Twilight and Chalotte will stay on the bank. If anything goes wrong, Chalotte, you'll have to create a diversion in the tunnels. Fuse the lights, shout, anything, only make the Wendles chase you.'

'Why leave us behind?' asked Chalotte.

Stonks grinned, not something he did often. 'Obvious,' he said. 'They won't spot Twilight in the dark and you can't stand Spiff so you're the best person to keep an eye on him. We don't know how far we can trust him now.'

'We never could,' said Chalotte, 'only we didn't know it.'

The insults rolled right over Spiff. He smiled ironically and helped himself to some food. 'You lot better eat up,' he said, 'because you're going to need every bit of strength you've got; and get some sleep too, you may not get any more for a day or two. I can tell you one thing though. I shall be watching your rescue attempt with great interest, and I shan't lift a finger to help you.'

It was the middle of the night and Bingo couldn't sleep. The ground was hard, but he was used to that. His blanket was grubby and smelt horribly, but he was used to that too. There was a song running round and round in his head and he could not banish it. It was the song the Wendles sang when they were in triumph:

We are the Wendles of Wandsworth Town,
We're always up and the others are down.
We're rough and we're tough and we don't give a damn,
We are the elite of the Borrible clan.
   Reach for your Rumble-sticks,
   Try all your dirty tricks!
   Nothing can beat us
   And none shall defeat us.
Say a wrong word and we'll hammer you down,
We are the Wendles of Wandsworth Town!

Bingo sighed and hoped the song wasn't an evil omen. He threw the blanket from his shoulders and sat up. In the pitch darkness he got to his knees, crawled to the doorway and went outside, turned left and immediately bumped his head against the shaft of a spear. There was someone sitting there, on guard. Bingo drew back and stared into nothingness. He could not see a thing; it was like being blind.

'Who's that?' he whispered.

A voice came back at him, a Wendle voice. 'You tell me who you are, mush, or you'll get two yard of spear up yer.'

'I'm Bingo,' said Bingo.

'All right,' said the voice, 'but don't creep about at night, you'll get yourself killed. I'm Norrarf.'

'I couldn't sleep,' said Bingo. 'It's so hot. I thought the air might be a bit cooler in the tunnel.' He leant against the wall, stretched his legs out and looked to where he thought Norrarf was. 'Can I ask you a question?'

Norrarf chuckled and it was no friendly chuckle. 'You can always try . . . Don't go in for idle conversation, us Wendles.'

'Oh, it's not idle,' said Bingo, his tone as cheerful as ever. 'I just wondered how long you've known Spiff. I mean, were you here when he was Borribled?'

Norrarf didn't answer for a while. Bingo began to think he'd gone but then the Wendle spoke.

'He was already here when I came, had been for ages, had more names than anyone else too, including Flinthead. A lot of people liked Spiff in those days, including me and Skug—still do—but Flinthead hated him, which was funny really seeing as the stories told how they were Borribled together, came from the same place and all that.'

'Did they quarrel?'

'All the time,' said Norrarf, 'but Spiff was always too smart so Flinthead started to spread rumours about him. He was jealous, see. Then he got a lot of cronies together and made them into a bodyguard and one day he had Spiff captured and staked him out on the mud and he left him there to drown at high tide. There was a sentry on duty to make sure he didn't get away, and nobody could do a thing about it—too scared, most of 'em.'

'Except maybe you and Skug,' said Bingo, beginning to understand a little of the friendship that existed between the two Wendles and Spiff.

'Me and Skug, we waited till the tide was right in, when Flinthead and the bodyguard thought it was all over . . . Spiff was almost dead, had the mud in his mouth, crawling up his nostrils, over his head. Then as the sentry walked away I did for him and Skug pulled Spiff out of the water; we brought him round and he went to Battersea.'

'And the sentry?'

'Dead. We put his body in Spiff's place and he was eaten by the eels. All that was left at the next tide was a skeleton. Flinthead was as pleased as a dog with two tails . . . There was no one to stop him taking the whole tribe under his control. Later he heard that Spiff was alive after all but he never knew how it was done. That's why he always has at least fifty of the bodyguard round him. He don't know who to trust. Not every Wendle likes Flinthead you know; they're just scared of him. Even Tron, I suppose, and he's pretty brave.'

'Tron doesn't seem to be so bad,' said Bingo.

'He's what he has to be, but what can he do? Flinthead don't trust nobody. He has three men watching Tron and three more men watching each of the men who's watching Tron . . . and so it goes.'

'Has Spiff got a plan, do you think?' Bingo didn't expect Norrarf to answer that question, but he did. Now that he had begun, he seemed to enjoy talking through the watches of the night.

'Well,' he said, 'if you're too thick to work it out for yourself then you must be dopey enough to tell. Spiff hates Flinthead, and perhaps he thinks that if he can get his hands on the treasure then most of the Wendles will go over to his side—that would be the end of Flinthead.'

'Yes, but if Spiff got the treasure he might become as bad as Flinthead,' said Bingo, 'and anyway money's not Borrible.'

'I know that,' said Norrarf, 'but Spiff thinks any method that gets rid of Flinthead is a good method. Spiff's craftier than anyone I've ever known. He can see round corners and tell you what happened tomorrow, he can. That girl with you says he ain't Borrible at all, but he's a damn sight more Borrible than Flinthead. Whichever way you look at it, getting his hands on that treasure is the only way he's going to get your mates out alive. Borrible or not Borrible, that treasure's a powerful weapon.'

'Is that his plan?' asked Bingo, his voice quickening with excitement.

Norrarf clicked his teeth in denial. 'Nah, that's just what I think, ain't it? If you want to know any more you'd better ask him, I've talked too much already. You'd better get back.'

Bingo could feel the Wendle studying him in the dark. He stretched his eyes as wide as he could but saw nothing more than the pulsing of his own blood.

'It takes years to get used to living down here,' said Norrarf. 'That's why we're the way we are, I suppose.'

Bingo got to his hands and knees and turned to crawl back to the guardroom. 'Thanks, Norrarf,' he said as he left, 'thanks a lot.'

Norrarf did not bother to answer.

The next evening, when it was time, the Borribles gathered together and made ready to set off. They had checked their catapults;

each wore an extra bandolier and carried a Rumble-stick as well. They were indistinguishable from any band of Wendle warriors.

'Right,' said Stonks, 'we'll march along the tunnels as bold as brass; that way we'll be taken for a relief guard on our way to a lookout point.'

Spiff sneered. 'And you'd better get me to walk in front,' he said, 'otherwise you'll get lost.'

'Wait a minute,' said Vulge, 'where's Norrarf and Skug?'

Spiff raised his eyebrows. 'How should I know, they can't nurse us all the time, can they? If we're going, let's go.'

It was a long trek across the underground citadel and the seven Borribles passed many Wendles on their way, but no one asked their business or stopped them to demand their destination. By the time Spiff marched them out on to the banks of the Wandle the Borribles knew their disguise was perfect and they were filled with confidence and determination.

They came to a halt near a small jetty where two skiffs were moored. These were the boats used by the sentries for travelling to and from the derrick. Everywhere, on both sides of the river, sat or stood small groups of Wendles, all of them waiting for the treasure to be unearthed. On the platform itself the great wheel turned and creaked as the buckets clanked and the mud-covered figure of Torreycanyon stumbled forever forward.

'Strike a light,' said Vulge, 'it don't bear thinking about, do it? Our mates working in that shit for months and months. Old Flinthead's got a lot to answer for.'

'That'll do,' said Stonks, walking up and down in front of his companions like a commander inspecting his troops. 'Remember everyone along here is watching us right now, so try to make it look as if you know what you're doing. When I give the order, Bingo, Vulge, Sydney and me will get into this boat here. You other three will make for one of those tunnels. You'll be able to see everything from there, and whatever you do, Chalotte, don't take your eyes off Spiff.'

'I ain't going anywhere,' said Spiff. 'I want to see what a mess you make of it,' and he did a right turn, saluted like a Wendle and stamped off towards the nearest corridor with Chalotte and Twilight following.

Stonks watched them go and then ordered his own contingent into the larger of the two boats. Vulge and Bingo took the oars and, shoving off, they rowed into midstream.

Sydney bit her lip as the water slipped by. 'Have we got a chance, Stonksie?' she said.

Stonks sat in the stern and gazed at the derrick as they approached it. 'Yes,' he said. 'If we're lucky with the four guards and if we can get the prisoners out of the mine before we're noticed, then we'll get away.'

Bingo and Vulge gave a few more strokes of the oars and their skiff arrived at the platform. One of the guards came to the edge of it and Vulge turned in his seat and threw him a rope. 'Tie us up, mate,' he called, and the guard knelt and hooked the painter on to a large nail, but there his friendliness ceased. As soon as Vulge made to climb from the boat the Wendle lowered his spear so that the point of it was only an inch or two away from the Stepney Borrible's face.

'Where do you think you're going, mush? You've got to have a special writing from Flinthead to get on here.'

Vulge hesitated; he didn't know what to say.

Stonks stood up in the stern of the boat, frowning. 'That's exactly it,' he said, 'we're special from Flinthead. It's an emergency. The off-duty guard told him about the shuttering in the shaft, said it was weak, likely to fall in and bury everything; we've got to inspect it.'

'I know nothing about that,' grumbled the guard. 'I've had strict orders.'

Stonks raised both arms. 'You do as yer please, me old china; you know what Flinthead will be like if we go back without having done what we were sent to do. If that treasure gets buried under a thousand tons of mud you can bet your ears you'll be down there with it.'

The guard paled and Stonks reflected, not for the first time, that Flinthead's strength was also his weakness. The Wendles were so scared of him that they had no confidence in themselves. 'It's up to you,' went on Stonks, 'but I wouldn't be in your waders, mate, if you send us off with a flea in our ear.'

'All right,' said the guard, 'but watch yer step or I'll skewer yer.'

Vulge leapt easily on to the platform, in spite of his limp, and held out a hand to pull the three others up to him.

'Thanks,' said Stonks, who came last, and he walked across to the great treadmill. Close to, it was a massive thing and inside it the tortured shape of Torreycanyon shambled along like a drunkard, tumbling forward at a dangerous angle, always on the point of falling over but never quite managing to leave his feet far enough behind. The cumbersome wheel turned, the heavy mud splashed down into the river and the yellow lights above sprayed a dismal colour over everything. As Stonks listened to the rumbling of the treadmill and the banging of the buckets his eyes began to burn with pity and a fearful anger gnawed at the back of his brain.

'I'll kill 'em for this,' he said, under his breath, 'I'll kill 'em, every last one.'

As he stood there one of the guards came up beside him and laughed. 'This is the way to treat 'em,' he said, and he cracked his whip, making it curl across Torreycanyon's shoulders. The captive Borrible lost his balance, tottered for a moment, and then ran on, just a little faster.

Stonks swallowed hard. His friend was a ghost, a shadow. His clothes were in tatters, he was barefoot and covered from heel to head in a dark stickiness, a mixture of sweat, mud and blood. There was slime in his eyes, slime in his hair. He was not far from death, ground down to nothing for the sake of the Rumbles' treasure.

'What's his name?' asked Stonks for something to say.

'Torreycanyon,' said the guard, 'and he's the lucky one. He's a bit like a pet dog to us, running round in his wheel. You should see the others down below, you'd have to see the state they're in to believe it. No fresh air, gasping for breath. If you could see their skin, which you can't 'cos of the mud, you'd find it had all gone green with mildew. I don't reckon they can live much longer, they may not live until they finds the treasure even.'

'Very interesting,' said Bingo, biting back his temper, 'but we're only here to see the shuttering.'

'Yes,' said Stonks, 'we'd better get on with the job.' He went past the treadmill and looked into the mouth of the mine. The chief guard was by his side.

'Well, that's it,' said the Wendle. 'About a quarter of a mile down they reckon they are now, wood planks all the way round the outside with two big beams going across every fifteen feet or so to stop the planks falling inwards, 'cos the weight of the mud and earth behind is enormous, and pushing in all the time. If that lot slipped I don't know what would happen, a bleedin' eruption I should think.'

The rescuers were silent. The shaft was about ten feet in diameter and, as the guard had said, the safety of the diggings depended on the solid beams that crossed at right angles to each other at regular intervals all the way to the bottom. Huge wedges held the first timbers in position; massive they were and rising above the level of the platform. Sydney sidled to the rim and peered down. Below her she saw an electric light and another platform, and below that another and another until they became so small they disappeared.

'Can't see anything moving,' said Sydney.

'And you won't,' said the chief guard, 'they're too deep; they've been out of sight for months. There's two at the bottom digging their hearts out, and another follows behind. Black feller!'

'He's black now all right,' said another guard and he laughed.

'He has to keep the whole shaft in good order,' continued the chief, 'otherwise, if those beams give way, any of 'em, why the whole shebang would collapse and kill 'em all, not to mention losing the treasure.'

'Still getting enough timber?' asked Vulge.

'We're having a bit of trouble since the SBG arrived outside, still we've got enough to be going on with.'

Stonks glanced at the banks of the river. No one seemed particularly interested in what was taking place on the platform. It was time to begin; he had to get rid of the sentries. 'Well,' he said, 'we'd better start our inspection.' He looked at the chief guard. 'Will you come to the first landing with me, I've already seen something there I don't like the look of.'

'Well, all right,' said the Wendle, 'but I'll be buggered if I'll go any further. I can't stand it in there, it gives me the creeps.'

Stonks winked at Vulge and whispered, 'You stay here and send me another one when I asks yer.'

Vulge perched on the coping of the shaft and watched Stonks follow the guard down the ladder. Bingo scrutinized the towpaths and Sydney placed herself near the treadmill. Whatever happened to her, she had decided, the guard with the whip was going into the mud. Her sharp knife was ready.

The moment Stonks arrived below he went to stand by the Wendle and called his attention to a split in the shuttering. The guard leant over to examine the fault and Stonks nudged him gently into space. For a split second the Wendle ran on thin air like a cartoon cat; his spear sprang from his grasp, his eyes bulged and then down he went, surprised, leaving only a small and diminishing scream behind him.

Stonks glanced up at Vulge and raised two fingers; he wanted another one.

'I think your mate's slipped,' said Vulge quietly. 'You'd better have a look.'

The guards who were nearest came to the shaft and bent forward to see.

'He's fallen to the next platform,' called Stonks. 'You'll have to come and help me fetch him up.'

'Dammit,' said the Wendles, but they laid their spears on the planking and climbed down the ladder.

'Blimey,' said Bingo, 'that first guard was a pushover.'

'No jokes,' said Vulge. 'Grab hold of one of them spears and pretend you're on duty. We don't want them Wendles on the shore to get suspicious. I'll watch Stonks.'

But there wasn't much for Vulge to see. The two guards arrived on the landing. Stonks got them to the edge, the Wendles stared downwards and the next thing they knew they were falling fast, rigid with terror, clutching their bodies one to the other in the hope that somehow they could alter the laws of gravity and so save themselves. The noise when it came was solid and sickening. Stonks looked up and raised four fingers; he wanted the guard with the whip.

'Here, mate,' said Vulge. 'Your two chums want you. I can't

make out what they're saying, got a speech impediment have they?'

The guard threw his whip on to a pile of tools near the treadmill and ambled over to where Vulge sat. 'They're a bunch of idiots,' he said, and leant over the parapet. Sydney had kept pace with him across the platform and as soon as he halted she hit him very hard in the kidneys, taking the breath out of his body so that he couldn't call or shout, then she bent rapidly to his heels, grasped them securely, and simply upended her victim into the mine. Fortunately he made no sound until his head hit the planks of the landing. There he rolled and groaned until Stonks helped him on his way with a soft touch of the foot, easing the unconscious Wendle into the shaft so that he could join his colleagues.

'My, my,' said Vulge as he watched the body swoop and dive like a swallow, 'he has gone down in the world.'

'Shall we tell Torreycanyon now?' asked Sydney.

Vulge looked at the river banks. All was quiet. 'No,' he said at length. 'He might get excited and give us away. Hurry, let's get on guard, them Wendles on the shore will get suspicious if there ain't someone walking up and down all the time. And keep cracking the whip.'

So the three Borribles seized their spears and stood sternly to attention or marched to and fro across the platform.

'I can hardly believe it,' murmured Sydney. 'It all seems to be going to plan.'

Twilight and Chalotte surveyed the river from the safety of a tunnel, staring anxiously across the Wandle to where the wooden derrick floated on the slow rise and fall of the black-green mud. Streams of darkness poured down between the yellow lights that the Wendles had raised and it was a darkness that was at one with the dingy waters of the river. Somewhere behind Chalotte sat Spiff, not watching, strangely melancholy, alone.

'They're going well,' said Twilight. 'Stonks has got three of them into the mine and no one on shore has twigged it yet, and Bingo and Sydney are pretending to be on guard.'

'I know,' said Chalotte, her voice hopeful. 'But it'll be a bit different when they bring the prisoners out; they'll have to go like the clappers then.'

Suddenly Twilight laid hold of Chalotte's arm. 'Listen,' he said. 'What's that whispering in the tunnels?'

Chalotte cocked an ear and the whispering, faint at first, began to grow more definite. It was a threatening and insistent noise, a soft squelching, a noise that brought fear with it. Chalotte was mystified, then she realized what it was; it was the sound of many scores of Wendles in supple waders running at a relentless speed. It was the sound that Flinthead's bodyguard made when it moved—direct, dedicated, unswerving and vicious—and when the bodyguard moved Flinthead moved with it, his shapeless nose sniffing the way.

'Oh, it can't be,' wailed Chalotte, 'it mustn't be.'

Her wishes made no difference. Within a minute or two a mass of heavily armed Wendles poured out of the tunnels on each side of the river, the light glinting on their spears and helmets. Many of them carried lightweight skiffs and their stride did not break as they reached the Wandle and ran on into it, launching themselves, their speed remaining constant as they went from running to rowing so that they flew on to the surface of the mud like black and orange water-bugs. Many more warriors spread out along the banks, prodding ordinary Wendles from the towpaths with the butts of their spears. Then came a clashing of weapons and a huge shout, and in the midst of fifty hand-picked soldiers Flinthead appeared, his golden jacket shining and his eyes brilliantly opaque with the coldness of his triumph.

'Dammit,' swore Chalotte, and she lifted her fingers to her mouth in order to whistle a warning, but strong arms seized her from behind and for a moment she thought she'd been captured—then she remembered Spiff.

'Keep yer mouth shut,' he said. 'It won't do anyone any good to let Flinthead know you're here. Just keep quiet and get ready to run for your life.'

On the platform, Bingo, Vulge and Sydney stood firm and made ready to defend themselves against the advancing warriors. It was pointless; the derrick was too large for three to hold against so many and the Wendle warriors overran the interlopers after the briefest of struggles. They were disarmed, bound and thrown to the floor. When all was secure Flinthead was rowed over and helped on to the platform by Tron, his captain of bodyguards, the stern fighter who had commanded and led the attack.

Then the Wendles waited, silent and patient until, in the end, Stonks climbed into view at the top of the mine shaft, pulling three exhausted and slime-covered slaves behind him. It had taken all his massive strength to bring them up from the bottom of the digging and so engrossed in his task was he that he did not notice the eager faces above him. He raised a hand for assistance and the Wendles grasped it before Stonks realized that things had changed. He was quickly made a prisoner himself, bound with ropes and pushed to the floor to lie by the side of his friends.

'Oh, Twilight,' said Chalotte, the tears flooding her eyes, 'this is awful, all of 'em captured. Look at those three covered in mud, the ones the Wendles are lifting out of the mine, that's Knocker and Napoleon and Orococco. Hell, they're so weak they can hardly stand.'

What Chalotte said was true. The captives swayed and blinked stupidly in the light. They were caked in mud, months of mud, it was ground into their skins like a paste of graphite. Their hearts had filled with joy at Stonks's unexpected arrival and in some unknowable and resolute part of their minds they had discovered strength enough to climb the long ladders upwards, only to find Flinthead waiting for them. It was one of life's rotten jokes and their dejection was total.

The Wendle chieftain laughed like a car-crusher. 'I knew well that something was happening here,' he crowed, 'and look what we have. Another four of them, brought here by greed, trying to steal what is rightfully ours. Well, brother Wendles, they will help us now, help us in our struggle to dig the mine.'

Stonks began to fight against his bonds and he swore at Flinthead. 'You snot-gobblin' little shit-eater,' he cried, 'you no-name pig.'

Flinthead was delighted and one of his guards kicked Stonks in the ribs.

'He's the strongest one, isn't he?' said the chieftain. 'I remember his name from last time . . . Stonks. He's the one who broke open the Great Door of Rumbledom, he'll be just right for the treadmill. Put a good man on the whip. I've waited too long for my treasure, maybe now things will move a little faster.'

'What do you want done with the old ones?' asked Tron. 'Shouldn't we let them go? They don't look as if they could work another day.'

'Send 'em back down,' said Flinthead, 'they can work till they die. Shackle 'em all up and over the top with 'em.'

The new prisoners kicked at their captors as their legs were manacled together with heavy chains, but the others, those they had gone to rescue, had not a word to say. Their muscles had striven beyond pain and their minds were submerged below thought. They knew how to dig and they knew no other thing. When they were ordered to clamber back into the mine they did so in abject silence. Flinthead watched and smiled; that silence was his glory! How were the mighty fallen.

'And let me warn you,' he said. 'If those buckets come up empty of mud I'll make an example of those two in the treadmill. I'll send 'em down to you headfirst, like you did with my guards. I want that treasure and I want it quick. You'll soon learn—no mud coming up, no food going down.'

'We'll get you one day,' shouted Bingo as he was forced on to the ladder with the others, 'and I'll have your nose off and slice it up like a side of bacon.'

Flinthead did not wait to swap insults. 'Double the sentries everywhere,' he shouted, 'twenty on each towpath too.' Then he stepped into his skiff and was conveyed to the river bank, his bodyguard following.

On the shore he was greeted by a multitude of excited Wendles. News of the attempted rescue and its failure had travelled fast. Flinthead was cheered till the roof resounded and there was great confusion as the crowd struggled to approach their leader, to touch him, to look at him.

Chalotte and Twilight had been completely disheartened by the turn of events but now they came out of their tunnel to stare as the bodyguard cleared a path through the mob. Chalotte fingered the knife at her belt and wondered if she should assassinate the Wendle chieftain there and then, but Twilight saw the movement of her hand and guessed what she was thinking.

'It would do no good,' he said, 'and would not help your friends; that is what we must think of now.'

Chalotte was about to answer when a sudden surge in the crowd plucked her from her feet and swung her against the firm flesh of the bodyguard. She looked up and saw that she was only a yard or so from Flinthead, dangerously close to that damp green skin, those lifeless eyes of power and the great shapeless nose. Chalotte shivered in spite of the warm crush of bodies all round her. She turned her head away from the hideous countenance and immediately saw two faces she knew. There, just in front of the chieftain, marched Norrarf and Skug, resplendent in brand new uniforms. They had not seen her; they were too busy smiling with pride.

'March on,' cried Flinthead. 'You did well, Norrarf and Skug; I will remember you when the treasure comes. March on I say, and sing the song of the Wendles.'

Chalotte turned her back to avoid being noticed and pushed her way through the crowd until she reached Twilight. Despair swept through her body and, amidst all the cheering and shouting, the tears ran freely down her cheeks.

'For Pete's sake don't do that,' said Twilight. 'The Wendles will wonder what's wrong with you, this is their celebration.'

Chalotte tried but could not stop her tears and Twilight guided her into a tunnel.

'I saw Norrarf and Skug,' she said miserably, 'in Flinthead's bodyguard. They weren't bodyguards before so that means he must have promoted them . . . It means they must have told Flinthead about us trying to rescue Knocker . . . That can only mean one thing.'

Now it was Twilight's turn to touch his knife. 'Of course,' he said, 'it means that Spiff told them about Stonks's plan, so now there's only the two of us against everyone else.'

A cool voice came to them from the darkness. Spiff's voice. 'If you'd listened to me none of this would have happened. I told you to wait.'

Chalotte wiped her eyes and blinked, trying to locate her enemy; it was impossible. 'You grassed on your friends,' she said, 'and now they're down the bottom of the pit and we'll never get them out.'

'I can get them out,' said Spiff, 'on my own if needs be.'

'Did you tell Norrarf and Skug to tell Flinthead about the rescue?' asked Chalotte. 'Because if you did I swear that I'll kill you the first chance I get.'

Spiff chuckled. 'You scare me to death. Yes, I gave Stonks away and I had good reasons for it. Flinthead knew there was something going on down here, he knew that someone from outside was inside. He'd already doubled the guards on all the exits and all along the Wandle. Stonks had no chance of getting anywhere, with or without the prisoners. He would have been killed; now at least he's alive, and all the others as well.'

'Alive like slaves,' said Chalotte, and she took her catapult from her belt and loaded it.

'Don't you realize,' Spiff continued, 'that I've been planning my revenge against Flinthead for years, every move, every detail. I didn't want it spoiled, so I put a spanner in the works as soon as I could.'

'Yeah,' said Chalotte angrily, 'and it didn't matter about our mates as long as your plan was all right.' She began to stretch the catapult rubber. If she saw Spiff she'd kill him.

'I'll get 'em out of here. Look on the bright side. Sure I had Norrarf and Skug tell Flinthead but now they've been made members of the bodyguard. Now I'll know everything Flinthead knows, but the best thing of all is that Flinthead thinks he's captured everybody. He's stopped sniffing; he doesn't know about us, we're a surprise.'

'What d'yer mean, we?' said Chalotte. She drew the rubber back to her ear and tried to judge Spiff's position from his voice. She'd let fly with the stone, she thought, and then run forward with her knife.

Spiff's voice floated through the darkness again, only now it came from a different part of the tunnel. 'If you put that catapult down, Chalotte, I'll tell you . . . and you too, Twilight.'

Chalotte cursed and lowered her weapon. She looked to her right and caught a glimpse of Twilight doing the same with his.

'You sod,' she said, 'you're about as straightforward as a left-handed corkscrew. Why didn't you trust us?'

'I don't trust anyone,' said Spiff. 'If you so much as pee against the wall down here Flinthead knows about it before you've finished. I'll tell you one thing and one thing only. You want your mates out and you'll have 'em out, that I promise you. What you've got to decide, Chalotte, is this. Do you forget about killing me or do I kill you, right now, because I can. I don't need you, I can do my plan on my own.'

Chalotte squatted on the rough floor, behind her the glow of the river bank and the noise of the Wendles as they dispersed, in front of her the blackness and Spiff's voice. There was no doubt that he could see her whereas she could see nothing. She would have to lie. She was determined to survive if only to make sure that Spiff got his come-uppance. She put her catapult away.

'I'd agree to anything,' she said, 'if I really thought you could still get them out.'

'And me,' said Twilight.

'You'll both have to do exactly as I say,' said Spiff, 'and no questions. I ain't telling anyone what my plan is.'

'Just tell me one thing,' said Chalotte, 'for the sake of curiosity. Was it you who arranged for the Borrible message to turn up in Neasden, the one that got Sydney so worried about Sam the horse, the one that made her come to see me at Whitechapel?'

'Yes it was,' said Spiff. 'I wanted to get you all here but I wasn't quite sure how to do it, then Sam and Sussworth and old Ben did it for me.'

'If your plan only needs you why did you need us?' asked Twilight.

Spiff chuckled, but with real mirth this time.

'Twilight,' he said, 'you're as bright as a new bar of soap. It was because my plan needed to lull Flinthead, which ain't easy. I needed someone to be captured, so he'd feel secure. Well he does now; all I've got to do is wait for the right moment.'

'And when's that?'

'I ain't saying. You can come along for the ride if you like or you can go away and hide in a corner till it's all over.'

'And the treasure,' said Chalotte, 'where does that come in?'

'Oh, it comes in,' said Spiff. 'That's power that is, not in a normal Borrible set-up, I know, but down here it is. I'll be honest with you; Flinthead is first, then your mates, then the Rumble treasure chest. All three together would be lovely, but I'll be happy to settle for the first one.'

Chalotte hesitated. She wished she had time to think, wished she had time to talk to Twilight, but there was no time. She sighed in the silence and said, 'All right, Spiff. I've got no choice, have I? It's Hobson's again. I'll go along with you, but when we get out of here, if we do, I might just stick my knife in yer.'

'Me too,' said Twilight.

'I wouldn't expect anything else,' said Spiff, and they heard him roll over and get to his feet.

The sly bugger, thought Chalotte, he's been lying on the floor, and she saw Spiff step into the light, holding a spear across his body.

'What do we do now?' asked Twilight.

'We go back to the guardroom and wait,' said Spiff. 'I'll ask Norrarf to get us a pack of cards. We can play patience.'

'And the others,' said Chalotte. 'I suppose we just leave them in the mine, digging and slaving for Flinthead, until it suits you, that is.'

Spiff smiled his most ironic smile. 'Well,' he said, 'at least we know where they are. They can't get lost now, can they?'

8

More than a week went by, a week that for Chalotte was made unbearable by Spiff's confidence and high spirits. It was as if he saw the future with complete clarity and knew that his long-laid plans were at last coming to fruition. But Chalotte had never been so unhappy. Every second she was awake she thought of the captives toiling in the humidity of the mine-shaft, digging their days and nights away, knee-deep in muck. She was homesick, a thousand miles from Whitechapel, and had it not been for the hope of rescuing her friends, she would have made her way to the nearest manhole and gone back into the streets, never mind the SBG; anything to get back to a normal life.

And so she waited with an ill grace. She detested Norrarf and Skug more and more, turning her head away from the sight of them each time they brought provisions and news to the guardroom. That was all she could do; she was helpless and she knew it. She was obliged to accept the situation for as long as it lasted, but she would not acquiesce. She spoke only in grunts to Twilight; Spiff she ignored completely and spent her time either scowling or sleeping. Her usual common sense had deserted her, banished by feelings of frustration and hatred.

Yet deep down, although the waiting seemed endless, Chalotte knew that soon it would have an end and that if there was any chance of freeing her friends then that chance lay with Spiff and the devious workings of his complicated and untrustworthy mind. On the morning of the eighth day after the capture of Stonks, Chalotte at last awoke in good heart; she took a deep sigh and decided only one thing mattered, and that was the deliverance of the enslaved Borribles.

As for Spiff, there was only one thing she could do. She glanced over to where he lay and studied his face, as crafty in sleeping as in waking. She could not fight him there and then, and anyway if the rescue attempt failed then Flinthead would kill them all. If it succeeded then there would be time enough to settle accounts. She would have to wait and see.

As she thought these thoughts Spiff opened one eye and smiled. He had a way of smiling that convinced Chalotte he could see right through her, and she knew he had realized, with his first second of consciousness, that she had come to a decision.

'It'll be all right,' he said, 'if you leave it to me.'

Whether her tacit acceptance had something to do with it or not Chalotte never knew, but from that day Spiff began to put his plans into operation. From then on they never stopped working. Spiff traipsed Chalotte and Twilight all over Wendle country, familiarizing them with the terrain, stealing systematically and making caches of provisions and weapons in likely and unlikely spots.

'Well,' he said in answer to Chalotte's questions, 'I'm not looking for trouble but when trouble starts it tends to get out of hand. Who knows which way we might have to run; we might have no weapons, no food, we might have to hide for days, weeks even. These supplies could be the difference between life and death.'

'But only if you can remember where they are,' said Twilight. 'That's not much good if we get split up.'

'It's good for me,' said Spiff.

And so he went on working away at his preparations until the fourteenth day and then he declared enough was enough. He and his two companions had just finished hiding their last Wendle skiff when Chalotte became aware of a figure leaning over her in the yellow half-light. She turned quickly in the water where she stood and pulled her catapult from her belt. Spiff waded ashore, laughing to see Chalotte so ready to fight on his side now. 'You still can't see in the dark,' he said. 'That's Norrarf.'

The Wendle threw three brand new orange-coloured jackets on

to the ground. 'I'm going to enrol you in the bodyguard today,' he said, 'all three of you, only you'll have to come right now.'

'That's good,' said Spiff. 'Plan A.' And he held out a hand to pull Chalotte from the water to the towpath, but he explained nothing.

'Put the jackets on,' ordered Norrarf, 'and as soon as you get a chance you'd better clean your helmets and waders. If you go round like that Flinthead will suss you for sure. And you'd best invent yourself a Wendle name too, just in case you're asked.'

Spiff slung his old jacket into the river. 'Right,' he said, 'as of now we're in the bodyguard. That means doing what you're told, Chalotte, when you're told, without question. We're walking on a knife's edge. If we get found out it's curtains.'

When Norrarf was satisfied with the look of his recruits he got them into line and marched them upstream until they came to the landing stage, the open space which was level with the mine and its platform. As always the noise of the treadmill and the buckets filled the whole cavern. Chalotte could see Stonks in the wheel with an arm round Torreycanyon, helping him along. Every now and then came the crack of the whip and Chalotte formed her lips to curse, but Spiff was watching and shook his head. 'Not now,' he said, 'not now.'

There were about twenty of Flinthead's bodyguard on duty in the area and their uniforms were spotless and their weapons clean. They leant casually against the brick walls or crouched on their haunches. From time to time, when they considered it necessary, they cleared the towpath of ordinary Wendles so as to make a way for Flinthead should he come. Apart from that they did nothing, though they gave the impression of being ready for anything at a moment's notice. Under the bright helmets their faces were hard; they did what they were told and they did it quickly.

Norrarf marshalled the newcomers on a flat space by the bankside. He clicked his fingers and a warrior brought him an assortment of sharp spears; he gave one each to the three Borribles.

'You have been picked to serve on Flinthead's bodyguard,' he said, loud enough for the nearest Wendles to hear, 'and you know what that means; you will be rewarded for instant obedience, anything less than that and you'll be staked out on the mud. Now dismiss . . . and get your weapons and uniforms clean.'

Spiff saluted and Chalotte and Twilight did as he did, then they turned and walked away to find an uncrowded spot on the towpath not too far from their new colleagues.

'I've seen a few Borrible tribes,' said Twilight, 'but I've never seen anything like Wendles, I mean obeying orders, cleaning clothes . . . How does Flinthead get away with it?'

Spiff spat on the point of his spear and polished it with his sleeve. 'Because he doesn't mind what he does or who he does it to, just as long as he gets his own way. It's also got a lot to do with living so near Rumbledom. Until the Great Rumble Hunt was successful your average Wendle never knew from one minute to the next if he was going to be taken over or not . . . . There was always a battle going on along the frontier. That made 'em suspicious of outsiders and always ready for a scrap, but then,' and here Spiff winked, 'so am I.'

During the days that followed Chalotte learned more about self-discipline than she had ever thought possible. She steeled herself to ignore the crack of the whip; she pretended to jeer and laugh with others of the bodyguard whenever Stonks or Torreycanyon fell to their knees in the treadmill; and she forced herself not to think of her friends, Knocker in particular, who were still toiling in the deep pit of the mine.

Most of the time she leant against the curved wall of the sewer and looked as ferocious and heartless as she could, or squatted cross-legged on the ground and played fivestones with Twilight, assuming an indifference to all that went on around her, though in reality her blood was seething with anxiety and impatience. Then one day, when she had almost forgotten who she was and why she was in Wendle country at all, Spiff came and sat with her and Twilight, resting his spear across his knees.

'Something's going to happen soon,' he began, 'I have a feeling in my water. Norrarf thinks they'll reach the treasure any day now and when they do he reckons Flinthead will go down to get it because he won't trust anyone to do it for him. He'll come this way, by the landing stage, and be rowed over to the platform, and then down he'll go.'

'Alone?' asked Twilight.

'Not bloody likely, he wouldn't be safe. Bingo, Vulge and Sydney are still pretty fresh, they might wind their leg chains round his neck and strangle him. He'll have to take some bodyguards with him . . . and we're bodyguards. Now whatever happens we've got to get over to the platform with Flinthead. Norrarf and Skug are in charge here and they are going to order us into the rowing detail. We must get to the platform.'

'Supposin' we don't?' said Chalotte.

Spiff dismissed the thought. 'We just have to, even if we take a separate boat. Once we get there you two line up with the Wendles and do as you're told. It's my job to see that I'm chosen as one of the guards to go down the mine with Flinthead.'

'Cripes,' said Twilight, 'you can't do that; it'll be you against all of them.'

Spiff turned his head very slowly and looked at the Bangladeshi, his blue eyes blazing with the bright love of danger. It was a light fuelled by hatred and Chalotte blinked in the glare of it.

'You're mad, Spiff,' she said very quietly, 'you're raving bonkers.' But although she meant it there was a note of admiration in her voice. His bravery burnt like a beacon.

'Maybe I am,' said Spiff, 'but when I get down there I won't let two or three little Wendles come between me and what I've been dreaming of for years.'

'What about when you come back up again?' said Twilight. 'We've got the whole Wendle nation to get past, remember. You said yourself they ain't going to sit back and let us go without a fight.'

'You don't have to know any more than I've told yer at this stage,' said Spiff. 'Just behave like regular bodyguards until I comes with the prisoners, then do as I orders and everything will work out fine.'

There was nothing more to be got out of him and he left them, ignoring them both in the days that followed and spending all his time with the troops of the bodyguard, laughing, joking and making friends. Indeed Spiff became very popular among the warriors, although it was obvious to Chalotte that if it became necessary he would slide his knife into any Wendle who upset his calculations. That was Spiff and he was not to be altered. So Chalotte gave up her contemplation of the strange un-Borrible Borrible and contented herself with counting the days . . . eighteen . . . nineteen . . . twenty . . . twenty-one.

An electric light flickered and Chalotte raised her head from between her hands. She was sitting on the towpath and Twilight sat nearby. In spite of her efforts she had lost count of time; there had been something like twenty-four days, she thought, since the capture of Stonks's raiding party.

Chalotte glanced into the roof vault. The light flickered again. Something was wrong in the citadel, there was something missing. Then she realized; there was silence everywhere; the buckets were not clanking, the treadmill was not creaking. Chalotte glanced across the river. Torreycanyon was a collapsed heap and Stonks was kneeling beside him. The guards were as still as stone carvings, their spear points unmoving. Everyone, standing or sitting, was motionless, their ears cocked, their eyes wide open. There had been a noise and they were listening to it. Chalotte herself, preoccupied by her own dreams, had let the sound slip by at first, but then her memory found the noise and brought it back to her and it merged in her ear with a real echo, and Chalotte recognized the sound and the echo for what they were and so did everyone else in the Wendle citadel.

A quarter of a mile below the surface of the River Wandle, at the very bottom of the mine shaft, in a pool of mud and filth, Knocker's spade had struck the steel lid of the Rumble treasure chest and the noise had rung in every Wendle heart, and it still rang and continued to ring as every heart stopped.

Down the corridors and tunnels the bitter noise echoed and no one moved while it passed them, but as it dwindled and died at last there came another sound, as chilling and as frightening as the first. A scream of pleasure rose from Flinthead's throat and rode along the dark passages of his empire. Flinthead had got his way.

Flinthead called again; his duty bodyguard gathered round him and all together they raced towards the river. The chieftain's face was crazed with greed and no one dared to look upon it in those first moments. But from the mouth of every tunnel that Flinthead passed came every Wendle who could move, eager to be with their leader, struggling with each other to be the first to see the box of treasure which they believed would change their lives.

Spiff rushed to Chalotte and Twilight and shook them hard by the shoulders, breaking the spell of fear that bound them. 'Come on,' he yelled. 'Today is the day of all days, follow me and think fast.'

Then Norrarf's voice came over the milling crowds on the towpath. 'Clear the banks,' he shouted, 'Flinthead is coming.'

'More room,' shouted Skug from somewhere.

'Follow me,' said Spiff, and with the haft of his spear he levered himself through a thick crowd of Wendles and Chalotte and Twilight went with him, shoving and kicking their way.

'Stand back for the guard,' yelled Spiff. Chalotte looked at him; he grinned and she grimaced in return, striking a Wendle with her spear. 'Stand back for the guard,' she shouted.

The three Borribles emerged at last on the landing stage where Norrarf and Skug and their platoon of warriors were fighting hard to keep a space open. Norrarf, who stood in the centre, was nervous, a sickly colour under his greenish skin. He blew his cheeks out with relief when Spiff and his companions arrived.

'You three,' he commanded, 'stand by the big skiff there; you will take Flinthead to the platform.'

Spiff, Chalotte and Twilight ran to the water's edge and stood by the boat. From everywhere came the sound of tramping and shouting, growing louder every moment. Spiff untied the skiff's painter and waded knee-deep into the mud, holding the rope in his hands.

'Stand smart on either side,' he said. 'Don't look at Flinthead; just obey orders and let's hope he's so excited that his nose don't smell us out.'

And then there came an increase in the rush of noise and it swept out of the tunnels like a wind and the Wendle chieftain, running at the head of his men, burst into view and strode to the landing stage, crossing it immediately and heading straight for the river where Spiff held the boat steady against the shore.

'You Wendles,' called Flinthead, addressing his bodyguard, 'you will hold this jetty until my return.' He stared towards the mine, his blank eyes burning. 'Who rows me to the platform?'

'Those three, Flinthead,' said Norrarf, his voice shaking, 'and me.'

'Very well,' said the chieftain. 'I shall need six or seven warriors to come with me to the bottom of the mine to help with the prisoners.'

'There are eight men on the platform now,' said Norrarf, 'ever since you ordered the guard doubled. They are eight of your best.'

Flinthead looked at his rowers and Spiff inclined his head and dragged the boat a little further into the mudbank. Chalotte and Twilight moved a little closer too, their bodies rigid with fear.

Flinthead stepped into the boat and it lurched. He strode over the seats and sat in the prow. Chalotte noticed the long knife in his belt; he kept his hand on it all the time.

'Hurry,' said Flinthead, 'or I'll know the reason why.'

Spiff shouted at Twilight and Chalotte, 'Quickly you two,' and they took their places by the slender oars. Norrarf followed and Spiff pushed the boat out into the flowing mud and leapt aboard expertly, like the Wendle he was.

'Row, you fools,' he shouted, grabbing an oar for himself, 'row, there's not a second to lose.'

The skiff breasted the current and floated slowly round to face the stream. On a word the four rowers leant to their task and the boat shot across the river. Flinthead turned in his seat and stared as the derrick drew near, his eyes steady.

In a moment or two the skiff bumped against the platform and the eight guards crowded forward to help their master disembark. Spiff was only a pace behind him, light-footed and tense like an alley cat.

The boat was firmly moored and Chalotte, Twilight and Norrarf clambered on to the wooden island while Flinthead himself shouted over the river to where Tron and his men stood in an orderly line on the far bank.

'Tron,' called the chieftain, 'while I am down below you will take charge; get over here with your three lieutenants. Anyone who breaks rank or disobeys orders will answer to me as soon as I return, and no one is to move while I am gone, do you understand?'

Tron raised a hand to show that he knew what Flinthead wanted, then he stepped into a boat, three warriors with him, and they began to row towards the platform. Meanwhile, Flinthead directed his attention to the eight guards and gave them their instructions.

'Two of you stay here,' he said, 'the other six will come with me. You won't need your spears, just knives and catapults. Norrarf, you will aid Tron and see that my orders are carried out.' And with one last bleak stare from his blank eyes the chieftain swung a leg over the rim of the shaft and went in search of his treasure.

As soon as Flinthead's face had sunk beneath the level of the planking Spiff pushed himself into the group of Wendle guards.

' 'Ere,' said one, 'he wanted six of us, not seven.'

'He gave me my orders earlier,' lied Spiff. 'I've got something special to do.'

'Oh that's different,' said the Wendle. 'You can go first then.'

'Not a chance,' retorted Spiff. 'I'm to bring up the rear; I've got to make sure you lot don't get lost.' This sounded so much like one of Flinthead's schemes that the guard believed it entirely and went quickly over the top, his five colleagues following him just as rapidly as they could. Spiff went last of all.

Chalotte watched him go. In that brief moment before he disappeared he glanced at her and she lifted a hand in farewell. She wanted to say something but dared not, for Tron was approaching the platform and coming within earshot. She smiled instead, for, when all was said and done and in spite of her dislike of him, Chalotte wanted Spiff to win, wanted him to conquer Flinthead and free the captives. But there was no need for words, Spiff knew what she was thinking and he returned her smile, his face looking as happy as she'd ever seen it. He was pleased with the danger and overjoyed at the unreasonable odds. That was how he wanted to live; and so he winked just once, ducked his head, and was gone.

Tron climbed on to the platform with his followers and went to stand by the mouth of the mine. On both sides of the river the bodyguards and warriors stood in ranks and kept the tunnel entrances clear. There were many hundreds of Wendles present and over the whole scene the tension tightened. Chalotte held her breath, waiting for the next stroke of her heart, willing it to come, dreading what it might bring. The world had slipped from its axis and was falling all the way down to the end of the universe.

Spiff reached the first landing and peered over the edge. Far below he could see the light reflected on Flinthead's copper helmet. The Wendle chieftain was already two or three storeys ahead of his guards and travelling as fast as he could. Spiff swung himself out on to the second ladder and went after him.

The mine was built from rough planks which the Wendles had taken from old packing cases; the black stencilled letters of the original destinations were still visible: Cardiff, New York, Calcutta. Every fifteen feet or so huge beams had been hammered and wedged across the shaft in order to hold the shuttering in place and to support the landings. It was the shuttering, or vertical planking, that kept the mud at bay, straining against terrific pressures. There were hundreds of thousands of tons of that mud on the other side of the planks and Spiff could hear it slide and slither, searching for a way in, the shaft itself shifting and swaying like a great eel in the currents that surrounded it. Every bit of wood in the construction creaked and groaned all the time, every strut and every joist. A thick slime oozed through the cracks and knotholes and trickled everywhere, saturating everything, dripping slowly from one surface to another until it reached the very bottom of that deep, deep hole in the ground.

The air was heavy and it became more and more oppressive as Spiff descended. It was wet too and clung to his limbs like sodden clothing. Sweat trickled down his face and stung his eyes with salt and the mud that covered all began to cover him, making him smell like a cesspool rat. Far above, the tiny blaze of light that marked the top of the pit gradually diminished; then it disappeared.

Spiff spat. 'I've got to overtake them guards,' he said to himself. 'Help them on their way.'

At the next opportunity he rested and stared down into the gloom. Every twenty or thirty feet the Wendle engineers had rigged an electric light and with their aid Spiff could see the figures of Flinthead's bodyguards hastening in pursuit of their master.

'This is no good,' said Spiff. 'I'll have to start moving, I'll have to jump.' Having made the decision he lowered himself over the lip of the landing, to the full extent of his arms, and allowed his body to drop the fifteen feet to the floor below.

He crashed on to the planking and rolled over. The thump of his fall reverberated and fell and made the bodyguards look up in fear. A gobbet of mud slopped and twisted through the air and struck one of the Wendles across the face. He screamed in terror, convinced that the mine was about to cave in and squash him. Then he stood motionless for a long moment, allowing his companions to go on, and as soon as they were out of sight he began to climb upwards, his knees weak and his lips trembling. But Spiff was relentless, thundering from one storey to the next, and the noise and the mud fell again and again; it was like the footfalls of a giant taking great and regular strides.

Spiff was travelling fast and he soon overtook the hindmost of the guards, diving past him as he cringed on the rungs of a ladder, petrified by the appearance of this mud-covered figure rocketing out of nowhere.

There was another crash as Spiff landed and rolled, getting to his feet to beckon at the Wendle in the most friendly manner.

'What you frightened of?' he said. 'We're all chums together, you know.'

'The mine's collapsing, isn't it?' said the Wendle, scrambling down to join Spiff. 'And it's so spooky. I don't care what I do as a rule but I wish I hadn't been picked for this job.'

'You will, certainly,' said Spiff, and with a straight right arm he pushed the bodyguard backwards from the platform.

The Wendle shrieked and the shriek stood across the darkness like a bright light. Even high up on the banks of the Wandle they heard it and there was not one person whose stomach didn't shrivel at the sound. Spiff himself listened to the cry with satisfaction but there was no time for such contentment; there were still five Wendles between him and Flinthead.

He came upon two of those five only a little later. Spiff's first victim, a dead weight plunging at great speed, had fallen on to them like a sack of spuds and had broken their bodies as effectively as any car crash. Now all three lay mangled together, groaning as the blood crept from their wounds to drip between the rough planks, and not far below the remaining guards knew the sticky touch of it on their hands and faces.

They were ready for Spiff when he appeared on the landing above them, and they were suspicious. They had heard strange bumps and bangs and had felt warm blood on their skins; something was wrong, very wrong. They loaded their catapults and aimed at Spiff's head.

'Gerrorf,' said Spiff. 'I'm just a member of the bodyguard, like you lot; you saw me at the top.'

'What's all this noise about?' asked the biggest of the three Wendles. 'And what's all this blood?'

'Ah,' said Spiff, 'you see one of your fellows lost his nerve and he's gone back up again. As for the other two, well, one of them slipped and fell a couple of storeys all in one go and as he went he pulled his mate along with him. They're a bit the worse for wear, they are, that's why there's blood about.' Spiff grinned and without waiting for the Wendles to come to a decision began to climb down towards them, talking as he went.

'This game don't half make your legs ache, don't it?' he said cheerfully. 'How much further do we have to go?'

'Effin' miles,' said the big Wendle when Spiff had joined him, 'and we'd better get a move on otherwise Flinthead will skin us.' He studied Spiff closely. 'Who are you then? You still haven't said.'

Spiff shut an eye and tilted his head to one side. 'My name's Ratrap,' he said. 'I've only just been made a member of the bodyguard.'

The big Wendle seemed satisfied with this explanation and he and his two colleagues stowed their catapults under their jackets and made ready to continue the journey. Spiff went with them to the top of the next ladder, making sure that he was the last in line as they each awaited their turn to go down. Then, as soon as the big Wendle had begun his descent, Spiff drew his knife, pressed his hand over the mouth of the guard who stood in front of him and quietly slit his throat.

By now the big Wendle had arrived on the floor below and was shouting for the others to follow on. Spiff lowered his victim's corpse to the planking and allowed the second Wendle to get his foot on the first rung, then he bent over and tapped him on the shoulder.

'Yes,' said the Wendle, raising his head. He was caught in an awkward crouching position.

'Aren't you the one with the whip,' asked Spiff politely, 'the one who's been bashing Torreycanyon and Stonks about?'

'Yes,' answered the Wendle. 'I'm good with a whip I am.'

'A-mazing,' said Spiff. 'Well, life is full of little surprises and here's one for you,' and he lashed out with a fist, striking his enemy hard and knocking him senseless. As the body fell it curved over backwards and dived gracefully on to the head of the big Wendle, smashing open his helmet, splitting his skull and casting him down into the half-darkness. There were no screams this time; there was nothing but a silent and elegant flight followed by a distant and mortal thud.

Spiff put his knife away. 'Beautiful flyers them two,' he said, 'just like the pigeons that live in Battersea Park . . . And now there's only Flinthead. He's got the treasure and I've got him.'

Spiff saw the lights at the end of everything long before he arrived there. He calculated that there must be at least four or five bulbs rigged round the perimeter of the diggings in order to make it easy for the miners to see what they were doing. Wherever the Wendles stole their electric power they certainly stole a lot.

Spiff was travelling slowly now, using the ladders rather than jumping, and all was silent again, except for the bellowing of Flinthead's voice at intervals, ordering his guards to hurry.

At last Spiff saw the chieftain's copper helmet. Flinthead was

waiting on the last landing of all, just above the very bottom of
the pit, and beyond him Spiff could make out the figures of the
Borrible slaves. 'Oh, boy!' said Spiff. 'This is what I've been
waiting for.'

Flinthead heard waders scraping across wood and he glanced
up. 'Where have you been, you fools,' he cried, but then he saw
one guard only and not the expected six. 'Where are the others?'
he asked. 'What are you playing at?'

Spiff pulled his tin helmet tight to his head and wiped a muddy
hand across his face in an attempt to disguise himself a little
more; it was hardly necessary. He was already covered from top to
toe in filth.

'I'm sorry, Flinthead,' he said, affecting a harsh Wendle voice,
'I came as quick as I could. One of the others had a nasty accident
and that held us up a bit.'

Flinthead swore and looked away and Spiff placed his feet on
the rungs of the ladder that alone separated him from the Wendle
chieftain. Down he went.

Here, where the shaft petered out, the protective shuttering had
a temporary and fragile appearance. The last landing was only
half completed, its planks loose and warped, and just one piece of
scaffolding board, with rungs nailed to it, led ultimately to the
floor of the mine.

Spiff gazed with horror at the scene he had journeyed so far to
see. It was bright with light and black with mud, the end of an
abyss, a cruel circle set in the still centre of the earth and dripping
with a poisonous heat.

The slaves stood or sat in a slime that was knee-deep and gur-
gled in from all sides. Spiff's eyes searched for Knocker and then
Napoleon and Orococco. They were difficult to distinguish, nearly
at one with the mud; their tattered clothes were welded to their
limbs, their hair was plastered flat on their skulls and they
crouched against the walls, thin and black, bodies drooping. Spiff
wrinkled his nose and even his stomach heaved; all the effluent of
Wandsworth came here.

Knocker raised his head, stared at Flinthead for a moment, then lowered it again. Spiff bit his lip, shocked for once. Knocker's face was lifeless, there was no blood left in it. Napoleon and Orococco were in the same pitiful state. Bingo and Vulge leant against the shuttering, holding their spades. Sydney sat on a piece of half-submerged wood, trying to keep dry. In the middle of the creeping sludge, gleaming at the corner where it had been cleared, was the brass-banded lid of the Rumble treasure box.

Flinthead squatted at the edge of the landing and pointed.

'You, Vulge, whatever your name is, take your spade and finish digging the box out.'

Vulge moved to a pile of spare timber, sat down and lifted his feet from the water. The iron fetters clashed on his ankles.

'Dig it out yourself,' he said.

Flinthead's voice hardened. 'I've still got two of your friends up top, remember, and I can still make them suffer. What's more I've got reinforcements on the way . . . I'll soon have you doing what you're told, you little rat.'

These threats did not alter Vulge's attitude. He was past fear and he made no attempt to move. It was Bingo, because he knew it would have to be done eventually, who swished his legs through the mud and used his spade to dig the chest free.

Flinthead turned his head from where he crouched and looked at Spiff's face and then up into the shaft. 'Where are those other guards?' he asked. 'They should be here by now.'

'They can't be far,' said Spiff, standing to attention like a good Wendle.

Flinthead lowered his voice to a whisper. 'As soon as they arrive,' he explained, 'I want you all to go down and kill the prisoners. They've done what they had to do, no point in taking them up again.'

'Yessir,' said Spiff. 'What about the two in the treadmill?'

Flinthead laughed. 'I don't need them either; when we get back we'll throw 'em over the top to join their friends.' He went back to watching Bingo and Sydney dragging the box clear of the mud. 'Right,' he said, 'bring it up here, just the two of you, no others.'

'Leave it be,' said Napoleon, 'he's going to kill us anyway.'

Flinthead raised an arm and pointed. 'You will die, Napoleon

Boot, certainly, because you are a traitor Wendle. The others I will let free if they do as I say; after all they have dug well and found my treasure for me.'

Napoleon lifted his gaunt face and stared at his chieftain. There was silence for a moment and in that silence a large round drop of rich blood fell from high in the mine shaft and landed on the back of Flinthead's hand, staining it red.

Flinthead brought the hand close to his eyes and stared at that blob of blood. The silence intensified. Slowly every head was raised to look into the darkness, every head except Spiff's. Instead he smiled a seraphic smile and removed his Wendle helmet; a life's work was nearing completion.

'I hate to disappoint you, Napoleon,' said Spiff in his old Battersea voice, 'but Flinthead ain't going to kill no one, I am.'

At these words even Knocker, Napoleon and Orococco found the strength to pull themselves to their feet. Their mouths dropped open with astonishment. Now they recognized Spiff's face: that cocky, crafty face, lined with double-dealing and artful treachery, and life drained back into their hearts.

Flinthead also recognized the face and, crouching as he was, knew himself vulnerable. He snatched for his knife and tried to get to his feet but Spiff was ready; he hooked his foot under Flinthead's behind and then shoved him hard, outward and upward.

The Wendle chieftain made a despairing grab at the air but it was useless. He flew like a bullet across the width of the shaft and his helmeted head rammed against the shuttering on the far side. There was a deep clang, a roar of pain and Flinthead's body jack-knifed and then plunged down the wall into the slop and slurry, crashing heavily across the box of treasure.

Sydney and Bingo toppled over too, diving joyfully to right and left to escape the falling Wendle. Then, in celebration, they slapped the mud with their hands, throwing it at each other and everyone else. Mud splashed over all.

'It's Spiff,' yelled Bingo, 'come from nowhere.'

'About time too,' said Knocker. 'He got us in here, it's only right he should get us out.'

'This is not the end,' screamed a voice, and the Borribles looked and saw that Flinthead had risen and though covered in sludge was standing astride the treasure box, the long knife in his hand.

'Let's get him,' shouted Napoleon. 'Quick.'

'No,' cried Spiff, 'you lot get up here out of the way, he's mine, he is, all mine.'

'My guards will be here soon,' said Flinthead, 'you'll sing a different tune then.' But Flinthead was deceiving himself. At that moment another blob of blood fell from above and slapped on to his dented helmet, and the sound rang in his ears like a death knell.

'Yeah,' said Spiff with a sneer, 'that's a bit of one of 'em dropping in right now.'

More blood fell and Flinthead realized that he was on his own, but he was not afraid. 'Even if you kill me,' he said, 'you'll never get out alive. The whole Wendle nation is waiting for this box of treasure.'

'Let him rant,' said Spiff, 'you Borribles start getting up here out of the way.'

The weakest ones, Knocker, Napoleon and Orococco, were the first to climb from the muck, hauling their bodies painfully from rung to rung, their leg irons banging. Bingo, Vulge and Sydney kept watch on Flinthead in case he should attack with his knife, but Spiff had drawn his catapult and there was a large chunky stone aimed at Flinthead's face.

'I've got him covered, Bingo,' he said. 'You and the other two can come up now.'

When Bingo reached his side Spiff handed him the catapult and his two bandoliers. 'You're a good shot, ain't yer Bingo?' he said. 'If I should lose this fight, kill him.'

Napoleon lifted his head; he lay stretched out and exhausted next to Knocker and Orococco. 'After what I've been through,' he said, 'I could kill him with my teeth.'

Spiff brushed past Bingo and went to Knocker's side. He took the weight of the leg irons in his hand and saw that Knocker's ankles had been rubbed raw by them. He looked into Knocker's tired eyes. 'Sorry mate,' he said, 'really I am . . . Things will be all right now, you'll see.' Then he took a deep breath and, not bothering to use the ladder, sprang from the landing.

The Borribles moved forward to watch, sitting or lying on the

loose planking. There could have been no more fitting place for
two such enemies to meet; a quarter of a mile of darkness above,
the slimy and treacherous mud underfoot, and the walls of the
shaft trickling steadily now with black water and red blood under
the bleak electric glare.

Spiff fell to his hands and knees, carried there by the impetus
of his leap. Flinthead stepped back from the treasure chest, there
was a flash of steel at his right hand and his long knife whistled
through the air.

Spiff knew the knife was coming and threw himself forward;
the dagger missed him and clattered against the side of the mine
and disappeared below the surface of the water. Spiff rose, the
filth dripping from him.

Flinthead looked round for some other weapon and saw one of
the spades, half submerged in sludge. He pulled at it with all his
strength and slowly it came away making a long sucking sound.

'Watch out, Spiff,' called Vulge. 'Get the other one, it's just behind yer.'

Spiff turned and grabbed the second spade. He grinned and his
teeth flashed white in his dirty face. He backed away, hefting the
weapon in his hand.

'So, Flower,' he said, 'at last we're alone, after all these years.'

'Don't you call me Flower,' said Flinthead, and he too tested the
weight of his spade.

'He doesn't like being called Flower,' said Spiff, 'that was his
nickname when he was a kid, before he was a Borrible even.
Everyone's forgotten it, except me, ain't that right, Flower?'

Flinthead leant against the wall and held the spade defensively
across his chest. His pale green face glowed with hatred but he
showed no fear. 'You're on your own, Spiff,' he said, 'and I've always been the better fighter. Those few up there won't stop me
getting out; they're too weak, and their legs is chained. You're going to lose, Spiff, killed by yer own brother.'

'Don't you brother me,' said Spiff.

Knocker pulled himself up on his elbows. 'Brother!' he cried.
'Brother!'

Spiff laughed but he did not take his eyes from Flinthead. 'You might as well know,' he said, 'it don't make no odds now. He's my brother all right . . . We came from the same family, ran away in the time of the old queen we did, became Borribles together. It was hard to stay alive in them days, so we came down here and took over the old tunnels. We did everything together, but then little Flower wanted to take charge of everybody and rule Borribles like they were never meant to be ruled. So they became Wendles and I became a nuisance and he had me staked out on the mudflats, his own flesh and blood, but I got away and now I'm back.'

'Back to be slaughtered,' said Flinthead.

'We'll have to see, won't we,' said Spiff. He lifted his blade and a solid lump of mud slid from it and plopped into the water and the fearsome cutting edge was suddenly revealed, shining with months of digging. The soft sand and mud had worked upon the tool and honed it to the sharpness of a razor.

'Well, brother,' said Spiff, 'I can dig your heart out with this.'

'And mine's as sharp as yours,' answered Flinthead, and the two Borribles moved into the centre of the arena. Spiff held his spade with both hands, his right grasping the handle, the left the shaft, aiming it at Flinthead's throat like a bayonet. He trod carefully, studying his opponent's every move.

The Wendle chieftain held his spade in a different manner, wielding it like a two-handed sword, swinging repeatedly at Spiff's unprotected head. The weapons clanged and clashed. Spiff defended himself well against Flinthead's massive blows, dancing and ducking round his antagonist like a boxer, lunging at him, trying every second to cut and wound. Twice Spiff rang his blade across his enemy's head and twice Flinthead's helmet saved him. Three times Flinthead caught Spiff with the flat of his weapon and three times Spiff rode the onslaught and dodged away before the Wendle could take advantage and go in for the kill.

From the scaffolding the slaves followed every movement of the struggle, their hearts beating against their ribs. Napoleon had scrambled to his knees and he swayed his shoulders in sympathy with every stroke Spiff made. All the months of his captivity rose up in his mind's eye and the hatred he bore his chieftain, for Napoleon had once been a loyal Wendle, was as great as Spiff's.

'Kill 'im,' he shouted. 'Kill 'im.'

Spiff pressed home his attack, beating and bashing, cutting and lunging, and he fought so relentlessly that at last he opened a way through his enemy's guard, and then, using every ounce of strength he possessed, he thrust his spade forward at shoulder height, holding it level, aiming at the heart.

Flinthead shouted and Spiff's weapon struck him fiercely in the chest, making a loud grinding noise like a metal hinge under strain. But it made no difference; the Wendle remained unharmed and Spiff's spade bent and quivered, rebounding from his grasp like a live thing, spinning above his head and splashing down to be lost in the mud. Spiff staggered backwards, dazed, both arms paralysed, his brain shocked.

Flinthead also staggered from the force of the blow but he recovered quickly and came on; he saw that victory was his for the taking.

'The bastard,' cried Vulge, 'he's got some special jacket on, look.'

It was true. Flinthead's golden coat had been cut open where Spiff had swiped him and the onlookers could see that underneath it he wore a garment of closely woven chain mail.

'I've heard about that,' said Napoleon bitterly. 'It's made out of spring washers, all lashed together; it's bullet proof.'

'I'll get him,' Bingo shouted, and he drew the elastic of his catapult tight, but Flinthead was not to be caught that easily. He moved his weapon so that the blade of it covered his face, and what with his legs being deep in the mud and his body protected by armour there was not one part of him that offered Bingo a reasonable target. The Wendle chieftain leered in triumph and went towards the defenceless Spiff whose death now seemed certain.

But Napoleon jumped to his feet. 'No,' he screamed. 'Never!' He ran off the scaffolding and hurled himself down on to Flinthead's shoulders, wrapping arms and legs around the chieftain's body as firmly as he could.

Napoleon was no longer strong. Lack of food had made him almost weightless, but for a second his anger gave him a furious energy and he bore Flinthead into the slurry.

Even so it did not take Flinthead more than a moment to free himself of his burden and he clouted Napoleon hard in the kidneys and thrust him into the mud. He swirled round to face Spiff, eager to finish the fight, but he was just too late. Napoleon's intervention had given the Battersea Borrible time to grope beneath the water, time to find his spade. When Flinthead moved to the offensive he found Spiff ready for him.

'So,' said Spiff, 'wearing a flak jacket, eh? Never take chances, do yer, Flower?' And, with a new determination born of his fortunate escape, Spiff advanced, now catching Flinthead in the teeth with his spade's wooden handle, now stabbing at him with the sharp steel.

The Wendle chieftain retreated round the wall of the pit and Spiff went after him, step for step, cold and deadly, smashing and banging with hatred until at last, in Flinthead's lifeless eyes, a distant red spark of fear began to gleam. The sweat of terror started to trickle under his armpits, his knees faltered and he stumbled. In desperation at last, he lifted his weapon above his head and kept it there. 'Enough,' he cried. 'I surrender.'

Spiff hesitated for a split second and in that second Flinthead whirled his spade in the air, hoping to bring it down on to his opponent's skull with all his might.

It was lucky for Spiff that he knew his man. He had hesitated but in that same moment he'd stepped backwards and sideways and Flinthead's blade ploughed harmlessly into the churned froth of the trampled sludge, the force of the swing yanking the Wendle from his feet and casting him to his knees. There he stayed, beaten, panting.

Spiff leant on his spade like a navvy at the end of a hard day's work. 'There, Flower,' he said, 'you've had too much of the soft life you have; slowed you down it has, and made you untrustworthy. You're going to have to make it up to us, you're going to make sure we get a safe conduct out of here . . . us and the treasure of course.'

Suddenly there was a violent surge in the mud and Napoleon rose from it like an underwater missile. He was unrecognizable.

He swayed and scraped layers of filth from his face with the back of his filthy hands. He spat dirt from his mouth.

'Never mind about getting out,' he said, 'kill 'im.'

'Napoleon's right,' said Knocker from the landing. 'I don't care if I don't get away, only killing will do.'

'Wait a minute,' said Sydney. 'There's not only you two to think of, remember there's Stonks and Torreycanyon up top, and Chalotte.'

'Chalotte,' said Knocker, 'is she here?'

'Listen to me,' said Spiff. 'The best chance we have of getting out is to use this twerp as a hostage. If we hold a knife to his throat they can't touch us, can they?'

'Don't be too sure that the Wendles will want him back,' said Napoleon. 'If they see him as a prisoner and realize that they can get rid of him they might just do for the lot of us.'

'On the other hand they might let us go if we hand him over all tied up,' said Sydney. 'How about that?'

'Don't be daft,' said Spiff. 'There's the bodyguard to think of, a couple of hundred of them; without Flinthead they're nothing, they'll want him alive if only to save their own skins, and I can tell you they're all waiting on the platform and along the river banks. No, we need him as a hostage, especially if we're to get away with the treasure as well.'

'The treasure,' said Sydney. 'I say leave the treasure where it is.'

'So do I,' said Vulge.

'Me too,' added Bingo.

'I say kill him,' said Knocker, 'and damn the treasure. I've learnt my lesson about that money.'

Spiff looked up at Knocker. 'I'd like to kill the old sod,' he began, 'but without him and the treasure we don't stand a chance of getting out, and besides—'

Spiff got no further with his explanation; Flinthead gave a loud cry, threw himself forward and with his spade held in his two hands charged at Spiff's throat. He knew that if he could kill his Battersea brother he stood a good chance of fighting his way past the others.

But Spiff was not known as the craftiest of Borribles for nothing. Talking to the others he had not forgotten his adversary; his ears had been cocked and he had heard the movement of the mud as Flinthead had sprung to his feet. Automatically he raised his own spade to protect himself and Flinthead's blow glanced off it, striking a spark as steel clashed against steel. Turning, Spiff saw that Flinthead was only a yard away, pulled off balance by the fierce lunge he had made. Spiff lifted his arms, holding the spade delicately between his hands as if about to throw it gently over a wall. He stood poised, briefly motionless, taking all the time in the world, waiting while Flinthead tottered and tried to draw back out of range—but now it was finished.

Spiff, his expression murderous, balanced his weapon at the level of his eyes and then punched it forward with all his power, guiding it with the left hand and shoving it from the handle with the right so that the bright blade cut into Flinthead's Adam's apple, through his windpipe and jugular, and out through the spine; and as it cut it made the sound of an axe slicing into soggy turf.

And the chieftain's head exploded from his shoulders and stood surprised in the air. Flinthead was slain and yet, for one instant, the opaque eyes of the Wendle shone at last, incandescent with the fire of death, and a red glow illuminated the whole cavern. Then a huge moan issued from the crimson lungs and the body fell, its blood mingling with the mud and water underfoot.

The severed head seemed to hang in the air for an age but at length it dropped into the sludge, facing upwards, staring sightless into the yellow blackness of the mine shaft, staring in such a way that Spiff could not bear the scrutiny. He raised a foot and slowly pushed the face under the mire and the thick and loathsome liquid crept across the eyes and closed them forever. And in his corner, where he swayed and clung in weakness, Napoleon Boot vomited.

But Spiff was aflame with pride, convinced of his magnificence and delirious with his victory. He threw down his spade and shook his fists at his companions and they stepped back in dismay, so terrifying was his face, so distorted with a terrible joy. And Spiff's voice sounded out in a hard and piercing yell of triumph. 'I am Spiff the Spifflicator, killer of Flinthead, stealer of the treasure. I have a hundred names now.'

When the shouting was past there was a great stillness and Napoleon crawled to the ladder and clambered up to join his friends on the scaffolding. While he did so Spiff seized Flinthead's helmet, just visible in the mud, and placed it upon his head.

'Strewth,' said Bingo. 'Brothers were they, and you can see it now he's got that hat on. You wouldn't know who was which, would you?'

Bingo's words made the others take heed and they could not help but see what he meant. The copper headgear made it almost impossible to tell brother from brother, the living from the dead, and Spiff stood like a statue, knowing the effect he was having, knowing how much of Flinthead there was in him. Then he glanced up and slowly the madness left his face.

'It is over,' he said, 'the long battle between us is finished; we must go.'

'How the hell are we to climb out of here?' asked Sydney, 'with Knocker, Napoleon and Orococco so weak they can hardly stand?'

'There's no other way,' said Spiff, 'but we'll go slowly, the stronger ones will pull the weak.'

'We'll make it,' said Knocker. 'We'll have to.'

'Yeah, maybe,' said Orococco, 'but what's to be done when we get to the top, man?'

'You leave that to me,' said Spiff and he groped beneath the mud and turned Flinthead's body over. In a moment he straightened and was seen to be holding the golden jacket, thick with slime. He laughed and threw it up to the landing. 'Here, Bingo,' he said, 'clean it while I get the money.'

'No money,' yelled Knocker. 'When Vulge was wounded in Rumbledom I wanted to leave him behind so that I could bring the treasure. Adolf wouldn't have anything to do with it and carried Vulge on his shoulders and saved his life. I did the opposite; I saved the treasure and got Adolf killed. He was a true Borrible, I wasn't. I won't make that mistake again.'

'We won't help you with that box,' said Bingo.

'All right,' said Spiff, 'have it your own way, but has any one of you smart alecs got a plan for getting out? There's a tribe of Wendles topside, just waiting. And what do you think they'll do when they see us arrive without the treasure . . . give us a round of applause and a free boat trip to Battersea?'

There was silence. The Borribles knew that Spiff was right but no one wished to agree with him.

Spiff laughed. 'Throw down that jacket, Bingo.'

Bingo did as he was told and Spiff slipped the garment over his shoulders. 'Now,' he said triumphantly, 'who am I?'

'You're Spiff,' said Vulge, 'but from here you could be Flinthead, alike as two gobs of spit.'

'Right,' went on Spiff, 'and who do Wendles obey, without question?'

Napoleon looked up. 'All Wendles obey Flinthead, especially if he's got the treasure.'

'Right again,' said Spiff. 'Now to get out of here we've got to give them something to occupy their evil little brains . . . When they see the treasure they'll be so happy they won't even look at me closely, they'll just see what they expect to see.'

'But they'll notice there's no guards; there won't be enough of us,' said Sydney.

'They won't at all,' said Spiff. 'Halfway up the shaft we'll find some bodyguard uniforms, on bodyguards I admit, and a bit damaged. Still, Bingo and Vulge can dress in those, the rest of you will act like captives. The Wendles will be too busy cheering and jumping up and down to start counting how many guards or prisoners there are.'

'Okay,' said Vulge, 'so you're Flinthead. What happens at the top?'

'Easy,' continued Spiff. 'I give orders, everyone else takes 'em. The treasure is locked in my apartments, the prisoners as well, ready for execution. But in reality, as soon as you're rested and got some decent food inside yer, we'll be off.'

'And the money?' asked Sydney.

Spiff grinned. 'Oh, I'll take that with me, there'd be no fun otherwise.'

Napoleon jeered. He might have been a slave for months but his mind had lost none of its Wendle suspicion. 'You expect us to believe that you're going to take Flinthead's place just for a couple of days and then walk away from all that power and take the money back to Battersea, share it out and settle down like a pensioner?'

Spiff shrugged. 'I don't care what you believe, you've got to do as I say or you won't get out at all.'

'Oh, I think you'll get us out,' said Napoleon, 'but I also think you'll stay behind and become Flinthead.'

Spiff ignored the remark and pulled at one of the handles of the treasure chest. It came out of the mud slowly and reluctantly but it came nevertheless. 'I reckon I can make the Wendles into proper Borribles again,' he said, 'even if I have to kid them along to do it.' He knelt and got the heavy box on to his shoulder and began to climb the ladder. No one moved to help him and Spiff's face grew red with the effort but he would not ask for assistance.

Napoleon and Knocker looked at each other. 'I don't like it much,' said Knocker, 'but he's right, as a plan it's all we've got.' He scraped the dirt from the palms of his hands and found the scars that the red-hot treasure box had scorched there when he had carried it from the burning halls of Rumbledom.

'You were given a second name you know, Knocker,' said Spiff as he arrived on the landing. 'Chalotte chose it, Knocker Burnthand.'

'That's just like her,' said Knocker, 'to give me a name that will always remind me of what an idiot I was.'

'All right,' said Bingo, 'we'll help you with the treasure, as far as the top, but only because it's part of the plan. Nothing after that.'

Spiff nodded and held up something small and bright. 'Good,' he said, 'and in return I'll give you this key. You'll find that it undoes those nasty shackles round your ankles. It won't half make climbing easier.'

'You sod,' said Napoleon, but he laughed.

Orococco laughed too. 'Once a Wendle, always a Wendle,' he said.

When everyone was prepared for the climb Spiff gave his last instructions. 'Let Knocker and Napoleon and Orococco go first,' he said. 'They're the weakest and we'll take their pace. The other four of us will take turn and turn about with the box. When we get to the top the captives will just behave like captives. The two dressed as guards will pretend to be guards. On the last landing I will take the treasure and come up behind you lot, that'll give the Wendles something to wait for, something to cheer. Don't forget at the top I'm Flinthead, so do as you're told. Let's go.'

The seven Borribles bent their heads backwards and looked up into the shaft at the long hard way they had to go. Mud and blood dripped in their faces; the rungs were square and rough.

'I wish,' said Knocker, 'that old Torrey was still working the treadmill, then we could have ridden up in the buckets like lumps of mud.'

'And why not,' said Napoleon, 'that's just what we look like.'

9

On the derrick platform at the top of the mine Chalotte stood next to Twilight and Norrarf. She was tense, so overwrought she could hardly keep still. Above her in the cavernous arches of the roof hung huge slabs of shadow, solid and black. Nearby Tron strode up and down, only pausing occasionally to look into the mouth of the shaft; time went by and he saw nothing. His three lieutenants leant on their spears and watched him, their faces blank.

On both river banks the bodyguards still held the towpaths clear, controlling the crowds who waited there. Most of the time there was quiet, sometimes there were shouts. Apart from sentries and lookouts every Wendle in creation was present, hundreds of them, all gathered to witness Flinthead's successful return. In the treadmill Chalotte could see Torreycanyon lying on the floor, exhausted and asleep; beside him sat Stonks, his head leaning against one of the rough wooden spokes.

Chalotte sighed. 'Why is it taking so long?' she asked Twilight in a whisper and Tron overheard her.

'Because the shaft is deep,' he said. 'They say a quarter of a mile, though that is hard to believe.' Tron studied her face and Chalotte hoped that he would not recognize her from the time of the Great Rumble Hunt. He didn't, and after a moment he resumed his pacing and the waiting went on; one hour, two, then three.

Once more Tron went to the rim of the shaft and Chalotte and everyone else studied him closely. This time the Wendle stiffened, he had seen something.

'They're coming,' he said quietly, and his three lieutenants straightened and twirled their spears above their heads. A cheer rose from both banks: 'The treasure, the treasure.'

Under orders from Tron every person on the platform was brought to attention and a buzzing quietness was imposed along the river banks, but there was still a while to wait. No doubt, thought Chalotte, they'd be climbing slowly because of the weight of that damn treasure box.

The thought of the treasure made her sick with anguish. She hated it more than anything or anyone in the world. It had ruined the last Adventure; it had killed Adolf and now it was coming back to trouble the Borrible way of life yet again. She bit her lip; who was returning from the bottom of that hellhole, Flinthead or Spiff?

Something stirred at the lip of the mine and Chalotte nudged Twilight's elbow. A black hand, caked in dry slime, grasped the top rung of the ladder and Orococco heaved himself into sight and tumbled out across the platform to collapse, apparently unconscious, by the side of the treadmill.

His arrival brought a mocking cheer from the watching Wendles, and laughter too. They shook their spears and stamped their feet in joy. Now Tron's three men were at the head of the mine shaft and with rough hands they hoisted Sydney from the pit and dropped her down to lie by the side of Orococco.

Next came two members of the bodyguard, their faces smeared with mud and daubed in blood. They strutted to the edge of the platform and gave a thumbs up sign and the crowds along the river went berserk with happiness. Tron's men leant into the shaft once more and when they lifted Napoleon Boot into the light a vicious jeering swelled up and resounded between the mudflats and the high roof, for Napoleon was a renegade Wendle, a traitor. Tron's lieutenants held him high so the crowds could see him and then, when they'd struck him several times, they threw him to the ground.

'Kill him, kill him,' the Wendles cried and shook their spears.

It took more than words to dismay Napoleon Boot; he crawled into an open space, levered himself erect and gave a two-fingered salute to the whole Wendle nation. And when the gesture brought shouts and threats in its turn he ignored them and wobbled back to his friends and collapsed across their bodies. He sighed and closed his eyes, groaning with the pain of extreme fatigue, but there was a hard and wicked smirk upon his face.

Eventually Knocker came and Chalotte's heart leapt, for she liked Knocker more than any other Borrible she had ever met, but her joy changed to pity in an instant for knocker was ragged and covered in sludge; his bones protruded through his skin like broken sticks in a sack and the lines of his features were deep enough to lose a finger in.

Tron's lieutenants had no such feelings. They seized Knocker by the hair and hauled him up and beat him to the floor and kicked him. The Wendles under Flinthead had been taught to hate Knocker for he had been brave and unflinching in his conflict with the chieftain and had almost succeeded in stealing the treasure completely away, only failing from ill luck. Again the cry rose from the river banks: 'Kill him, kill him!'

Suddenly Tron held up his hand and all noise stopped. Knocker dragged himself out of the way like a half-smashed cockroach, trailing blood, and Flinthead's copper helmet appeared at the rim of the great pit. At last the whole host of Wendles saw the chieftain climb back into their sight; on his back he carried the great burnt box of Rumble treasure and they lifted their spears high in the air and with one voice they shouted: 'Flinthead, Flinthead, Flinthead!'

The noise was overpowering, Chalotte could hear nothing but noise. She looked at Twilight in confusion. 'It's Flinthead,' she cried, 'he must have done for Spiff. He's got the treasure too; he'll kill us all.'

Twilight could not hear Chalotte's words above the din of the mad rejoicing that rang along the river banks. He pointed to the shore. 'There's too many of them,' he shouted. 'Just keep quiet and hope for the best.'

Chalotte scanned Norrarf's face. Would he betray them now? It certainly seemed likely; he was laughing and shouting with the rest. He half turned towards her. 'It's all right, it's Spiff,' he said, but Chalotte, in that clamour, did not catch his words. She glanced at the treadmill where her friends cowered, beaten and battered. It was heartbreaking. They stared at Flinthead, abject, like slaves about to be sold.

Chalotte gritted her teeth and decided; whatever happened, whether she died or not, she wouldn't allow Flinthead his triumph. The treasure must not return to destroy the Borrible way of life. She and her companions were as good as dead anyway, but if they had to die it was better that Flinthead should die with them.

Another great shout rolled across the river. Flinthead stood on the last rung of the ladder, a crazed smile on his blood-covered visage and smudges of gore on his gold-coloured coat. Chalotte heard him raise his voice.

'I am Flinthead, here is the Rumble treasure and it is mine again . . . Now the prisoners can die.'

'And so can you,' cried Chalotte and, unnoticed in that great commotion, she leapt forward and seized a mallet from among a pile of Wendle tools. Twilight went with her out of a feeling of loyalty, not knowing what she had in mind but eager to help. Tron pivoted on his heel but Chalotte was upon him and he had no opportunity to defend himself. She bashed the mallet against the side of his helmet and Flinthead's second-in-command collapsed, unconscious. Before Tron's lieutenants realized what she intended Chalotte had climbed the parapet of the mine and was hitting out with all her strength, loosening one of the wedges that held the mighty cross-timbers in position. The wedge swivelled, Chalotte clouted it again and the block of wood flew free, clattered against the side of the shaft and then fell away out of sight in a spinning blur.

'Chalotte,' yelled Spiff, 'don't be a fool, it's me.'

For a moment Chalotte did not understand. 'Damn you, Flinthead,' she cried. 'I won't let you bring that money back.' Then she thought that maybe Flinthead was not Flinthead and that perhaps she'd made a mistake, but in the same instant she decided that it was not a mistake and that anything, even Spiff's death, even her own, was better than the recovery of the Rumble treasure. With a cruel determination in her heart she raised the mallet above her head and swung it like a pick to strike at the shifting timbers beneath her feet.

Tron's men sprang at her but Twilight got in front of them and struck out, tugging, tripping and punching. Bingo and Vulge, still acting the part of Flinthead's guard, caught their breath in fright and stretched their arms to pluck Chalotte from where she stood on a cross-beam, shouting for her to stop, dragging her at last to the safety of the platform—but those heavy blows had been enough. The main beam jolted sideways and the tension that had held it in position for months was released and the timbers of the mine shaft lurched, the mud squeezed in and a wild wrenching sob was torn from the heart of the wood. So loud was it that the sound of cheering was stilled and the watchers on the towpaths realized that something had turned their triumph sour; danger had come to take the place of pleasure.

Bingo shook Chalotte as hard as he could, anger and fear mingled in his weary face. 'You damn fool,' he said, 'now we're all dead men.'

Chalotte stared at Bingo like an imbecile, alarmed and fearful. She opened her mouth to speak but now there was no time. Another grinding scream was wrung from the mass of splintering timber, the very grain of it was riven and rent asunder and the great beams at last plunged downwards, their massive weight twisting and gathering momentum to smash and destroy the landings and scaffoldings below.

Spiff called for help but his ladder veered away from the wall of the mine shaft and teetered, becalmed for a second, standing on nothing and near the point of falling. The blood drained from his face, he clung frantically with one hand to a rung, and with the other he grasped the treasure box. It was a long stationary moment; it was almost his last and Spiff knew it.

'Damn you, Chalotte,' he yelled.

Then came another cracking and another rumbling as more scaffolding dropped into the shaft and the shuttering that held the mud back began to slip and great streams of black sludge surged forward. The mud was thick and muscular; it could strangle and it could suffocate, it wanted to drag everything down to the darkness at the centre of the earth.

The top section of the shuttering now collapsed completely and fell inwards, the huge planks coming together like rigid fingers, smashing Spiff's ladder to smithereens and pinning his body in space. Spiff screamed in pain and the treasure box dropped from his grasp, disappearing into the ravenous mouth of mud. Spiff struggled against the timber, trying to push it away, trying to stop it crushing him. His efforts failed; he was held too tightly, like a wireworm in steel tweezers. He raised his head in his agony, but he could not scream. There was no breath. His eyes glazed over until there was no sight left in them and then slowly the timbers slid down into the mud and, inch by inch, they took Spiff with them. He was gone.

Now all around; apart from the soft surging of the thick waters, there was no noise. The Wendles on either towpath stared in disbelief as the Borrible they believed to be their leader died before them, while the Adventurers knew only too well that it was Spiff who had died there, his eyes blind with terror, his lungs empty of air.

Chalotte shook herself free of Bingo. 'Oh, Spiff,' she cried. 'Oh, Spiff.' And the hot tears ran down her face for what she had done.

'Get back,' warned Vulge. 'Get back, or you'll be dragged in too.'

Bingo pounced on the unconscious Tron and hoisted him to his feet. The Wendle rubbed his eyes.

'Where's Flinthead?' he asked.

'Dead,' said Bingo, 'the way we're all going to be in a minute.'

Tron looked about him and took in the situation. The platform was sinking and the mud was rolling inwards, unstoppable. Only the treadmill seemed solid and even that was beginning to go under.

'Quickly,' Tron shouted. 'The wheel. Get those two prisoners out of it and turn it over, it'll float.'

Suddenly there was another grinding lurch and the platform settled a foot into the mud. Tron's lieutenants and the two Wendle guards threw down their spears and dived into the river in panic, making for the shore.

'Come back you fools,' yelled Norrarf, 'the mud'll swallow yer.'

'Never mind them,' said Tron, 'let's get this wheel over.'

It was no easy matter. By the time Stonks and Torreycanyon had crawled between the spokes the platform had sunk so far that the Borribles were up to their waists in a quicksand that sucked at every movement they made. Yet somehow, and all together, they bent and groped below the surface, grasping the bottom of the treadmill and heaving it upwards with such energy that it rose for an instant above the mud before splashing down on to its side.

'Come on,' shouted Tron again as soon as the wheel was floating. 'Everyone aboard, it's our only chance.' just as they felt the platform plunge away from beneath their feet the Borribles managed to scramble up on to the solid spars of their makeshift raft. But no sooner had they gained this temporary safety than a new danger threatened them. The mouth of the mine, now clear of debris, had become a mouth indeed; it gaped and pulsated, the centre of a slow whirlpool, a black vortex that waited to devour everything: mud, timber, Borribles and all.

'We must do something,' said Knocker. 'We'll be drowned in a minute.'

'Is there any chance of your blokes getting a boat out to us?' asked Bingo.

Tron stood on the rim of the wheel and looked towards the shore. 'There are no boats,' he said after a while. 'The currents have swept the banks clear, half of my men have gone too.'

'What about a long rope then?' said Stonks. 'Couldn't they pull us in?'

Tron shook his head. 'They don't have a rope that long, and even if they tied several ropes together we'd be at the bottom of the shaft before they'd gone and got them. The river is falling into the mine and we're going with it.'

A muffled scream came from somewhere, then another.

Norrarf pointed. 'That's them bodyguards,' he said. 'They've had it; swimming out there must be like swimming in cement.'

But the Borribles had no time to think of others, their own plight was too desperate. The whirlpool churned on, round and round, and the treadmill went with it. Air bubbles, escaping from below, erupted and threw sludge into the air so that it rained down with a vicious force and made the surface of the Wandle froth and seethe like a volcanic lake. It was a scene from the heart of hell.

And the mud flowed on into the pit, sometimes oozing, sometimes swirling, but at whatever speed it moved one thing was certain: the wheel to which the Borribles clung was steadily dropping into the centre and nothing in the world could reverse its progress.

'We've had it,' said Vulge, 'really had it.' But as he spoke the spate of the torrent eased and in a little while it halted altogether.

'The hole must be full up,' said Bingo, a note of hope in his voice. 'We've stopped moving.'

'It can't be full up,' said Napoleon, 'that mine's a quarter of a mile deep.'

'What is it then?' asked Twilight. He glanced at the shore. There the currents had not stopped and the powerful rise and fall of the waves kept the Wendles high on the banks, watching silently, the warriors resting on their spears.

'This is our only chance,' said Napoleon, 'we oughta swim for it.' But before anyone could move the mouth of the shaft opened again; there was another rush of mud towards it and the treadmill dipped and reared like a switchback.

The Adventurers cried aloud, convinced that their moment of death had come. The great wooden wheel toppled into the very eye of the storm and, half submerged, it tilted sideways and the Borribles were swung above the abyss but, as they swayed there on the brink, a surge came from beneath them and the wheel spun once more, swooped, and finally stuck, wedged across the wide mine shaft.

'What's happened?' asked Twilight; his teeth chattering. 'Are we still alive?'

'Yes,' said Napoleon, 'but the future don't look bright.'

The mud and water raced by like a waterfall, tearing at the Borribles, trying to smash them into the stream. The treadmill was under intense pressure; it cracked and creaked, its timbers began to give and nails and screws loosened and fell away. Then, just as suddenly as it had started, the down-flow ceased. The gaping mouth of the mine became covered and the Wandle drifted over it once more.

'Is it full up now, d'yer reckon?' asked Sydney.

'I told yer before,' said Napoleon, 'it can't be full.'

'I know what it is,' said Knocker, 'it must be an airlock. I think the first lot of mud must have gone down so fast that it trapped a big bubble at the bottom . . . If it stays this way long enough we might have time to get to the shore.'

'We're too weak to swim,' said Orococco. 'It'd be certain death out there.'

'And what do you think it is here,' retorted Napoleon, 'gracious living?'

'I'll tell you something,' said Tron sombrely, 'if there is an airlock down there, sooner or later it's going to explode, and when it does it'll be like a nuclear bomb going off. There'll be shit and slosh going in every direction at once, and bits of us with it.'

No one answered the Wendle; there was no need and no time. From some faraway part of the earth came a great rumbling sound. The vaulted roof of the cavern shook and bricks plummeted from it. The river boiled like hot pitch, faster and faster, releasing a vile gas which from its stench might have been nurtured for months in the reeking flesh of a corpse long dead.

'I can't breathe,' cried Sydney. 'I can't breathe.'

'Don't worry,' said Vulge, wiping the smoky vapour from his eyes, 'in a little while you won't have to.'

The rumbling grew louder. A tidal wave of silt reared up and billowed along the river banks, and the Wendles standing there turned and ran into the tunnels, trampling each other underfoot in their eagerness to be gone; and gone they all were in a few turbulent minutes, leaving only the injured and unconscious behind them, some to crawl away and some to be pulled under by the raging waters.

Still the rushing and the roaring came nearer and the whole world shook and a great explosion hurtled up the mine shaft like a locomotive, and the Borribles crawled towards each other on the wheel and flung their bodies together for protection.

Then the explosion burst out in a mighty upheaval and the

treadmill was cast aloft like a pebble, borne upwards on a twisting column of slush that spun and whirled and dipped and swayed like a huge tornado, and the Borribles fought for each breath in the gyrating mud and fought even harder not to be thrown from the wheel and off into the spinning darkness.

Upwards and upwards they went, soaring and gliding a hundred feet high until the wheel was resting lightly on the outermost upthrust of a great pillar of filth. It hovered there for an eternity, balanced between down and up. Then at last, dipping and skimming once more, it swooped away on the crest of a wide and indolent wave that carried it back to the surface of the Wandle flats, where it plunged deep into the river, only to leap into view a moment later with the slime-sodden Borribles still clinging to it; poor black scarecrows coated in muck.

One of the scarecrows weakly raised an arm and tried to shout above the din of the mud storm. It was Knocker and his voice could barely croak. 'Look, look where we are!'

The others scraped the sticky mire from their eye sockets and saw that the wave had brought them more than two hundred yards downstream and near to the north bank. They struck out with their legs and found that their feet could touch the river bottom.

'We're safe,' cried Chalotte, speaking at last, happiness in her tone now that she realized that she had not killed her friends after all.

Napoleon staggered away from the treadmill. 'Don't waste time,' he shouted. 'Get out before the explosion stops.'

He was right. Once the great geyser collapsed the mud would flow back into the mine with even greater power, and everything in the Wandle would flow with it until the shaft was full.

Stonks was still the strongest of the Borribles. One by one he grabbed the most feeble of the Adventurers and dragged them to the shore and shoved them up on to the bank. Napoleon first, then Torreycanyon and Orococco, Knocker last. While he did this the others waded to dry land as best they might, stumbling, floundering, leaning on each other until they all fell together in a heap.

'Never mind resting,' said Napoleon urgently, and finding the strength from somewhere he forced himself to his knees and laid hold of the lump of mud next to him. 'This is Tron, get the other Wendle quick.'

Stonks knew immediately what Napoleon meant but it was impossible to tell one slimy shape from another. It was Norrarf himself who gave the game away, leaping to his feet in panic, and Stonks seized him roughly by the neck and squeezed hard.

'Don't let the Wendles get free,' he yelled, 'or we've had it.'

In spite of Napoleon's efforts to hold him down Tron stood up easily. 'Wait a minute, Napoleon,' he said. 'Flinthead is dead now, there will be no more war between Borrible and Borrible.'

'I'll believe that when I'm out of here, and not before,' said Knocker.

'Don't be idiots,' said Norrarf, struggling in Stonks's grip. 'I was helping Spiff all along wasn't I? Why should I give you away?'

'Everything's changed now,' said Tron. 'Besides, you can be sure that the whole Wendle nation thinks we're dead; nobody stayed to watch exactly, did they?'

Knocker and Napoleon looked at each other. The mud spattered around them and the tornado thundered.

Napoleon shook his head. 'We've been through too much to take any chances . . . Hold 'em fast and keep yer eyes on 'em.'

Tron shrugged. 'I don't blame you,' he said, 'but I can show you that I mean no harm. I'll take you to a safe way out, a secret way out that only Flinthead and I knew.'

'Where is it?' asked Vulge, shouting through the storm.

Tron jerked a thumb over his shoulder. 'That way, along that tunnel; it's a manhole that comes out next to the cranes on Feather's Wharf. It's not far.'

'We'll have a look,' said Stonks, and he began to help his friends to stand, but before they could set out the depths of the mine reverberated and a second air pocket was heard booming its way to the surface. The swirling geyser faltered and dipped for a moment as if about to break, but then it surged upwards with an even greater strength than before and the Borribles fell back, folding their arms over their heads for protection against the mud that pelted them with the force of hailstones.

Chalotte screamed. 'Look,' she gasped, 'look there!'

Her companions peered through the steady barrage of slime and what they saw harrowed their blood and, after all they had endured, warped their sanity to breaking point.

Rising gracefully up the side of the great whirling tornado, turning slowly as if in some grotesque dance of death, the body of Spiff appeared and close by him came the headless trunk of Flinthead, his brother. Languidly they drifted upwards, changing positions unhurriedly, and just below them floated the box of Rumble treasure, so near that at times the two bodies seemed like effigies standing upon it. Spiralling round and round the tableau ascended, moving to the far side of the whirlwind only to reappear a few seconds later, travelling at the speed of the cyclone but seeming uncannily motionless to the eyes of those who watched.

Chalotte touched her face with shaking fingers. 'It's a nightmare,' she said, 'a horrible nightmare.' No one answered her. They stood quite still, all of them, but the horror had not ended. As Flinthead and Spiff revolved in their deathly dance, the lid of the treasure box eased open and, one by one at first and soon in hundreds, bright gold and silver coins began to appear, spread themselves in spangled swathes across the surface of the cyclone and glittered there.

Then the lid of the box opened completely and a thousand banknotes detonated into gaudy streamers and fastened themselves on to this great spinning wall of sewage that turned and turned and drew everything irresistibly towards it. And the paper money shone in all bright colours: green and orange, violet and yellow, amber and pale blue; and the whole whirlwind was festooned with it and so were the bodies of Flinthead and Spiff. It was beautiful.

Chalotte shrieked and the noise shook the Adventurers from their trance.

'It will suck us in if we stay here,' she cried, 'we're too close; run away.' In that instant the mine shaft expelled a long and tumultuous sigh. The last of the imprisoned air escaped from the bottom of the pit and the tornado at last stood still, all power gone. Then its outside skin of slush began to slip and slide until finally it fell with a loud crash back into the depths, burying the bodies and the treasure for ever in the Wandle under countless tons of mud, and huge cowpats came raining down and swamped the Borribles with such a persistent force that they were thrown violently to the ground. Wave after wave reared from the Wandle and threatened to bear them away but they dug their hands into the earth and clung to each other for dear life, and so tightly did they cling that although the river surged and tore and plucked at the Adventurers it could not claim them for all their weakness.

Slowly the clatter ceased and the currents of the river calmed. The tide receded from the banks and the Borribles could raise their heads and look about them. Knocker pushed himself on to his hands and knees; water and slime poured from his limbs.

'I've spent months in this Wandle mud,' he said. 'I've got to get out of it before I go really and truly mad.' He stumbled among the others, looking for Tron.

'Tron, which one are you? Get up.' Tron rose and Knocker went to him. 'Get us out of here, just as quickly as you can.'

The remainder of the Borribles struggled upright and Norrarf went to stand by Tron. 'You can trust us,' he said. 'Honest.'

'Yes,' said Tron. 'Follow me, it is not far.' He put his arm on Norrarf's shoulder and the two Wendles, walking side by side, led the way into a narrow tunnel.

As Tron had said, the secret escape hole was at no great distance. In less than a quarter of an hour's march Tron brought everyone to a halt and pointed at the roof. 'There it is,' he said.

'I don't see no manhole,' said Bingo.

'You won't,' said Tron. 'It's meant to be secret but it's there and it hasn't got an SBG man standing on it, neither.'

'That's as may be,' said Stonks, 'but I'd better go out and have a scout round. If I'm not back in ten minutes you'll know there's something wrong.'

'Suit yerself,' said Tron, 'but be careful, it might be daylight.'

'There's only one way to find out,' said Vulge. 'Let me and Bingo make a step.'

When they were ready Stonks climbed on to their clasped hands and they lifted him into the roof of the tunnel. There was no noise while Stonks groped above his head, but soon his feet shifted and there came the sound of iron grating upon iron.

'Got it,' Stonks grunted, and as he spoke a cool draught carved its way into the stinking atmosphere of the underworld. Each of the Borribles took a long deep breath. It seemed like years since any of them had breathed untainted air.

'Cripes,' said Torreycanyon, 'that's beautiful, like drinking cold water; almost knocks yer unconscious, don't it?'

Stonks's feet disappeared and a second later they heard his voice. 'I'll be back in a few minutes,' he whispered, 'and if I ain't, scarper.'

The Borribles waited and said nothing. Their minds were too full of what they had seen and suffered to allow them to think of talking for the sake of it, but eventually Chalotte did speak and she asked Tron something she thought she ought to know before they parted company, perhaps for ever.

'Why are you letting us go like this, Tron?' she asked. 'Why aren't you calling for your warriors?'

'Well, look at us,' answered the Wendle, 'nearly dead, almost were dead, covered in slime, and for what? The proverb says that fruit of the barrow is enough for a Borrible, yet we seem to have forgotten all that. We've been through something really rotten and it should never have happened, but it did and we were to blame, I suppose, all of us.'

'Funny really,' said Knocker. 'Once it all began it was too late to stop, but I don't mind admitting . . . that mud has taught me a thing or two I won't forget.'

Tron nodded. 'Flinthead wanted power and money, that's where it started, and he made a lot of Wendles think the same, me included . . . Spiff wanted revenge on Flinthead for things that happened long ago, things that we didn't even know about; bloody ridiculous when you think of it.'

'Still,' said Chalotte, 'the Rumble treasure's gone now, and so much the better. That's how it should be with us. It's people like Flinthead who bring trouble, greedy sod, and Spiff was greedy too, in a different way. I don't think it was only revenge he wanted; could have been lots of things, glory, another name. Maybe he did want to take what Flinthead had and keep it. For all we know he really might have wanted to take the money back and share it out equally, but even if he did it wasn't a good idea; it wasn't Borrible.'

'There's enough Rumbles to fight without fighting among ourselves,' said Tron, 'that's plain madness. Anyway, with Flinthead gone I reckon there'll be a lot of Wendles who'll realize they can go back to being Borribles plain and simple, Norrarf here for one, and Skug, and there'll be others.'

'There'll be lots all right,' said Norrarf. 'They didn't dare do anything before because of Flinthead and the bodyguard. You know, just because of the way things were.'

'That's it, though,' said Napoleon. 'I'm a Wendle, remember, or was. I know the bodyguard, they won't let you have everything your own way.'

'We'll have to see,' said Tron, with a sigh. 'We others outnumber them after all. I tell you one thing though, I won't let anyone take over where Flinthead left off, that's for certain.'

And that was the end of it. Stonks's voice dropped down into the darkness and brought the discussion to a close. 'It's nearly dawn,' he said, 'but there doesn't seem to be anyone about. There's a light in Ben's shed. Best thing is to come up quietly; you never know, Sussworth may have a Woollie hidden, waiting for us.'

Tron linked hands with Norrarf to make a step, and one by one the Adventurers said goodbye to the Wendles, friends now, and jumped upwards to grasp the rim of the manhole and haul themselves out into the cool of the summer dawn.

At the very end Knocker stood ready to go. He raised a weary foot and placed it in the Wendles' hands. 'Perhaps,' he said, 'we shall meet again.'

'Sometime,' said Tron, 'when things have gone one way or the other. If I'm still alive I'll come and tell you the story of what I did.'

'Do that,' said Knocker. 'I like a good story.' He turned to Norrarf. 'I didn't get to know you Norrarf, but thanks. Remember, real friends will come when you call . . . and both of you, don't get caught.'

'Nor you,' said Norrarf, and he thrust with his hands and Knocker found himself shoved up through the manhole and pulled over and on to the ground by the strong arms of Stonks. Then he heard a clang and the iron cover slid into its grooves behind him.

10

For a long time the Borribles lay on the uneven and rubbish-strewn dirt. They listened and they heard the sound of the Wandle where it met the River Thames. A tug hooted out on Wandsworth Reach and an early car swished along on Armoury Way. It was warm. The London heatwave had not relented but the outside air felt deliciously cool after the triple-baked temperatures of the underground mine.

Knocker relaxed flat on his back and gazed into the sky; the sky that he had thought never to see again. He smiled and the drying mud cracked on his cheeks. It made him glad to see the pale yellow stars and the deep blue of the night fading into grey on the horizon as the dawn came. His breast swelled with a pleasure he felt he could not endure: the simple pleasure of being alive, of being thankful for it and knowing he was. The tears trickled down the side of his face and into his hair, but nobody could see them, lost as they were in dirt.

He sat up. The mingled odours of river and rubbish were wholesome after the smell of the sewers. He turned his head and saw that he and the others were right by the two steam cranes that guarded Feather's Wharf.

Napoleon sat up too. 'Well, what do you know?' he asked of no one in particular.

'Man,' said Orococco, 'it's like breathing for the very first time.'

The Borribles looked above their heads. In the moments that had elapsed since the closing of the manhole the stars had gone from the sky, a quiet traffic noise was growing and bright squares of electric light were appearing in tall and distant buildings; holes cut from the black sides of Wandsworth. A breeze was riding in on the back of the river and a loose flap of corrugated iron banged on the side of a shed somewhere. In a few minutes the rubbish men would be arriving to work on the dump, digging and delving into the loose mountains of trash and loading the river barges until they almost sank, while the tipper trucks roared in from all over London. It was a new day.

'Let's go to Ben's,' said Sydney. 'I'd like to find out what happened to Sam.'

'Ben?' said Knocker.

'Sam?' said Torreycanyon, who had forgotten all about the horse.

Chalotte pulled Knocker to his feet. 'There's new stuff to tell you—there's Twilight here, and Ben and Sam. There's Sussworth too, and Hanks and the SBG.'

'Sussworth,' Napoleon spat out the word. 'Straight away I don't like the sound of him.'

Stonks swore. 'You won't like the look of 'im either,' he said, 'especially if he catches us out here. Let's get out of sight.' He set off into the mile of space that lay between the Wandle and Wandsworth Bridge, followed by the others along a path that wound between the piles of discarded washing machines and broken refrigerators. They walked quietly in file until they came within sight of Ben's hut, and there they saw a light flickering behind a threadbare sack which hung for a curtain at a lopsided window. They took cover and waited while Stonks went to the door. Carefully he lifted the latch and poked his head inside, then after a moment, he beckoned to his companions, indicating that all was safe.

'This is Ben,' he explained to those who had not been to the shack before, 'and Ben is the only grown-up Borrible in the world.'

The interior of the hut was gloomy, lit only by one oil lamp. Ben was discovered sprawled asleep in a low broken-backed armchair and he looked just the same as he had always looked: covered in many overcoats, his beard spreading over his chest, his long black hair tumbling to his shoulders and his skin pitted and filthy. He smelt just the same too: awful.

'Blimey,' said Orococco, 'he's blacker than I am.'

Sydney closed the door and the slight noise made Ben stir in his sleep. He belched and opened one eye, then the other. Slowly he came awake and shifted in his chair, rubbing his hairy face with a soiled hand.

'Well,' he said, 'strike me purple.' The old tramp shook his head, surprised, but then a broad smile began to grow behind his beard. 'Well, I'll be damned,' he went on. 'I thought Sussworth had got you for sure. Not my business of course, but I didn't like it, didn't like it one bit.' He reached for the beer bottle on the table and took a long swig to reassure himself that the world was still in the same place. 'There's more of you, though,' he said. 'Found some friends ain't yer? What you kids get up to is nobody's business, but whose business is it if it ain't nobody's?'

Sydney, who had spent more time with Ben than any of the others and therefore knew him better, stepped up and touched him on the hand. 'We've had the most terrible time, Ben,' she said. 'Could we hide here for a few days maybe, get some rest? We're dropping on our feet.'

Ben rummaged in his overcoat and began to produce bottles of beer one by one. 'Stay, sunshine,' he bellowed, 'why of course you can,' and he wagged his beard like he was chewing a tough bit of meat. 'Get this sherbet down yer, that'll straighten you out a bit. Strewth, look 'ow muddy you are, and them clothes, waders and orange jackets . . . You've been thieving again.'

Stonks found a bottle opener and passed the bottles round. The Borribles drank and allowed the strong ale to trickle down their throats, but they stood awkwardly in the hut. After all, Ben was an adult, and Knocker and Napoleon kept near the door in case they had to run.

The tramp hoisted himself upright. 'Blimey,' he said, 'you must be tired; I've never known you so quiet. You look dead on yer feet.

Why don't yer get into the other rooms and spread out on the mattresses, get some sleep? It'll all be better by the time you wakes up, you'll see.'

Twilight looked around. 'You've changed all the furniture,' he said, 'and all your things are different.'

Ben placed his hands on his hips. 'That was your friend Sussworth,' he said. 'He will have his little joke. The day you left he smashed all me bits and pieces, all me bottles, threw me locks and keys into the barges. It was worth a lot of grub that stuff was. He said he was going to scrub me clean, give me a shave, put me in a home. Bleedin' little Hitler he is. Kept asking me where you'd gone.'

'What happened?' asked Vulge.

'Well, I kept saying it was none of my business and eventually they let me go with a kick up the arse.'

'And all this stuff,' said Chalotte, 'where'd that come from?'

'Oh, that's easy,' said Ben. 'If you live in the middle of the world's biggest rubbish dump you want for nothing, do yer? There's plenty of beds and blankets; I've got more bottles. I'm rich I am, Sussworth can't bother me.'

'Where is he now?' asked Stonks.

'Ah,' answered Ben, 'that's the trouble. He's got the whole of Wandsworth surrounded. He knows you haven't gone home yet. Don't know how he knows, but he knows, but then he makes it his business to know, don't he?'

'Then everything's just as bad as it was before,' said Bingo.

'And so it may be,' said Ben, 'but we've got to look on the bright side, ain't we? Well what is it to be, sleep or eat?'

'Sleep,' said the Borribles.

'Right,' said Ben, 'you know where the beds are, just like before. You show your mates. When you wake up I'll 'ave a feast ready for you, a regular feast. You'll wonder what's hit yer, see if yer don't. Now off you go and get yer heads down.'

The Borribles needed no second bidding. They filed from the room and within a minute or two were all in a deep slumber, dirt, slime and everything. Only Sydney lingered.

'Ben, how's Sam, the horse, is he all right? Has Sussworth found him?'

Ben shook his shoulders loosely by way of a laugh. 'That there horse,' he said, 'is as snug as a bug in a rug. Five-star hotel he's in, first-class oats and hay, fresh water, lots of other horses for company. Saw him only yesterday, hardly recognized him, did I? Knibbsie likes him so much that he never lets him out of his sight, and Sussworth, like I said, never thought of looking for him in a stable; too subtle, that is.'

Sydney sniffed. 'Thanks, Ben,' she said, holding down the lump in her throat with difficulty. 'Thanks.'

Ben spat into a pile of coal. 'I don't often make things my business,' he said wisely, 'but when I does, I does.'

Sydney smiled and went to find somewhere to sleep. Now that the tension of the escape was over she found that she could hardly stand. Ben waited until he was alone and began to feel in his pockets for a pipe. It took him a long time. 'Them bleedin' kids,' he muttered, 'they're something special they are, something really special.'

And so the Adventurers slept and slept again. They were to stay with Ben for more than a week and for most of that time they woke only to eat. Every time they opened their eyes Ben was there with more food.

'Eat up,' he kept urging them, 'eat up, you're all so skinny. Plenty more where that came from, all the rubbish in the world here.' And from the depths of his overcoats would come forth packets of this and bottles of that.

During this period the Borribles were quite content to leave their safety in the tramp's hands. 'Sussworth's out there,' he told them, 'him and the SBG, but they don't take no more notice of old Ben.' He'd swig from a bottle and tell them not to worry about the dried mud that was flaking off their bodies and into the blankets. 'I don't care about a touch of dirt,' he insisted. 'A good bit of dirt never hurt anyone except the old lady who broke her back scrubbing the floor.'

Towards the end of the week the Borribles began to recover.
Knocker, Napoleon, Torreycanyon and Orococco were the last to
get on their feet but then their captivity had been long and ardu-
ous. When they finally emerged into the daylight of Feather's
Wharf the mud had gone from their skins if not from their clothes.
They looked pale and thin but there was a new light in their eyes
and the sparks of a new energy could be seen in their movement
and thought; they started to exchange their stories, as Borribles
love to do.

Vulge told how Sydney had come to Whitechapel, and how
Twilight had saved Chalotte from a Woollie that very same day.
Sydney spoke of the strange message telling of Sam the horse and
how she and the others set out to find him, and Stonks explained to
Knocker about the formation of the SBG and who Inspector Sussworth was and how the Adventurers had been captured at the Battle of Eel Brook Common. Then Bingo took up the tale and
recounted Ben's rescue of them all and the newcomers looked at
Ben with a deep admiration.

'That was the best of it,' said Chalotte, 'but the worst of it was
what I discovered when I talked to Spiff while you were all down
the mine.

You see he'd planned the whole thing; it was him that sent the
message to Sydney, just to start things going, so that he could get
back at Flinthead.'

'He was devious all right,' said Knocker, 'double devious.'

'I dunno,' objected Torreycanyon. 'Whatever you say about him
he got us out of there alive remember. I don't reckon anyone else
could've.'

'That's right,' said Napoleon with respect in his voice. 'He
fooled Flinthead all the way, and that's not easy, and what a scrap
with the spades. He was Spiff the Spifflicator, there ain't no doubt
about that.'

'Wait a minute,' said Knocker darkly. 'If it hadn't been for
Spiff we wouldn't have been down the mine in the first place. He
owed us a rescue . . . and we might not have got away at all if
Chalotte hadn't knocked the wedges out.'

'Of course we would've,' said Napoleon. 'Chalotte nearly got us all killed. All Spiff had to do was pretend to be Flinthead; he could have got us out whenever he liked then.'

'Ah,' said Knocker, 'that's it. Would Spiff have done that? Who knows what he might have done once he found himself in power? He might have let us go, he might not have. There was nothing to stop him kicking us out into the street either and staying behind himself to become Flinthead, swapping identities, like.'

'He wouldn't have, would he?' asked Twilight, his eyes round.

'Spiff was capable of anything,' said Knocker. 'that was part of his strength, that's why he was a danger. What's more that box of treasure did things to people, changed 'em. It made Flinthead worse than he was before, it tempted Napoleon once, it certainly made me ambitious for more and more names. Who knows what it was doing to Spiff, eh, who knows?'

There was so much to think of after what Knocker had said that there was silence for a while. Then Sydney raised her eyes and said quietly, 'So Chalotte was the only one of us all to see it, and when she saw it she destroyed the mine, destroyed the money . . . and killed Spiff.'

Chalotte stared at the floor; her face reddened. 'I didn't know what I was doing,' she began, 'and I don't want to take credit for it. I didn't want to kill Spiff; he was brave, he did save us all in the end, but he never told us what he was doing, you never knew which way he was going to jump. When you came out of the mine I wasn't certain of anything. One moment I thought it was Flint-head climbing out, then I wasn't sure. There was so much noise, so much shouting. I was frightened of what was happening and what might happen. All I know is that I didn't want that money back among Borribles again . . . Knocking out the wedges was the only thing I could do, it seemed like the right thing.'

'I think it was,' said Knocker. 'I think it was, even if it nearly killed the lot of us.'

'She was bloody brave anyway,' said Vulge. 'There was a lot of certain death flying about for a quarter of an hour.'

Chalotte shook her head. 'I wasn't brave,' she said, 'just scared out of my brains.'

'What a great story it will be,' said Twilight. 'It will be the greatest Borrible Adventure ever told, better even than the Great Rumble Hunt, maybe.'

Knocker looked stern. 'I don't know about you others,' he said, 'but there are some things about this Adventure I don't like. Perhaps we shouldn't tell this story, we should keep it secret among ourselves.'

'A secret story,' said Chalotte. 'Well you might be right, you might not. We'd have to think about it.'

Knocker gazed at the scars that were burnt into the palms of his hands. 'You know, Chalotte, I'm glad you gave me that second name, Knocker Burnthand. I'm proud of it in a funny back to front kind of a way . . . but I don't want another. I've had enough adventures to last me a Borrible lifetime.'

And so they talked on and Ben sat and listened with great interest and passed bottles of stout to each speaker in turn so that they could build up their strength, and the Borribles came to accept the tramp as one of their very own. Indeed it was a mark of the confidence they felt in him that the Borribles told their stories in front of an adult at all, for it had never been done before.

It became obvious to them that Ben would have had the Borribles live in his lean-to for ever, but as the Adventurers felt their limbs grow stronger they began to worry about getting home, back to their tumbledown houses in their own areas of London.

'It won't be easy,' said Stonks, when he had explained to Knocker how determined and well trained Inspector Sussworth and his men were. 'The SBG know that we had something to do with Dewdrop's death and they won't give up till they've got us and clipped our ears.'

Ben knocked his pipe against the side of his chair and allowed the ash to fall to the floor. 'Every time I go out,' he said, 'I see coppers everywhere; like a bloody coronation it is, except they're searching for you lot, and they look like they're ready to wait for ever, day and night and mainly between here and Battersea, which is where you want to go, ain't it? We'll have to think of something really good this time.'

The discussion went on and on and got nowhere. Some thought it would be a good idea to make a raft and drift down the river in the dark. Others suggested that it would be safer to walk along by the river's edge and get round the police cordon that way. One or two argued that they should stay where they were and wait until Sussworth gave up his task and moved away, but then it was pointed out that there was no guarantee that the SBG would not pay Ben another visit and catch them all there, say, sleeping in the middle of the night. It was dangerous to go and every hour it became more and more dangerous to remain; the situation looked hopeless until one day Ben returned from the outside world, emptied his pockets of provisions, banged a bottle on the table and called for silence.

'I've been thinking,' he said, 'and swipe me if that ain't given me an idea. None of your plans is very good, none of 'em, but I reckon I can get you out of Wandsworth in style and comfort, the horse as well.'

'The horse as well,' said Sydney, her face happy. 'How?'

Ben squinted and filled his eyes with mystery. 'Ha,' he said, 'you'll have to wait and see. Let's say the day after tomorrow, very early in the morning. Get plenty of rest, you may need it.'

For the whole of the intervening time the Borribles could hardly contain themselves. Ben came and went on several occasions and laid in a great stock of rations and swigged from his beer bottles ceaselessly. On one of his appearances he staggered into the lean-to carrying a huge bundle of second-hand children's clothes and threw them down on to the floor.

'Best get out of that Wendle stuff,' he said panting, 'you look like a bunch of bandits. I've got some lovely gear here. Real posh you'll look in this little lot, like bleedin' choir boys . . . and girls o' course.'

Bingo held up a clean shirt that had once been very expensive. 'Where'd yer get it?' he asked.

Ben raised his eyebrows. 'Where'd yer think? It fell off a lorry, just like that. Wonderful thing gravity, I don't reckon we could live without it.'

At five in the morning on the day of departure Ben crept into the room where the Borribles were sleeping and shook them gently awake.

'Come on, mates,' he whispered. 'It's time.'

As usual the tramp had sat in his armchair all night with a fire going in spite of the heatwave, drinking and thinking, and although the dawn was warm and sticky he still wore all his overcoats, just like he always did.

The Borribles stretched, rolled from their mattresses, dressed quickly in their new clothes and made their way to the kitchen.

'Got some tea for you,' said Ben as they appeared one by one, 'and there's a kettle on the hob, look, if you want more. Bacon sandwiches on the plate . . . get stuck in.'

It was just light when they left the lean-to a little while later. Two or three seagulls were tearing at piles of offal near the river and Ben looked up at the sky.

'It's going to be as hot as 'ell again today,' he said, and pulled his collars tighter to his neck.

In single file the Borribles followed the tramp over the rough terrain of Feather's Wharf. Across broken and deserted factories, through abandoned houses where glass crunched underfoot and where rotten floors threatened to snap and fall, Ben stepped out, travelling in safety by unmapped and forgotten ways, ways that were known only to himself and which no ordinary adult or policeman had ever seen. Over the railway line they went, along the Causeway by the River Wandle, and finally they stumbled across a dusty field of crumbling bricks and corrugated iron and found themselves on the edge of the broad thoroughfare of Armoury Way.

Ben looked up and down carefully; the Borribles stood behind him. The pavements were grey and empty and stretched for miles. Ben gave the word and he and the Borribles rushed across the road in a gang. When he was satisfied that no one was watching he grinned and pushed against a plank in the high advertising hoarding beside him. The plank swivelled on a loose nail and the Borribles saw a large hole appear.

'This is how I gets into Young's Brewery,' cackled Ben. 'This is how I goes to see my mate, Knibbsie, and this is how I brings me beer out. In yer go.'

When everyone had passed through Ben replaced the plank and breathed a sigh of relief. 'We're safe now,' he explained. 'We're in the back of the brewery, private property, no Woollies here. Knibbsie and me used to be draymen together once, as well as being on the road. He looks after the horses now, 'cos they still delivers their beer with horses and carts you know; you ever seen 'em?'

'Seen 'em,' said Bingo. 'I should think so. Bloody great animals, big as double-decker buses.'

Ben nodded. 'Come on then, no time to lose.' He shuffled on through the yards and alleys of the brewery and the Borribles went with him. Everywhere they passed stood gigantic wooden drays, high, like carriages for kings, with massive steel-rimmed wheels painted in bright fairground colours.

The tramp stopped by the side of one of these carts and pointed up to the polished seat that must have been a good fifteen feet off the ground.

'That's where the driver and his mate rides,' he said. 'It's like flying, it is. You can see everything for miles up there. You can look into upstairs windows as easy as winking, and see people having their breakfast . . . And all the traffic has to stop for you. The hooves clip-clopping, the leather creaking, the brasses swinging and clanking. I tell you, if you have to work, and I don't wish that on anybody, but if you has to, well that's the best job in the world, and the beer's free too. You just sniff the air in here, for example, and see. Why that air's so heavy with ale that it's good enough to make breathing a crime.' And as if to prove his point Ben sniffed deeply and philosophically before continuing on his way.

They were very nearly at the end of their journey now. Ben took them into a wide stable yard and there, at the far end of it, stood a man in a long leather apron, leaning on a broom. 'That,' said Ben, 'is my mate, Knibbsie.'

Knibbs had obviously been waiting for them for he showed no surprise at their appearance. Sydney, who had last seen him on the misty night of the escape from Fulham police station, looked at him closely.

She remembered the face now: pale, with strange spiky hair sticking out horizontally under a flat greasy cap. His nose was hard and bony, his eyes dark. He wore a big fluffy moustache too and it was stained with brown beer. His face looked glum until he smiled but he smiled now and his face changed and became warm. He beckoned and the Borribles and Ben went towards him.

On either side as they walked were huge yellow doors, divided in half, and the top half of each stall was open and the great shire horses that pulled the drays stood there as solid and heavy as mammoths.

'Swipe me,' said Vulge, 'look at the size of 'em; imagine having one of them step on your toe.'

'And look at their teeth,' added Twilight. 'One mouthful and you'd be gone.' But the horses showed no sign of hostility, they were not interested in a band of insignificant children. They simply shook their heads, snorted, stamped their feet and waited for their early morning feed.

When the Adventurers were standing before Knibbs he leant his broom against the wall and crossed his arms. He looked at Ben and then at the children. 'Borribles, eh? Well I've heard of 'em; never thought I'd see any, knowingly like.'

The Borribles tensed. Knibbs, after all, was an adult.

'Don't worry,' he said. 'Ben's told me all about it. All I want to do is get you out of sight before anyone else gets here. I don't mind helping, but I don't want the sack on account of it, eh, Ben. What would we do for beer then?'

'What indeed?' said Ben sagely. 'What indeed?'

'Wait a minute,' said Sydney, 'don't you remember me? I met you before, that night in the fog. I brought you a horse . . . What's happened to Sam?'

Knibbs looked down at Sydney. 'Sam,' he said, 'why Sam's lovely. You never seen such a horse, not in all your natural you ain't.' He went to a nearby stable door and unbolted the lower section. 'I 'as to open the bottom bit,' he explained. 'Sam isn't big enough to look over it, not like the others.' With that the stableman opened the hatch and there stood Sam. But such a Sam. He was so sleek and well fed. His hooves glittered like anthracite and his coat was so polished that Sydney could see her face in it. No longer the dingy downhearted nag that had once pulled Dewdrop's cart, Sam had been transformed into an aristocrat of a horse, small but distinguished.

The Borribles cried aloud with surprise and pushed forward to stroke and pat the animal and Sam neighed gently and nuzzled them all one by one, recognizing them.

Sydney turned to look at the stableman. 'It's Sam all right,' she said, 'and he looks lovely. But he used to be brown, now he's black.'

'So he is,' said Chalotte. 'I hadn't noticed.'

'Ah,' said Knibbs, 'that's a disguise, that is. We've got to get him past Sussworth today and that's how we're going to do it. If Sussworth recognizes that horse he'll know that you ain't far away; that's it and all about it. Now all of yer, outside and out of sight.'

Back in the yard Knibbs took them to one of the huge drays that stood near the stable office. 'This one's already loaded,' he said, 'and me and Ben are taking it out today because they're short-handed. Now see that ladder, well you lot get up it. Lively!'

The Borribles did as they were told and found themselves on the very top of a mountainous load of wooden barrels that had been piled one on another across the length and breadth of the cart, except that in the middle Knibbs had left a space big enough for the Adventurers to jump down into and hide.

'Don't make a sound,' Ben shouted. 'Don't come out again till I tell yer it's safe.' He threw a square of canvas up to them. 'And cover yourselves with this so yer ain't seen from a buildin' or a bus.'

'Where's this cart going,' said Orococco, 'not Tooting by any chance?'

'No,' said Knibbs. 'Battersea High Street, that's why we're taking you. We're delivering to a pub called the Ancient Woodman. No more noise now.'

The Borribles grinned at each other and scrambled into the centre of the cart and found that they were hidden on all sides by the towering beer barrels. They sat and pulled the tarpaulin over their heads.

'Just think,' whispered Twilight, 'we're on our way home.'

'You ain't home yet,' said Stonks. 'There's still Sussworth and Hanks to get past.'

'Yeah,' said Vulge, 'and just think what they'll do to Ben and Knibbs if they finds 'em smuggling Borribles . . . They'll send 'em to prison for years and years.'

Outside, beyond the barrels, the brewery went about its business and the noises they heard told the Borribles what was happening. First, one of the stable doors was opened and Knibbs and Ben emerged with two shire horses and buckled them into the shafts of the great cart. Then came the light step of Sam as he was brought out too and tied behind. A little later there was more noise as other drivers and draymen arrived to groom their horses and back them into the carts ready for the day's work. Then the foreman came and checked the loads and told the teams which part of London they were to go to, and where they were meant to deliver their barrels. He called out the names of the pubs from his order book: the Fallen Tree, the Old Goat, the Jolly Sailor, the Apple of My Eye, the Garden of Eden, the Charcoal Burner, and many more.

When the foreman had reached the end of his list he rolled out a firkin of beer, lifted it up on to a wooden trestle, broached it and then handed every man present a pint mug of ale so that they could drink to the new day. As soon as their glasses were empty the draymen smacked their lips, shouted goodbye to each other, climbed to the pinnacle of their high carts, cracked their whips in the air and at last allowed the giant horses to move forward.

Now Knibbs cracked his whip and spoke to his horses. 'Come on up, Donner, my beauty; come on up, Blitzen, my girl,' he called, and Ben wrapped his legs in a huge leather apron and the great dray rumbled over the cobbles.

'We're off,' cried Ben, and there was a clashing of horse-brasses as well as a racket of horseshoes and the cart charged down the yard and out through the brewery gates like an engine of war on its way to do battle.

'It's now or never, all right,' said Bingo, jolted so much that his voice shook. 'If we get caught this time there'll be no getting away from in here. It'll be ears clipped for sure.'

Knocker smiled. 'As the proverb says, "There's a time for fingers crossed and mouths shut." This is it.'

It was eight thirty in the morning now and the rush hour traffic in Wandsworth High Street was heavy, not that traffic made any difference to Knibbs. The law of the land gives horse-drawn vehicles right of way over motor cars, and so they were all made to stop and wait as the drays clattered from the brewery to head in different directions, out over London. Knibbs touched on his reins and the great horses strode proudly on, and behind the cart trotted Sam as dainty as a thoroughbred. Into Wandsworth Plain they went, round the one-way system, back into Armoury Way, past the traffic lights and on to the great modern roundabout where Sydney had walked in the mist with Ben, and finally into York Road, towards the line where Wandsworth meets Battersea, where Inspector Sussworth waited in ambush with Sergeant Hanks and the men of the SBG.

And along each road the traffic yielded before the steady progress of the magnificent horses, car drivers leant on their steering wheels and peered up through their windscreens to savour a moment of beauty to take to work with them, and passengers in the hot smoky upstairs of the buses gazed stupidly across at Knibbs and Ben and wondered why they looked so free and piratical, never guessing for a moment that within a secret space, deep among the barrels, lay the Adventurers, escaping across a frontier.

Halfway along York Road the stream of cars and buses slowed to a halt and the horses stopped too. Ben stood on his seat and tried to make out what was happening in the distance. A second later his voice drifted back to the Borribles.

'Steady, mates, I can see a blue van up front . . . It's them all right. They're searching all the cars, they've got a barricade across the road. Keep yer 'eads down.'

Pace by pace the dray advanced and the Borribles bit their lips and waited. They couldn't see and they daren't look but Ben told them that there was a dark blue Transit van parked halfway across the road and two or three policemen were filtering the traffic past it in the direction of the city. Slowly the horses stepped, responding patiently to the commands of Knibbs, until at last they came level with the policemen and there was Inspector Sussworth, standing on the pavement, watching everything with his bright dark eyes. His long coat swept the ground, his buttons shone and the two sides of his square moustache twitched up and down like the wings of a dying moth. Beside him, forever faithful, stood Sergeant Hanks, forever fat, his tunic stained with months of food, greasy layers of it. Sussworth gestured and one of his constables stepped to the side of the cart and gazed up into Knibbs's face.

'Pull that cart over here, out of the way,' said the policeman roughly. 'You're causing an obstruction.'

'Wouldn't be if you didn't have that stupid van of yours halfway across the road,' said Knibbs. 'Broken down, have yer?'

'Watch yer tongue, chummy,' said the policeman, and he made Knibbs bring the cart to the kerb where Sussworth stood, his hands clasped behind his back.

'And where are you going with this lot?' he asked, his manner argumentative and superior, his head pivoting dangerously on his neck.

'We're going to a bottle party,' offered Ben, 'and we don't want to look mean.'

'Don't be smart,' said Sussworth, then he looked again. His expression hardened. 'Well, well,' he said, 'that's old Ben, the tramp. I've had trouble with you before. Didn't think you worked, Ben. I had you down for one of them welfare scroungers. You know, half the year on the dole and the other half in an alcoholic haze.'

'I'm a part-time drayman,' said Ben haughtily, feeling quite safe on his lofty perch. 'It's my trade.'

'Drinks more than you sell, I'll be bound,' said Hanks, and he took a boiled sweet from his pocket, unwrapped it with his teeth and sucked it into his mouth. He licked the paper then let it flutter to the ground, wet with his saliva.

'I asked you where you were going,' persisted Sussworth, 'and if I don't get a proper answer you'll bloody well stay here till your beer goes flat.'

Knibbs said, 'We're delivering in Battersea High Street, the Ancient Woodman, down Church Road to the Swan and then back up Battersea Bridge Road.'

'Hmm,' said Sussworth, not convinced, and the Borribles heard his little dancing steps come nearer to the cart. Behind him thudded Sergeant Hanks, cheeks slobbering noisily at his sweet. It sounded like someone with a bad cold sniffing loose snot.

Suddenly Sussworth took a truncheon from one of his constables and began tapping all the barrels he could reach, one after the other. Fear grasped the Borribles by the heart and they held their breath. Slowly Sussworth worked along the dray, down one side, across the rear, then up to the front. When he'd finished he stood in the roadway, dwarfed by the horses, so small that he could have walked under their bellies without removing his hat.

'What's that horse doing at the back? Stolen is it? Looks familiar to me.'

'Well,' said Knibbs, 'one horse does look very much like another.'

'That's the trouble,' said Ben, looking astute, 'seen one horse, seen 'em all.' And he nodded his head as if he'd been grappling with the problem all his life.

'And why is it so small, then?' asked the inspector. 'Couldn't pull a cart this size, could it? So what's it doing with you?'

'Cor,' said Ben, blowing his cheeks out with indignation, 'give an 'orse a chance. He's little, certainly, but he's learning to be big, ain't he? Still growing, still training. I mean you went to night school, didn't yer?'

'Don't you get uppity with me,' said Sussworth angrily and a dark cloud passed over his face. 'If that horse weren't so black I'd swear it was the little brown job those Borribles nicked.' As he spoke an idea came into his head and he went to the back of the cart again and studied Sam very closely, wiping his hands down the animal's legs. Sam trembled with fear and distaste. He needn't have worried though; the dye that Knibbs had used did not come off on the policeman's hand in spite of the fact that he rubbed as hard as he could. The stableman was a wily old horse-trader and had lived with the gypsies for many years in his younger days. He knew all about disguising horses.

Disappointed and still suspicious Sussworth returned to the front of the cart and stood by the tail of the offside shire horse, the one Knibbs called Blitzen.

'Now listen here, you layabout,' he said to Ben, 'have you seen anything of them kids since I asked you last? There's a reward out for 'em you know, five hundred pounds. Just think what you'd be able to drink with that.'

'Oh,' said Ben, clasping his hands together and lifting his eyes to heaven, 'five hundred pounds, such money. You know I dreams of money, every night, in banknotes mostly. I sees myself stuffing me mattresses with it, and me pillows. I've got my eyes peeled like spuds for them kids, Inspector, sir, honest I have. I'll find 'em out for yer, bet yer boots I will.'

Sussworth thought for a moment and Sergeant Hanks stuck a fingernail into his nose. There was silence as everyone waited for the inspector to come to a decision. The rest of the morning traffic moved slowly past the barrier.

At that moment Blitzen arched her massive tail with an elegant slow grace and a soft wide cable of freshly plaited manure appeared, rolling out of the great body in a heavy lump of steaming brown flecked with straw. It flopped moistly to the ground and exploded over Inspector Sussworth's shoes and trousers.

The inspector cried aloud and jumped backwards immediately, prodding his sergeant in the stomach with a sharp elbow.

'Ouch,' yelled Hanks. His boiled sweet slipped into his throat and stuck there and his fingernail scraped the inside of his nostril and drew blood. Unable to speak a word he staggered to the nearest policeman and, going redder and redder in the face, begged, with gestures, to be thumped hard on the shoulders before he died of a seizure.

Sussworth went frantic; he could not abide dirt. He stamped and scraped his feet on the edge of the kerb, he shook his trouser legs, he shouted and screamed.

'Get those horses away from here, get my car, take me home. I must get changed, I must have a new uniform, I must have a bath. Take those animals away, have them shot. They're disgusting, unhygienic, there ought to be a law against them. I'll have 'em turned into catsmeat, take 'em away.'

Knibbs winked at Ben and shook the reins. Blitzen turned her huge head and gazed with disdain at the prancing figure of Inspector Sussworth and, as the horse moved out into the stream of traffic, she twitched her tail once more and farted loudly, like a cannon.

Sussworth's legs shook in temper, he felt weak with the vulgarity of it all and he covered his face with his hands. 'Hanks,' he moaned. 'Hanks get my car, take me away. I'll kill that horse if you don't; I won't be responsible for my actions.'

Knibbs held up his whip, the slow traffic stopped and the dray pulled round the SBG van and into the open road beyond. The barrier had been passed, the frontier had been cleared. Down among the beer barrels the Borribles clasped each other in jubilation.

'We've done it,' said Chalotte.

'And with Sam too,' said Sydney. 'We escaped with Sam.'

Knocker grinned and grinned. 'I never felt better in my life,' he said. 'Home, sweet home.' And he threw his head high and sang a song of triumph, not loudly, for he did not want to be heard outside the barrels, but with feeling and gratitude warm in his voice. And his friends closed their eyes, both to concentrate on the words and to keep back the tears of joy. This was Knocker's song.

> *'Hip hip hooray—we've won the day!*
> *We ride victorious from the fray!*
> *Three cheers for Knibbsie! Three cheers for Ben!*
> *And Donner and Blitzen, three cheers for them!*
> *Defying the odds they've brought us free*
> *Of Sussworth, Hanks and the SBG.*
> *Toast them in beer for all they've done—*
> *Honorary Borribles, every one!'*

Donner and Blitzen rattled their brasses as if in answer and trotted on at a fair clip. Past the lights at the end of Plough Road they went, past Price's candle factory and finally into Vicarage Crescent and to the bottom of Battersea High Street. Only then did Knibbs and Ben stop the cart and, to the astonishment of passersby, they stood on their seat, doffed their hats to each other and gave three cheers.

'You're a gentleman, Ben,' said Knibbs.

'And you're a scholar, my dear Knibbsie,' said Ben.

While the two adults were exchanging these compliments the Borribles climbed out of their hiding place and sat on top of the barrels in order to contemplate their freedom.

'And Ben,' said Sydney, 'you're a real Borrible.'

'And you too, Knibbsie,' said Chalotte, 'a real, real Borrible.'

'Thank you,' said Knibbs. 'I must say I've always felt like one.'

Ben wagged his beard. 'Don't you lot get careless now.' He looked down the street. 'You'd better scarper before you're spotted.'

'But will we ever see you again?' asked Chalotte, her face creased with worry.

Knibbs smiled. 'I should think so. I'll give a whistle every time I come down here with a load, and bring Ben sometimes, when he's sober, that is!'

'Fair enough,' said Napoleon, screwing his face up like a conspirator's. 'And if you two ever need help, no matter what, Napoleon's yer man.'

'And us too,' said the others, and they climbed down the great cartwheels and gathered together on the pavement while Sydney went to Sam the horse, untied him and stroked his neck. The Adventurers looked at one another, suddenly concerned.

'That's a point,' said Vulge. 'What are we going to do with him? We haven't thought of that, have we?'

'That's no problem,' said Bingo, 'there's stacks of empty houses down here. We'll get him into one of those for the time being and then we'll . . .' His voice faltered.

'Exactly,' said Napoleon. 'And then what do we do?'

Sydney tossed her hair. 'Don't you fret,' she said. 'I'm going to take him back to Neasden as soon as I'm ready. I've got a special place all fixed up.'

'Neasden!' shouted Torreycanyon. 'Strike a light, that's right over the other side of London.'

'I know where it is,' said Sydney, 'I live there. Besides I haven't asked you to help, have I?'

Ben called down from the top of the cart, 'Hey you lot, if you've stopped arguing, we're off.'

Knocker waved a hand. 'We've finished and we're going as well. Goodbye you two, and don't get caught.'

Ben hooted with laughter. 'You're the ones as better watch out,' he cried. 'They can't clip my ears any more, only yours. Keep yer eyes skinned for Sussworth, and take good care of Sam, he's a good 'un.'

Knocker looked at Chalotte and smiled. 'Don't worry, Ben,' he said, 'we'll watch out for him.'

Then Knibbs spoke to Donner and Blitzen; the great horses leant into the traces, their hooves struck white scars on the black tarmac and the cart moved up the street to begin its deliveries, leaving the Borribles standing on the pavement with Sam.

'Come on,' said Bingo. 'We have to find somewhere to hide this horse before a Woollie spots us.'

'There used to be an old factory behind the scrapyard,' said Knocker. 'We could get him in there, yards of space there is.'

'But there's a better place up by the market,' objected Bingo. 'It'd be easier for stealing carrots and stuff.'

'It don't matter where we go,' said Stonks, 'as long as we go. I didn't rescue you lot just to get caught by the Woollies again.'

'That's right,' said Napoleon. 'And think what will happen if we try to take a horse to Neasden in broad daylight. It's mad. I thought we were going in for the quiet life now, no more high adventure.'

'You can't desert Sam,' protested Twilight. 'He saved your lives on the Great Rumble Hunt; you owe him. He's a kind of horse-Borrible, and Borribles stick together, that's what we said.'

'A horse-Borrible,' sneered Napoleon. 'Well, I knew Pakis were barmy but—'

'Don't you Paki me,' retorted Twilight. 'I'm a Bangladeshi; and at least I'm brown, not green like a Wendle.'

And so they crossed the High Street in an untidy group and went towards the derelict factory, quarrelling on the way about which was the best building for hiding horses, and how impossible it was to smuggle a horse the length and breadth of London, especially in the teeth of Sussworth and the SBG, not to mention all the other dangers too, like Borrible-snatchers and undiscovered tribes of Rumbles who might be lurking in unexplored parks.

Sydney refused to budge from the pavement. She put her arms round Sam's neck and tears ran down her cheeks. 'I'm not scared,' she said to Chalotte who had stayed by her side. 'I'll take him all the bloody way on my own, you see if I don't.'

Chalotte laughed, really laughed. 'You mustn't be daft,' she said. 'You know what they're like, that's just the talk talking.'

'But listen to them—arguing, shouting—they can't agree about anything.'

'But the Borrible who doesn't quarrel is no Borrible,' said Chalotte. 'Look, I wasn't keen on going to look for Sam in the beginning, was I? But now we've got him, well, that's different. Like Twilight said, he's one of us, so we'll just have to do something about him, won't we? It's a rule.' She grinned and nudged Sydney with her elbow. 'Besides, there's no rush, mate; it's a long way to Neasden, a very long way.' And without another word she took Sam's halter from her friend's hand and led the horse across the road, following the others.